D1304627

PRECINCT 13

TATE HALLAWAY

BERKLEY BOOKS, NEW YORK

THE BERKLEY PUBLISHING GROUP
Published by the Penguin Group
Penguin Group (USA) Inc.
375 Hudson Street, New York, New York 10014, USA

Penguin Group (Canada), 90 Eglinton Avenue East, Suite 700, Toronto, Ontario M4P 2Y3, Canada (a division of Pearson Penguin Canada Inc.) • Penguin Books Ltd., 80 Strand, London WC2R 0RL, England • Penguin Group Ireland, 25 St. Stephen's Green, Dublin 2, Ireland (a division of Penguin Books Ltd.) • Penguin Group (Australia), 250 Camberwell Road, Camberwell, Victoria 3124, Australia (a division of Pearson Australia Group Pty. Ltd.) • Penguin Books India Pvt. Ltd., 11 Community Centre, Panchsheel Park, New Delhi—110 017, India • Penguin Group (NZ), 67 Apollo Drive, Rosedale, Auckland 0632, New Zealand (a division of Pearson New Zealand Ltd.) • Penguin Books (South Africa) (Pty.) Ltd., 24 Sturdee Avenue, Rosebank, Johannesburg 2196, South Africa

Penguin Books Ltd., Registered Offices: 80 Strand, London WC2R 0RL, England

This book is an original publication of The Berkley Publishing Group.

This is a work of fiction. Names, characters, places, and incidents either are the product of the author's imagination or are used fictitiously, and any resemblance to actual persons, living or dead, business establishments, events, or locales is entirely coincidental. The publisher does not have any control over and does not assume any responsibility for author or third-party websites or their content.

PUBLISHING HISTORY
Berkley trade paperback edition / August 2012

Library of Congress Cataloging-in-Publication Data

Hallaway, Tate.
Precinct 13 / Tate Hallaway. — Berkley trade pbk. ed.
p.   cm.
ISBN 978-0-425-24779-2 (pbk.)
1. Coroners—Fiction.   2. Psychic ability—Fiction.   I. Title.   II. Title: Precinct thirteen.
PS3608.A54825P74   2012
813'.6—dc23   2012003994

PRINTED IN THE UNITED STATES OF AMERICA

10   9   8   7   6   5   4   3   2   1

ALWAYS LEARNING   **PEARSON**

For Shawn and Rita. Two awesome moms.

ACKNOWLEDGMENTS

As always, I must thank my conscientious and devoted editor, Anne Sowards, and my massively supportive and understanding agent, Martha Millard. My writers' group, the Wyrdsmiths, helped tremendously, including newest member Adam Stemple, whose suggestions made me angry, but were ultimately worthwhile. Another Wyrdsmith I must pick out to honor is Kelly McCullough, who graciously allowed an homage to one of his Urbana critters, the "skitter." Also, speaking of such matters, I must thank Rachel Gold for letting me "steal" her tough-guy fairy idea, as well as a lot of the brainstorming that went into this novel.

Naomi Kritzer and Eleanor Arnason get my gratitude not only for their work in the writers' group, but also for their friendship and the lifeline that is our Wednesday Women of Wyrdsmiths gathering. Sean M. Murphy, also, for all his last-minute critiquing, even though this time he didn't get much of a chance to do so.

My family, Shawn and Mason Rounds, are my biggest fans, best supporters, and, in the case of Shawn, co-conspirators. This time, however, it was my mother, Rita Morehouse, who gets the honor of Muse, since she told me, "Why not just go for it?" and I did. My father, Mort Morehouse, spent much of the writing of this book sidelined, but happily will return to his duties as "stage mom" now.

ONE

I never dreamed of being a coroner. No, when I was a little girl, I wanted to grow up to be a fairy princess or maybe a dragon-riding warrior queen. Turns out, however, there's not a lot of call for either in the real world.

So how did I end up in Pierre working with dead people? As the newspaper's headline read on the day I was elected: "Double-Dare You: Alexandra Connor Wins Coroner Position on a Bet."

That pretty much sums it up.

Several months ago, after too many beers, my roommate, Robert, told me that the solution to my financial woes was in the newspaper. I thought perhaps he'd found me work as a cashier or something, but he pointed to the upcoming spring election roster where the position of coroner was listed.

Despite seeing it in black-and-white, I didn't even believe that you could run for such an office. We Googled it. Turns out in some states, including South Dakota, you campaign for the position, like you would city council.

Robert and I also discovered online there weren't a lot of requirements. Almost zero medical expertise was required for the job. I already had a degree in forensic science and had started medical school. Though I'd been on a, shall we say, "extended hiatus" from school due to a health crisis . . . of the mental kind.

I guess I never *quite* let go of that fairy princess thing. Let's just say the *real world* isn't always my best friend.

At any rate, Robert and I had laughed all night about the idea of me becoming county coroner. At some point he said he'd put down twenty bucks if I'd actually put my name in the hat for the job. I almost gave him his money back the next morning. Yet when I woke up, deeply hungover, the idea was still stuck in my head, bouncing around, making more and more sense, at least financially. The position paid nearly sixty thousand dollars a year. No small potatoes and one hundred percent better than the negative numbers I was pulling between my lack of employment, student loans, and, er, those medical bills.

Thus, two weeks later, completely sober, I filed paperwork and took Robert's twenty.

Afterward, I promptly forgot about it. I mean, it wasn't like I was going to campaign. I couldn't just go knocking on my neighbors' doors and say, "Hi, I'm Alex Connor, and I want to cut up bodies for the county. Please vote for me next Tuesday!"

But, I won. I fucking won the election.

Who knew that the previous coroner was completely corrupt? Not me. But apparently plenty of the voters who'd shown up that Tuesday had at least heard the rumors involving that secretary and all the cases that just happened to favor the chief of police. The guy was a dirty old man on the take and, despite being a lifelong politician who ought to have known better, he'd managed to piss off more than his share of regular voters.

It was insane, but here I was, standing in a morgue waiting for my first case.

I'd been really rather hoping to go the whole year without one. Sixty thou for doing nothing would be a pretty good gig. And, totally possible; there aren't a lot of suspicious deaths in Pierre. In fact, in the last two years there were exactly zero homicides.

The lack of action might explain why the morgue wasn't very spacious or fancy.

The thing that dominated the area, to which most people's eyes were instantly drawn, was the stainless steel table. There were holes and drains and faucets that tended to fascinate and horrify any visitor to the morgue. Mostly, that was all anyone ever noticed about the place. After a good, long look at that table and even the tiniest bit of imagination, they wanted to flee.

A stalwart visitor might next see the nearby double-basin sink area. It was polished steel as well, with a few cabinets above and a counter big enough to set out all the equipment needed to perform an autopsy. Right now, laid out on a sterile white towel were a pair of dissecting scissors that looked far too much like pruning shears for most people's comfort; surgical knives; a gallstone scoop; a cavity mirror; a few probes; and a number of double-prong flesh hooks.

If the visitor had not yet run screaming in abject horror, they might spot the wall of body freezers against the far end of the room.

No one would ever detect the cozy corner that I'd made into my makeshift office. It had been a workstation with the barest minimum equipment: a phone, space for a laptop, a chipped and rotten corkboard full of outdated safety warnings and office memorandums. I'd brought in a little, cheery area rug to go over the painted concrete floor, a spider plant, and a cheap poster of Monet's water lilies. It was nearly comfy. I even had a chair for someone else to sit in.

Not that I got a lot of visitors.

The only other body in the morgue besides my own belonged to poor Mrs. Finnegan, who'd died peacefully in her sleep of old age. She took up one drawer in the row, waiting for her family in Minnesota to get the paperwork together to transfer her remains. She'd been fine company, not bothering me in the least, just cooling her heels patiently.

I'd been left alone here for almost three weeks, drawing pay and doing a lot of dusting and rearranging. My easy days were about to come to a bitter end, however.

I was going to miss the quiet, too. I'd needed this time alone, honestly. The last year had been *so* hard. My doctors told me that the best thing I could do was leave Chicago, sever all my ties to my past, tell no one where I was going, and start over somewhere new. Quit "old people, places, and things," like Alcoholics Anonymous preached. It sounded like good advice, but I missed him . . . I missed Valentine.

My psychologist told me I would, but that it was a crutch. He was bad for me. He enabled my sickness.

I took a deep breath and tried to do what my therapist always said I should. Focus on the present. Focus on what was *real*.

I checked my watch. Where was everyone? I was supposed to have an assistant, though I had yet to really meet her. We'd pressed palms briefly at my orientation/welcome party. I had a vague memory of a fortyish brunette in a black dress with a sloshing glass of wine in one hand. She'd been the one to perform all the autopsies for my politician predecessor, and I'd hoped she'd walk me through this one.

Her loyalties had been pretty obvious at the party, the way she stage-whispered drunkenly that I looked "awfully young and inexperienced," and, given my weird haircut, probably a lesbian.

I guess it wasn't a really big surprise she was AWOL this morning.

Luckily, I'd enjoyed doing autopsies in med school. Most of my colleagues freaked out about touching dead people, but I found them to be like Mrs. Finnegan—uncomplaining and patient. Besides, there were worse things than being dead.

I wasn't supposed to think about those options anymore, though, was I?

Outside the door, I heard the squeak of wheels. I pushed open the double swinging doors to look down the hall. The walls that formed the entry to my cave were unadorned plaster. Bare bulbs surrounded by safety cages ran down the center of the ceiling. The wires were exposed. It was ugly, but it was honest.

Two cops wheeled the sheet-covered cart down the hall. The pair seemed like the classic odd couple. He was shorter and lither, and probably in his mid-forties. She was taller, but built more like a rectangle, and looked younger, though I couldn't say why. In fact, if it wasn't for the messy ponytail, I might have mistaken her for a man. I couldn't distinguish their words in the echo chamber, but the guy seemed to be telling some wild tale, punctuated by a lot of chuckles.

Typical cops, in other words.

Frankly, I preferred corpses.

I steeled myself for the inevitable interaction as they came within range.

"Where's the coroner?" the guy cop asked, looking around me as if hoping for someone more impressive.

No one expected a petite, twenty-six-year-old to be in charge of anything, much less the county's morgue. This was heightened by the fact that I was in the process of growing out a very punk hairstyle, and still had spikes and a streak or two of blue. I also tended to dress in clothes that could get dirty, so I had on blue jeans and a cotton T-shirt. Knowing I was going to have company, however, I'd tossed a white lab coat on for that extra air of authority. I pointed to myself and tried to sound confident as I said, "That would be me, Alex Connor."

"Oh, Alex, as in short for Alexandra or something," he said, squinting at my shaggy hair. "I thought you'd be a dude."

And, yet, somehow I knew you'd be an asshole, I managed not to say. Instead, I murmured, "Uh-huh." I looked down at the outline of the figure underneath the white sheet. There was a manila folder on his chest. "Anything you want to tell me that's not in this?" I picked up the file to show them.

When he didn't answer right away, I set the folder back down and glanced up. The guy cop had his arms crossed in front of his chest, an almost defensive posture, and was looking to his partner. So, I glanced over at her as well.

She was the flintiest woman I'd ever seen. I suspected a smile might actually crack that stern face of hers. Generally, she was built like a block. Everything about her was very squared away, too. Well, except her hair. Wild, dark curls sprung out in every direction underneath her cap, defying the ponytail, and completely covering her forehead and ears. She just stared at me with an unreadable face.

Even her name was solid. The embroidered name under the badge said, simply: STONE.

"You guys *have* some information, right?" I prompted when neither of them said anything. "I know my predecessor was a crook, but, you know, we're on the same team here."

"Are we?" the guy cop asked. I noticed his name was Jones, and he didn't look at me when he asked the question, so I wondered if he was really quizzing his partner about her loyalty for some reason.

"We should tell her," Stone said in a voice very much like the rest of her: solid and deliberate.

"Yeah, you really should," I agreed.

"You tell her," Jones said gruffly.

To my surprise, he turned and walked away. His boots clomped in the corridor. The door at the far end of the hall squeaked when he pulled it open, and slammed shut hollowly, as he left.

Okay, this was getting very strange, very quickly.

I scanned the remaining cop's face for some clue. What the hell was going on with the corpse that this Jones guy just recused himself from discussing it?

When the silence had stretched to an almost unbearable length, Stone finally asked me in a serious voice, "Do you believe in magic?"

Oh, shit. Of all things to ask . . . when I'd just been thinking about Valentine, too.

Breath caught in my throat so suddenly I nearly choked. All the blood drained from my face to collect in my hammering heart.

"I've had a . . . complicated relationship with magic."

I'm not sure why I even admitted that much, but it seemed to be the answer she was looking for. The corners of her lips turned up slightly, and her eyes softened a tiny amount. "Good. Then I must tell you to be careful with this body," she said, matter-of-factly. "There's magic in it. Do you understand?"

"No," I admitted, my voice little more than a hoarse rasp. I was having trouble remembering to breathe. "Not in the least."

"We suspect this man was a necromancer. A bad magician." She spoke slowly, carefully, very coplike, as if explaining the situation to a frightened child. I had to admit that wasn't too far from the truth, given how small I felt and how much my body was shaking. "Someone who uses the dead for rituals."

I nodded, despite myself. I did know what a necromancer was, even if I wasn't ready to talk about it.

She continued, "There may be a booby trap, a spell inside him that might—"

At the word *spell*, I held up my hand. "Stop."

She waited while I tried to compose myself. It wasn't easy. My entire body quivered with each heartbeat.

Finally, I was able to muster enough righteous indignation to sputter, "Spell, huh? Now I know what's going on."

"I don't under—"

I grabbed the gurney from her with a violent jerk. "I know what you're doing," I said more firmly than I felt. "This is some sort of cruel joke and I'm not falling for it. I don't know how you found out about my problems, but it's not cool to poke at . . . sick people, okay?"

"I'm not—"

"Shut up," I snapped, which surprised even me. I wasn't usually in the habit of disrespecting the uniform, but she'd really pushed my buttons. "You are making fun of my illness, and I would appreciate it if you and your partner, Jones, or whatever his name was, would knock it off. I'm sure it's all over the department by now, but you can just let everyone know that I am perfectly fine these days and haven't seen a fairy in months."

"Actually, you just—"

"I don't want to know," I cut her off quickly, and put my hand up again. I wheeled the stretcher around and turned my back on her.

"Just don't crack the rib cage," Stone shouted.

Oh, like I could perform an autopsy any other way. "I'll take that under advisement," I said over my shoulder as the doors slammed behind me.

Once I could no longer hear the sound of footfalls in the hall, I leaned on the cart, breathing hard.

What I couldn't understand was how anyone had found out such specific details of my delusions. What the hell happened to doctor-patient confidentiality?

Oh, crap, the court case. Of course the police would have access to all my insane ramblings from Valentine's trial, when I tried to convince the world that his aggravated assault on my stepmother was justifiable because she was an evil demon who'd cast spells on me.

Not one of my finer moments.

With my luck, they probably had the court transcripts super-sized and posted on the bulletin board in the staff lounge for everyone's edification and amusement.

Fuck.

So much for starting over fresh.

I hugged myself and wished it was Valentine's arms around me. Which I supposed was a foolish thought, given that he was part of the problem. Or so all the doctors told me.

Why did I still miss him so much, I wondered.

Letting myself go, I blew out a steadying breath. Well, what did all those group therapy sessions teach me? One thing at a time.

I had a body to deal with. That was the first order of business. I took what comfort I could in the cold metal and simple, rough furnishings of the morgue. I moved one of the adjustable floor lamps off to the side and wheeled the body next to the mortician's table.

I stared at the sheet-covered corpse. The police file on his chest had his mug shot paper clipped to the outside, so I checked it out.

What had Stone said? He was supposed to be some kind of a necromancer? That was clearly a joke. The guy looked like a hippy Jesus. Hell, he'd even smiled pleasantly for the camera—not in a serial-killer creepy off-kilter way, either, just nicely, as if happy to oblige. Blond and Vikingesque, this necromancer of Stone's looked like half the guys I went to college with at the University of Minnesota.

Thumbing through the file also revealed that he was just under six foot and a hundred and ninety-odd pounds.

There was no way in hell I'd be able to move the body off the stretcher without help.

I looked around the empty space again.

Where *was* my assistant? I shook my head in frustration. I was going to fire her if she ever showed up for work.

Returning my attention to the dead man, I asked, "So, what's your story? Your *real* story?"

I thumbed through his file. There were a lot of reports of domestic squabbles. A woman with the same last name had briefly had some sort of restraining order against him. It wasn't just his wife or whoever that he liked to threaten, though: He seemed to love a good brawl. If there was a bar fight on any given night, it seemed my friend here had been pulled out of it and set to cool his heels in the city jail.

On paper, he seemed like a pretty bad guy: violent, destructive, and dangerous.

But I knew all about labels, and how they could stick to you, even when you didn't deserve them. Somewhere in a precinct in Chicago there was a file like this on Valentine. It only told half the story.

So what was the rest of this guy's?

My iPhone beeped. I fished it out of my pocket to see a text from someone named Boyd with a Pierre Police Department address informing me a preliminary report was ready for me to look at. I left the body where it was for a moment, and went over to my little office space to fire up my laptop. I opened the e-mail. This was what I needed.

Most cops are terrible writers, I've discovered. Grammar isn't always their strong suit. But this one had done a pretty good job of describing the scene. The officers had responded to a neighbor's complaint of weird noises—moaning and groaning. When the police arrived at the apartment building the sounds were still going strong. They knocked, but no one answered. The noise got stranger and louder, until the police fetched the super to open the door. They found the guy hunched over some kind of altar. The cop stopped short of using the words *black magic*, but he did describe an awful lot of disturbing figurines, candles, silver skulls, etc. Anyway, despite all the racket the guy had been making seconds ago, he was dead. A cup was found near his hand, the contents of which smelled of rat poison. The paramedic was called. The paramedic had declared it a suicide by poison.

All I had to do was confirm it.

I swiveled my chair around and gave the body an appraising look. *Rat poison, eh?* I could *do* this.

With my shoulders back in determination, I walked over to the gurney and pulled the cloth away from his face.

Yeah, he looked dead to me.

I wondered if I should presume the paramedic did all the classic tests? No breath, check; no pulse, got it. His eyes were glassy and empty. His skin was already taking on that grayish hue favored by corpses, though it hadn't yet settled into the "clammy" temperature range.

No doubt that was because he hadn't been dead very long.

I could tell right away that my job was going to be a lot harder than I was hoping. Rat poison's main ingredient is warfarin, which, among other horrible things, acts like a blood thinner. People who have accidentally ingested rat poison bruise easily and get bloody noses. I could see no trace of blood in the hairs of my corpse's mustache, but he might not have had time to develop one.

I pulled the sheet the rest of the way off, ready to look for more confirmation for the poison theory. It was almost impossible to tell if he had bruises because his body looked like someone's doodle pad. Very little of the ink made any sense, either. I thought I recognized Hebrew characters in a band around his left wrist, and the squiggles around his thigh might have been Arabic. Or Sanskrit. Or Greek, for all I knew.

There were a few pictures interspersed among the nonsense or foreign words—a nude female demon with bat wings over his heart, a human skull on his bicep, and, over his stomach, a devil doing rude things to a woman with his tail.

Okay, I was getting why Stone thought she could pull my leg with the whole black arts/necromancer thing. There were all the creepy artifacts found at the scene, and, while he might have Jesus' face, dude had Satan's tats.

Of course, he also seemed to be wearing Tweety Bird jammie bottoms, but that just added to the scary.

I was sure that the CSI team at the scene had taken pictures of his body, but I wanted my own documentation. Using my key, I unlocked the desk and found the giant analog camera used for documenting autopsies. After determining there was plenty of film still in it, I brought it over to the body. I adjusted the floor lamps to illuminate the body, and so I was surprised when the flash went off. "Dang it," I cursed under my breath.

As I was getting ready to move to take a close-up of the stomach art, I stopped. The letters on his wrist—had they shifted? Of course, what did I know from Hebrew, but I would have sworn it was different a moment ago.

I took another picture, forgetting about the stupid flash again. *Pop!*

Now I was sure the tats had moved. The rude devil was in a completely different position. The last pose had been plenty memorable; I didn't think I'd imagined it.

I rubbed my eyes. No time to start with this again.

Pushing down my rising blood pressure with effort, I

concentrated on taking slow, steady breaths. I needed to be rational, scientific. Scientists didn't believe in magic.

"Complicated relationships" aside, magic *wasn't* real.

Besides, I was safe here in my basement, far away from other people, distractions, and the world. If I thought I saw something, then I needed to prove it to myself.

So I fished my phone out of my pocket and took a picture. Nothing moved.

Either I *had* imagined it, which would be an enormous relief, or the phenomenon had been caused by the bright light. So I pressed the button on the analog camera to trigger the flash.

I compared the body to the image stored in my phone.

It *was* different.

I did that routine—flash, click, flash, click—about six more times.

When I flicked through the digital images the differences were clear. Some words had changed completely. The gross devil bucked and swayed. In one particularly disturbing picture, it seemed to wink at me.

Stepping back from the corpse, I looked around the room. I half hoped a troupe of cops would jump up and yell, "Surprise!"

You can't even imagine how disappointed I was when they didn't.

A shiver shook along my spine. The temperature in the basement space seemed to drop a degree or two.

I would have been a lot happier thinking that the shifting, changing tattoos were some kind of super-elaborate hoax to flummox the new girl. My finger slid through the photos again, marveling at the articulation of the rude devil and the changing facial expressions of his sexual partner.

Turning my phone off, I stuck it back in my pocket. I very carefully set the other camera on the mortician's table.

Things like this shouldn't happen.

Yet they always seemed to. To me, anyway.

Snapping the phone off, I shoved it resolutely into my pocket. I was going to pretend that none of this had just happened.

If I didn't, I'd have to admit Stone was right and this guy was magical.

I couldn't believe that.

Taking a deep breath, I closed my eyes. I'd just keep them shut for a moment and it would be a little "do-over." When I opened my eyes, I'd be a rational scientist again. I wouldn't be a scared girl totally willing to believe crazy Officer Stone's babbling about booby-trapped corpses.

That would be *crazy*, and I wasn't crazy. Not anymore.

Okay. Two more calm breaths and I'd be okay.

I opened my eyes.

The body still lay on the stretcher next to the mortician's table. He looked very dead, at least. The tattoos continued to stare at me, but I ignored them. Instead, I smiled again at the PJs.

Before trying to move him, I pulled up the corpse's lip. The gums were pink. With rat poisoning, they should have been white.

I was going to have to do a full autopsy, after all.

Which meant I was going to have to get the body onto the table . . . all 190 pounds of it.

I knew I should have stuck with that weight-lifting resolution Robert and I made last New Year.

It took me twenty minutes, but I managed, incrementally, to nudge his body onto the mortician's table. I was glad there was no one around to watch me grunt and swear. Sweating and straining, at least, made me feel normal, grounded. Work did that for me.

The crack of the ribs was an ominous sound. I'd been so absorbed in the autopsy that the sound startled me out of a deep concentration. There was no evidence of internal bleeding, which would have been consistent with rat poison. In fact, I was having trouble finding anything wrong with the guy, other than the fact that he was quite obviously dead.

This corpse was so healthy that he didn't even have any plaque buildup in his arteries. Frankly, that spooked me almost more than the shifty tattoos. Nobody was this healthy and dead. It was unnatural.

The contents of his stomach, which often told you a surprising amount about a person, their whereabouts and general habits, revealed a very mundane mixture of microwave popcorn and soda, brown—probably something like Coke or Pepsi. It seemed he'd died from a home movie night. I did take a sampling of the liquid to send to the lab to make sure there wasn't any rat poison in it, but that was looking less and less likely in my mind.

"What killed this guy?" I asked out loud, for the benefit of the tape recorder on the table. Maybe I'd actually have to look for some kind of brain aneurysm, though his pupils hadn't looked particularly dilated.

When my hand closed around his heart to check it for signs of trauma, something moved. Quite distinctly, I felt something slither along the back of my glove. I made a grab for it. I thought it might be a giant roundworm. It wouldn't be completely out of place as they hang out in the lungs during part of their lifecycle.

But, as gross as a giant roundworm is, it doesn't bite. Nor does it make a wailing hiss, like some kind of banshee from hell.

When sharp teeth penetrated glove and flesh, I screamed. I pulled my hand out with a jerk. When it hit the air a sound echoed through the warehouse morgue like rending metal.

A black snake gripped my hand between its jaws. The scaly reptile twisted and curled around itself, as I pulled thirty inches of it from the corpse's body. Its beady, black eyes fixed on me intelligently. Once free from the corpse, the snake entwined around my arm, almost like a python, squeezing.

I screamed continuously, bashing its head against whatever surface I could find. Instead of loosening its hold, every bang seemed to push the snake into my skin. It collapsed in on itself, flattening to become two-dimensional. Soon, a black-and-white picture of a snake formed tight circles from my wrist to my shoulder. The only thing that still appeared to be alive was the eye that gleamed maliciously just under the surface of my skin.

The sound of medical equipment hitting the floor with a clatter made me look up. The corpse sat up. I would have mistaken it for ill-timed rigor mortis, but his gaze was different. He looked straight at me, with eyes completely black and hard like the snake's. Despite his body, open and ruined by the autopsy, he spoke. The words were foreign and strange. I thought that somewhere in all the gibberish, I heard a name. He said it again, much more clearly: "Spenser Jones."

Swinging his feet off the gurney, he grabbed his liver from where I had left it in the scale. He scowled at the shreds of the PJs I'd had to cut away, but took the plastic bag I'd put them into.

The toe tag made a scraping sound as he walked out the door.

TWO

Instinct propelled me to the sink, where I attempted to wash off the snake. Peeling off the shredded remains of my glove, I scrubbed with surgical soap. I rubbed my arm with paper towels, frantic to remove the image.

The lidless eye glinted menacingly at me. Though unmoving, I could tell it was alive.

I screamed at it and poked it. Nothing worked.

In utter desperation, I grabbed a bottle of formaldehyde and splashed it right into the eye just below my pointer finger. "Die, you creepy fucking thing!"

The tattoo hissed. I felt a tightening, and saw the image wiggle on my skin. I didn't know if it was the shouting or the chemical that seemed to work, and so I squirted more of the liquid on it and continued to yell. "Take that, you evil bastard!"

My arm flailed around like some kind of isolated seizure or a bad comedy skit. I just kept swearing and squirting until the light went out in the snake's eyes. The tattoo faded so that it looked like I'd had it for years, but it didn't disappear entirely.

My knees buckled and I collapsed onto the floor, "Ohshit-ohshitohshitohshit!"

I cradled my arm against my chest. My eyes flicked from the empty gurney to the monochrome tattoo on my arm. I kept hoping one or the other would return to normal.

No luck.

This *couldn't* be happening again. I was supposed to be in a safe place, damn it.

I closed my eyes and concentrated on calming my breathing—a difficult feat considering how close to hyper-ventilating I was. I rocked back and forth until I stopped shaking. Fumbling in my pocket, I found my phone. I should've called my therapist.

Why was it, then, that my fingers automatically dialed Valentine's number, instead?

Was it because I needed the way he picked up on the first ring or the breathless sound of relief in his voice?

"Alexandra," he said, with that tiniest trace of a Russian accent that made the vowels of my name sound aristocratic, precious. "I've been waiting for your call."

"It's happening again." I whispered a choked sob into the receiver.

His response was exactly why I didn't call a psychologist. There was no hesitation, no question of my sanity.

"Are you in danger?"

"I don't know," I admitted, looking at the hideous black marks on my arm. "I mean, I don't think so—at least not at the moment. There was a dead guy . . . a necromancer, that, uh, just walked away."

"You were hit by a spell." It wasn't a question. Somehow, hundreds of miles away, Valentine *knew*.

I pulled the cell away from my ear and frowned at it. I could see his face in my mind with its hard, sharp lines and *that* look in his storm-colored eyes—the one that bordered on a fanatic sort of protectiveness, the one that often preceded . . . violence.

"I shouldn't have called," I said almost to myself.

"If there is magic, you need me there."

"Don't talk about magic, please." I whispered. Then my mind hit on the rest of what he'd said. "Wait. Are you saying you're coming—here?"

"Of course. If you call, I will always come."

Coming? Had I told him where I was? "Valentine, you can't come. I don't have a guest bedroom, and don't you remember all the trouble we got into last time we talked about spells and magic? It wasn't just trouble, either, it was really fucked-up." My voice bordered on a kind of desperate screech.

He laughed kindly. "Yes, I'd say. But I sense this time is different. At any rate, I'm already on my way," he said, full of calm reassurance.

Then air, like a hurricane wind, roared through the speaker.

I pulled the phone from my ear again when the sound became deafening. "What's all that noise? Valentine! What about the body? I mean, I'm kind of responsible for it, and it's wandering around town and no one is going to believe me . . . *again*. I can't take that. I can't." My fingers on the phone were turning white from the pressure with which I gripped it.

My phone . . .

I had pictures.

Proof.

I sat up so suddenly that I banged the top of my head on the bottom of the sink. He was right. This time *was* different: I had photographic evidence.

"It's okay," I said quickly. "I'm going to be okay. Never mind. You don't need to come. It's not magic. It's . . . it's . . . Well, I've got pictures at any rate. And, really, I'm not sure I'm ready to see you again and, uh, South Dakota really isn't your scene. Too quiet."

My voice trailed off when I realized he'd hung up some time ago.

Valentine was coming.

I wasn't sure how I felt about this. Part of me was excited, of course. This place had never felt like a home without him. Hell, I'd been missing him from the moment I'd left Chicago and run out on him while he was still serving time.

I hated leaving him in prison—without even a note of explanation. I'd changed my number and done all the things the psychologists told me I had to do in order to start over, but I felt like a heel.

Yet, he hadn't had an angry word for me. He said he'd been waiting for my call.

I'd tried to explain this to other people, but Valentine was different with me. Never once had his darker side ever spilled over onto me. The only time I ever saw his fierce nature was when he was protecting me.

My therapist, however, was going to be furious. For some reason, every mental health professional I ever dealt with hated Valentine. Their abhorrence increased if they met him, it seemed. All I ever heard was how much healthier I'd be without him. I was going to get an earful if I confessed to calling him.

Well, I'd deal with that later.

I rubbed my head where I'd bumped it. I took a deep, steadying breath and pulled myself up on shaky knees. Opening up the pictures, I reassured myself that they were still there.

There was always the possibility that the chief of police would look at my phone's images and tell me he only saw the same photo twelve times. He could look at my arm and see nothing.

But I couldn't get away from the fact I was going to have to explain the missing corpse. I could lie, I supposed, but whatever I said I'd end up in the same amount of trouble, possibly worse if I told a bad lie. Unfortunately, I had a lot of experience with that as well. If I was going to get fired or sent to the loony bin, I might as well get there honestly.

I straightened my apron and caressed the tattoo on my arm where it tingled uncomfortably under the lab coat. "Okay," I said out loud to help steel myself. "I can do this."

"Of course you can, dearie," said a muffled female voice somewhere in the room.

"Hello?" I looked at my phone, briefly thinking I must have butt-dialed a number by accident. Seeing that it was off, my next thought was of my assistant. However, a quick scan of the room showed me it was still empty. "Where are you?"

"Not sure myself. It's dark and cold."

The freezers. "Mrs. Finnegan?"

"Yes, hon?"

I rushed over to wrench open the drawer. I pulled it open, expecting to find Mrs. Finnegan miraculously recovered. Instead, she was still very much dead. Her lips were a deep shade of blue. I stared at her for a long time before working up the courage to poke her on the cheek. She didn't flinch. In fact, her skin was stiff and hard.

"I liked you better when you were quiet," I said to her unmoving form.

Thankfully, she had no response.

Even so, I waited several more minutes for signs of life before sliding her back into the freezer.

After, quite calmly, vomiting my breakfast into the stainless steel sink—pop tarts and cranberry juice redux—I washed my face. I scrubbed my cheeks and hands again, giving my new tattoo another rubdown to no avail. My skin was red, but the snake stayed firmly under it.

Stripping off my apron, I tugged my T-shirt over my hips. I picked up the tape recorder; it had been rolling this entire time. I rewound it. My finger hovered over the PLAY button, but I was afraid I'd hear only my own voice.

I clicked it on.

And turned it off instantly when I heard garbled hissing.

Bad batteries—or messed-up magical shit?

Either way, I decided it was better to focus on the immediate concern, the necromancer . . . or whatever he was.

Shoving the tape recorder into my pocket, I marched determinedly out the door, leaving behind what remained of the necromancer as evidence. I was comforted by the blood congealing on the table and the spatters in the scale where the liver had been.

Mrs. Finnegan's new conversational skills would be my little secret.

THREE

My resolve weakened as I climbed the concrete stairs from the basement to the main floor. Leaving behind the comfort of the morgue, I passed the office suite I'd ignored since the election. My predecessor had procured a fancy section of the first floor. There were gilt letters on the glass door. It belonged to a career politician—someone confident, unafraid, and powerful. I felt none of those things, especially not while clutching my phone like a talisman to ward off danger and insanity.

The higher I rose, the more cops I saw.

Police stations made me nervous. I avoided the cops' curious glances as I threaded my way through their desks. In no time, I found myself standing in front of the chief's office door.

Everybody knew Chief Stan Krupski because he was an avid fisherman and a collector of classic cars. He was a politician's politician—handsome and charismatic. People told me he was a pretty good cop, even though he and my pre-decessor had conspired to make their lives more comfortable. I knew he didn't like me much. He'd called me a blue-haired freak when we first met, but I figured it was still my duty to inform him that there was a corpse wandering around town. In case, I don't know, they needed to put out an APB for a gutted guy carrying his liver.

Okay. Keep the nervous laughter to a minimum, Alex. That was going to be the hard part: telling.

I had trust issues with the truth.

Sensing me hovering nervously on the threshold of his office, the chief looked up. Stan was in his forties, but still looked boyish. If it wasn't for the salt in his pepper hair, he could pass for a guy half his age, easy. The only thing wrong with him as far as I was concerned was his fondness for Texas-style gigantic belt buckles. I found them disconcert-ing because they drew my eye to his crotch. Of course, he stood up to usher me inside. I focused on his face, which was currently smiling, but I could see it falter around the edges.

"Something wrong, Connor?"

"You could say so, sir." I didn't know him well enough to call him by his first name, and was not nearly cool enough to get away with "Chief." Technically, he was my colleague, not my boss, since he worked for the city and I for the county. I shouldn't be deferring to him, but I didn't know who else to go to with something like this.

He leaned over and shut the door, before propelling me into one of the uncomfortable chairs he kept in front of his desk. "You'd better tell me what's going on," he said.

I gaped for a moment as I tried to decide how to broach the subject. How did you explain something like this with-out sounding insane?

A little laugh escaped before I could stifle it. If I knew how to talk about magical goings-on without sounding insane, I would never have spent time in a locked psych ward and Valentine wouldn't have gone to prison.

I opted for just blurting out the truth. "The corpse is gone. He got up and walked out. With his liver."

Stan leaned against the edge of his desk, so I couldn't help but blink stupidly at the gaudy silver buckle. Seriously? A steer's head? At least it wasn't a skull. I couldn't take anything vaguely spooky right now. I gripped the edges of the seat, like I was trying to literally hold on to reality.

His arms crossed in front of his chest as he waited for me to say more. "You misplaced a corpse? Are you talking about Mrs. Finnegan?"

"No," I said, dragging my eyes away from the steer horns. "I should start at the beginning. Uh, you know Stone and Jones, right?"

I was relieved to see him nod. I never knew at what point in the story people would stop believing me.

"Okay, well, they brought this body in, some guy they said was . . ." I couldn't say "necromancer," it was just too weird. ". . . dead."

God, of course he was dead, Alex. You're the damn coroner! I looked up at the chief nervously, but he just nodded encouragingly.

"Anyway, I was in the middle of the autopsy when . . . something happened."

When I found I couldn't say more, he prompted: "Something?"

I nodded mutely.

"What?" he asked. The chief was watching me carefully, waiting for the rest.

Crazy shit, I thought, but couldn't quite bring myself to say.

Yet this was the moment, wasn't it? I had to say something.

I held up my arm to show the snake. "Do you see this?"

Again, the nod came.

"Okay. This was in his chest cavity, only three-dimensional and squirming, but somehow it's on me now. At least it's not alive anymore. I think."

"Uh-huh. Jones, you said?"

Was the chief about to tell me this was all a joke and that Jones was known for pulling off real kickers? My throat was dry and scratchy. "Uh, yeah, he and Stone brought the body in."

"Stone. Right."

Oh no. I'd heard the skeptical tone in Stan's acknowledgment far too many times before. "Is there some kind of problem with them?" I asked far too quickly.

But he'd turned his back to me already. He was walking behind his desk and pulling out a notepad.

Even as I watched him scribble something down, I was trying to make myself believed. "You know, I have pictures," I said, pulling my phone out. "Those tattoos on the body were definitely not normal."

Stan looked up at me then, but didn't say a word. He just reached his hand across his desk, offering me the note he'd written.

I took it. "What's this?" I asked.

"I want you to talk to these people. They can help."

Oh great, more psychologists. I didn't need that. "I already have a therapist."

"These aren't shrinks," the chief said. "They can *really* help."

I felt miserable. I didn't want any more help; I wanted all this to be normal and okay. "I swear this is true this time."

Stan shocked me by saying, "It's not that. I believe you. It's out of my jurisdiction is all."

He believed me? "Oh."

I looked down at the note. He'd written an address and the words *Precinct 13*.

I wandered out into the melting snow of the capitol grounds in a daze. I used my cell to call the courier service to come pick up the lab work I'd done on my AWOL patient, and nearly told the receptionist I loved her, I was so happy.

Coming to South Dakota hadn't been a mistake; things *were* different. Someone believed me. Or at least pretended to. I supposed Precinct 13 could be code for "the guys with little white coats" that would take me to the padded room, but the chief had shaken my hand pleasantly and wished me good luck. That didn't seem like the actions of a guy setting me up. I decided to remain cautiously optimistic.

Even though it was mid-April, spring was returning slowly to Pierre. Patches of snow still covered the lawn in front of the capitol building. Meanwhile, the branches of the tall maples had begun to green with buds. I walked along the sidewalk that led along the riverfront. Whitecaps flashed on the Missouri, which had swelled with snowmelt.

I pulled the collar of my coat up against my ears to ward off the chill. The pavement was wet with slush, and the sky was gray and heavily overcast. A group of life-sized bronze soldiers saluted me from where they stood on a wooden dock. Seagulls circled overhead.

My foot slipped, but I managed to catch myself before I stumbled. I looked down, expecting a patch of stubborn ice, but found a cardboard rectangle. Picking it up, I recognized it instantly as the necromancer's toe tag. He'd come this way!

Though I knew it was probably useless, I looked around for other signs of his passage. Hardly anyone was outside. I could see someone sitting on a wooden park bench closer to the capitol, but otherwise I was alone. Clutching the toe tag in my hand, I headed that way. As I drew closer, I could see that the person was an older woman and probably homeless, given the matted state of the gray hair that frizzled out from under a knit hat. She wore an oversized parka that had been patched in places with silver duct tape. A large army pack sat beside her. Though I was less than a foot behind her, I hesitated, especially since I could hear her muttering to herself about the government and space aliens.

I turned away. Shoving the toe tag into my coat pocket, I continued toward the address on the slip.

Even if the old lady *had* any information, I wasn't prepared to do anything with it. Let's say I had caught up with the reanimated corpse; then what? I wasn't even sure what a person did when confronting a naked dead guy. This was the sort of thing I desperately hoped that the people at Precinct 13 specialized in. Best to let the experts deal with it.

It didn't take me long to find the address.

I'd walked as far as downtown. It was about three blocks up from the waterfront. The trees had disappeared as I left behind the river. Many of the buildings were box stores, unadorned concrete with big, asphalt parking lots around them. For a Chicago girl like me, the squat buildings spaced so far apart were disconcerting, as if I were exposed in all the emptiness.

The address directed me to a group of buildings that had a more old-fashioned, frontier-town look. Built of red brick with white stone trim around the windows, they were two stories tall. On the side of one, paint peeled off an advertisement for Coca-Cola featuring a woman with a 1940s hairdo. I stopped in front of the street number that matched the one on my slip of paper.

Considering I walked from the station house, I couldn't quite see how this was a new "jurisdiction," as the chief implied. In fact, the place to which he'd directed me appeared to be an empty storefront. A dusty film covered the windows, and an OPENING SOON sign was propped against the sill. I double-checked the address. This was supposed to be the place. Despite my better judgment, I knocked. The head of the snake was just visible peering out from under the cuff of my coat sleeve.

Cupping my hand, I peered into the storefront. No one seemed to be around, but it looked as though someone were renovating the place. There was an ancient, paint-spattered boom box stereo plugged into an outlet, and one of those massive floor polishers propped up against a wall.

My earlier euphoria began to drain. Maybe the chief *was* just being polite and was giving the crazy girl somewhere to go while he called in the city council or whatever it took to fire me. What if, when I went back, there really *were* men in white coats waiting for me?

I shook my head. *Thinking like that is real paranoia, Alex. Don't go there. Not yet.*

"Hello?" I said to the door, knocking again. "The chief sent me!" I plastered the slip of paper up against the glass door as proof, even though there was no one to see it.

I nearly jumped when I heard the sound of sleigh bells as the door opened. "You must be looking for Precinct Thirteen."

With the whole "precinct" part, I expected a cop. The guy who answered the door looked more like a—well, like he could be a friend of mine.

He wore mostly Goth gear: a lot of black on black. Underneath his leather jacket, his T-shirt . . . glowed. It looked like the icon on my laptop that showed how many bars my Wi-Fi connection had. Plus, he'd accessorized with a multicolored striped scarf that was completely oversized on his slender frame, which reminded me of old-school Dr. Who. So what did that make him? Gothy geek? Nerdy Goth?

His hair was short and either badly slept in or a carefully stylized mess. He was pretty enough that it could have been the latter, but the earrings and the nose ring made me lean toward the former.

"I'm Jack," he said. "You must be Alice."

"Alex," I corrected.

"I was making a literary reference," he said with a sniff and a London accent. He stepped aside to let me in. "Because, *Alex*, you're about to enter Wonderland."

I stepped over the threshold. The coil of the tattoo tightened slightly, squeezing my arm painfully.

The interior transformed completely. Gone was the empty, half-painted space; people bustled everywhere. There were cops in uniform, detectives with gold badges on their hips, and people dressed in street clothes.

The scene was reminiscent of an old-fashioned newsroom. Desks were scattered throughout the room; some had actual typewriters, others modern computers. Books were piled everywhere, like a library had exploded—a really old library. As Jack led me to the center of the room, I realized that many of the books had vellum or leather covers, gilt lettering, and . . . runes?

Every desk had a potted plant, a bouquet of fresh flowers, or a mini fishbowl on it; I'd never seen such a green office space. A row of flat-screen TVs lined one wall. They showed several different channels, including some foreign ones and a video feed to the front of the shop where I'd been standing.

"What *is* this place?" I asked.

"It's the situation room in the war against the unnatural," he said dramatically.

"There's a lot of that in South Dakota?" There were a lot of other things I probably should have asked first, but, honestly, it just sort of slipped out.

"South Dakota. South Hampton. South Wales." Jack shrugged a delicate shoulder. "The unnatural is everywhere. Anyway, you're the one knocking at our door. What do *you* think?"

He had a point there. I smiled. "I think it's a pretty neat trick what you did with the storefront. How did you get it to look abandoned?"

"Magic," he said simply.

My breath caught. I'd hoped he'd go into some kind of elaborate explanation of the holographic technology involved, not suggesting in such a laid-back way that he'd . . .

I stumbled a bit when my knees weakened. I had to catch myself on the nearest desk.

"What?" I asked, gulping for air. "What did you just say?"

He stared intently into my face as I slowly pulled myself upright and tried to get my breathing back under control.

"Are you sure you're in the right place, miss?" His voice took on a sudden formality, and he looked around the busy office space nervously, as if searching for help.

With shaking hands, I pulled out the chief's note again. I read off the address carefully.

"Right. That's us," Jack said, his gaze continuing to skim through the room hopefully. Not finding any relief, he shifted back to me, grimacing at the awkwardness. "You, uh, do understand what it is we do here, don't you?"

"No," I admitted.

"I see," he said, clearly not comfortable being the one to have to explain it to me. "Um, well, you were sent here for a reason, right? Something unnatural must have happened."

I liked the solid, normal sound to the word *unnatural*. My face brightened. "Yes," I said. "A couple of uniformed officers brought me this body this morning and the corpse, well, he—"

"Oh, I see! You're the coroner? Brilliant! Spense will want to hear all about whatever happened. Come on, I'll introduce you."

He brought me over to where a group of people stood looking down at a map spread out at a table. "Alex, this is—"

"Hey, I know you!" I interrupted, recognizing the police officer who'd brought the necromancer into the morgue. "And you!" I said to his stony partner.

"—Spenser Jones and Hannah Stone," Jack continued.

The moment he saw me, Officer Jones's face crumbled into a frown. "This isn't good." He turned to his partner. "You did *tell* her, didn't you?"

"I did," she said very cautiously, not looking at me. "You

know it can be very difficult for me to explain these sorts of things to humans."

Humans?

"You warned her about the rib cage, though, right?" Jones barked at his partner.

"Yeah," I interrupted. "How *did* you know about that?"

"Spense can smell a spell a mile away; it's in his blood, you see," Jack said. He was watching the two officers with the expression of a gleeful spectator.

With effort, I held back another choke at the word *spell*. Sweat prickled under my arms. In my heavy coat, the room felt stuffy and hot. Gripping the back of the office chair in front of me, I looked down at the beady, black eye of the snake on the back of my hand. "So, uh, anyway," I said, my eyes still glued to the snake. "Thing is," I continued. "That body you brought in, the necromancer? Well, he got up and walked away."

I looked up when Jones swore under his breath. His fist crumpled the edge of the map he'd been consulting.

His partner seemed surprised by his reaction. "We should have expected something like this. This is why we need a magically aware person in the coroner's office. I've been saying that for years."

"There isn't a huge pool to choose from, is there?" Jones snorted. "This is just great." With effort, he released his death grip on the paper. Smoothing it out, he looked at me. "He walked out? Are you saying the necromancer is still alive?"

"I was halfway through the autopsy. His liver was in the scale. I don't know how he could be."

"Well, then, how did he walk out?" Jones pursued.

Holding back a hysterical giggle with effort, I offered lamely, "Through the door?"

Jones failed to see the humor. "I meant, by what magic?"

I swallowed hard.

Stone put a hand on her partner's elbow, as if holding him back. In reality, he hadn't moved any closer to me, but I cowered as if he loomed over me. "I don't think she knows, Spense," she said calmly.

"Right," he said, letting out an exasperated breath. "You'd better start at the beginning."

He gestured for me to take a seat. Fishing into his pocket, he pulled out the kind of notebook detectives always had in the movies. He stole a pen from the cup on the desk. "Tell us what happened."

Jack started to park his butt on the edge of a nearby desk, as though intending to settle in to listen to my story. Officer Jones gave him a sharp look. "Why don't you fetch our guest a cup of coffee, Jack?"

Jack's crinkled nose clearly said "why don't you do it yourself," but his mouth managed a very terse, "Certainly. Do you take milk or sugar, miss?"

I smiled at the incongruous image of this nose-ringed, leather-jacketed, scruffy man playing butler. My stomach growled at the thought of coffee, but the back of my throat still burned from my recent bout of nausea. From an industrial coffeemaker in the corner of the room wafted the aroma of stale, burnt coffee, so I waved away the offer. "I'm fine, thanks."

"At least let me take your coat," Jack offered, still playing Goth butler.

Considering how much I'd been sweating with all this talk about magic, I happily agreed.

He stood up and held out a hand, like a gentleman.

I shrugged out of my coat. When I gave it to him, our

fingers brushed. My tattoo squeezed sharply. I gasped and broke contact. My skin buzzed angrily, and I cradled it to my chest gingerly. Jack jumped back, just as startled. The coat fell to the floor in a heap.

"Bloody hell!" Jack shook his hand out like he'd been zapped by a joy buzzer hidden in my palm. Then his eyes zeroed in on the tattooed arm I had pressed against my chest protectively. He pointed with his uninjured hand. "What's that?"

FOUR

All eyes focused like lasers on the snake tattoo on my arm.
None of them seemed to approve. In fact, Officer Jones
seemed disgusted to the point of hostility. His fingers strayed
to his gun.

Was he going to shoot me for having an ugly tattoo?

Stone backed up a step. It was less a gesture of fear than
one making ready for a fight.

In fact, the entire office hushed. All eyes turned toward
me and I heard whispers of, "Maleficium."

"Is that what I think it is? What's your game?" Jack
demanded, moving in closer, as if protecting his colleagues
from me. "This is natural space. You trigger any kind of
maleficium in here, you're going down."

"What? Trigger 'mal'—what? Do you mean this?" But
when I raised my arm to show them the snake, Jack's hands
went out protectively in front of Jones and Stone.

Jack pulled something from the inner pocket of his leather

jacket. I half expected a gun, but instead it was one of those whip-thin, segmented car antennas. He pointed it at me menacingly, the button tip waving from the sudden movement.

People around the office ducked behind desks or took up other defensive postures.

It was like I had a bomb strapped to my chest, not just a butt-ugly tattoo around my arm.

Meanwhile, Jack began tracing a series of lines and circles in the air with his car antenna. Underneath his leather jacket, the Wi-Fi indicator on his T-shirt pulsated brightly.

My skin itched under the tattoo.

"What's going on?" I asked, my eyes frantically searching for a sane answer to this sudden, bizarre turn of events.

"You don't know?" Jack paused in the middle of his fourth downward swipe. He shook his head, as if he'd lost track of something. "Bollocks. Do you know how hard it is to spell in binary? Now I'm going to have to start over."

"Start what over?" I was so confused that I was on the verge of weeping from frustration.

Jack must have seen the tears I held back glistening at the corners of my eyes. He dropped the point of the antenna, and frowned into my face, "Are you serious? You have no idea what's happening?"

"No," I said. "You're all acting like I'm the mad tattooed bomber, and I don't know why, especially since I had nothing to do with this stupid snake on my arm. One minute, I was doing a normal autopsy like a regular, sane person, and the next this . . . this . . . thing jumps out from behind the heart and now it's on my arm." I looked to where Officer Jones glared at me from behind Jack's shoulder. "You should understand," I said to Jones. Turning to Stone, I added, "You, too. You're the ones who brought him to me."

"Who?" Jones asked.

"The body! The necromancer, of course!" I yelled.

"The necromancer," Officer Jones said slowly, his brows still knit tightly, as if he was trying to unravel a particularly difficult puzzle. "You're saying this spell isn't yours? That it came out of the necromancer?"

Spell?

Not *that* again.

"Can we please have a conversation that doesn't use the word 'spell'?" I asked.

"Not until you explain that," Jones said, pointing to my arm.

Explain it? How could I?

Slowly, so as not to alarm anyone, I lifted my arm to inspect the ink. I tried to see what it was that had armed police officers cowering behind their desks. The snake's eye stared back at me with a kind of dark, unblinking intelligence. I had to admit that, if I were looking at this several months ago, I'd have had no trouble believing it was an evil spell.

All around the room, people held their breath. A blond woman crouching behind her chair watched me with wide eyes and her hand clasped over her mouth, as if holding back the urge to scream. Were they all afraid of the tattoo because they thought it held some kind of magic? Magic that I was assured by many doctors wasn't *supposed* to be real?

The two uniformed cops and Jack waited for my response to their question. I didn't have an answer I felt comfortable giving. I had no experience with people asking me the details of my delusions and treating them as though they were real or important.

Finally, I said, "I don't really know anything about all

this. I mean, I really, really don't like to think about this too hard, but this thing on my arm started out three-dimensional and came out of the corpse sort of"—what was that word Jack had used?—"unnaturally. Like, as an attack snake."

When everyone continued to look at me as if they expected me to explode, I finally gave an exasperated sigh. "Believe me, I don't like this any more than you do. I mean, look at it! This thing is like some kind of prison tattoo on steroids, for crying out loud. Do I look this hard core? Seriously? The only ink I have is a tramp stamp of a butterfly I got when I was too stupid to know better. It's pink for fucksake."

Jack's tight expression melted into a smile at my words. His eyebrow quirked as if to ask: "A tramp stamp? Really?" Lifting his car antenna again, Jack placed the flat of his palm on the button tip. With a deft movement, he collapsed it between his hands. He stowed it back into its spot inside his jacket. The Wi-Fi icon on his T-shirt dimmed to two bars.

As if following Jack's cue, the others began to relax a little as well. Officer Jones's fingers left his holster. Stone dropped her shoulders, too. People around the office let out their breath. A few cautiously stood up, though no one went back to work yet. The office remained hushed, though the timbre changed from fearful to curious. The only voices were muted ones coming from the reports or whatever streamed on the video screens.

"You say the snake came out of the necromancer?" Jack asked again. When I nodded, he shook his head. "I don't understand how it ended up on you. If it was protecting him, it's done a piss poor job of it. I mean, that is"—he ran a hand through his mess of hair and gave me a half-apologetic, half-thoughtful grimace—"since you're still alive and all."

"You sound disappointed," I noted, unable to keep from smiling at him.

"It's not that," he assured me quickly with a bright, disarming smile of his own. He shoved his hands into the pockets of his jeans. "It's just very unusual that, well, it seems to have transferred its loyalty to a . . . uh, that is, someone nonmagical."

"Or, woefully unschooled," Jones muttered.

Jack started at that comment, and shifted his attention to Jones. I followed his gaze, and gasped in surprise. For a brief second, I thought Jones's eyes glowed bright green with an inner light. At my sound, he blinked and the brightness instantly faded.

I took a step back, and nearly collided with a nearby desk. I shook my head, as if denying what I'd just seen. *No glowing eyes*, I admonished myself. All the rest of this stuff, sure. But no glowing eyes. That was too much like what got me in trouble back in Chicago.

I tried to refocus the conversation on something, anything else. "You said something about loyalty?" I asked Jack. "You make it sound as though this tattoo is alive," I said, trying to keep myself, unsuccessfully, from looking into the tattoo's glittering eye again.

"You should let me look at that." Stone came out from behind the desk she'd put between us, and held out her hand. I pulled the sleeve of my T-shirt over my shoulder to let her see all the damage.

She took my wrist without hesitation. I nearly jerked away, expecting another painful response from the snake, like what had happened at Jack's touch, but it didn't come. Her hand on my skin was cool, but solid.

The tension I'd carried in my shoulders drained at her

touch. It was like she grounded me. I sank back against the edge of the desk that had nearly tripped me, letting my butt rest against it.

"It's very attached to her," she told Jones, letting go of my arm. My arm flopped at her release. I blinked, shaking off the uber-calm her touch had inflicted.

Officer Jones's hands hooked on his belt. "You're sure?"

"I'd tell you to test it for yourself," Stone said, "but considering what it did to Jack, it would probably knock you out."

"I don't get it." Jones crossed his arms in front of his chest. The stiff fabric of his uniform bunched up and caused his silver badge to reflect the fluorescent light. "How could the spell attach so easily to an *ordinarius*?" He looked like so many police officers I'd seen in my life, standing there; it was getting harder and harder for me to cope with the fact that everyone seemed to be talking about magic like it was real.

Finding a nearby chair, I swung it around. I let myself drop into it. "It would be really awesome if someone would tell me what the hell is going on. Or at least, you know, tell me that I'm not going crazy. Again. More."

Surprisingly, it was Officer Jones who spoke first. His voice was still as gruff and abrupt as ever, but the certainty in his tone was reassuring. "You're not crazy. Something very weird is going on here."

I shut my eyes and let his words wash over me. *Not crazy.* I liked the sound of that.

I was just about to let out a sigh of relief when he added, "Something went wrong with that spell, at the very least it should have knocked you out. That's what I was expecting when I smelled it on him. I can't understand how you countered it."

Squeezing my eyes tighter, I tilted my head until it rested against the back of the chair. A perfectly sane police officer did *not* just suggest that he knew that there would be some kind of magical booby trap inside that corpse. I should count to ten. Maybe when I opened my eyes again, I'd be sitting in the middle of an empty store.

One . . . two . . .

"I said we should have tried to defuse the protection spell before we handed it over to an unprotected human. What if it had been set to kill?"

That must be Stone with her weird use of "human." I'd lost count. Better start over with one . . . Okay, breathe slowly.

One . . .

"She clearly took care of herself."

Two . . .

"I'm not sure that's Hannah's point, Spense," Jack said. "You kind of took a big risk with someone who is completely helpless."

"Is she, though?"

Through my closed eyes, I sensed a shadow looming over me. I opened them in time to see Jones stepping closer to me. He knelt down, looking at where my arm was cradled in my lap. He inspected the snake as closely as he could without touching. At his nearness, the snake buzzed angrily. Jones seemed to sense the hostility and rocked back on his heels, putting a bit more distance between himself and the tattoo. He looked up into my face, and seemed to study me, as if for the first time.

"You're *not* an *ordinarius*, are you? You're not normal."

Wow. A stab right to the heart of my greatest fears. "What's that supposed to mean?"

Jones squinted at me in that penetratingly suspicious way cops had that always made me feel guilty of something, even when I wasn't. "Are you magic?" he asked.

"No," I said quickly and perhaps a bit too loudly. I looked him hard in the eyes, and repeated myself very clearly, and as calmly as I could, "I am definitely not."

"All right. Was someone else there when this happened?" Stone asked.

I shook my head.

Jones continued to scrutinize me, as if he didn't believe me in the slightest. This close, the overhead lights reflected the amber highlights in his green irises. They flashed, almost glowing, and I tried desperately not to notice.

"Someone must have countered the spell," Jones insisted. "Did anyone intervene or interrupt you in any way? Did you hear a curse?"

"Curse? You mean like swearing? I was defiantly swearing up a blue streak," I said with a little, slightly hysterical laugh.

"Someone *besides* you," Jones insisted, his tone clearly chiding me for not taking all this seriously.

I cleared my throat. "I was alone. I mean, I was the only living person in the room. Mrs. Finnegan didn't start talking until later."

"Who's Mrs. Finnegan?" Jack wanted to know.

"Ruby Finnegan," Officer Jones supplied over his shoulder. "She's been in the morgue waiting for a transfer to wherever her family has their plot."

"Minnesota," I said absently.

"Was she one of ours?" Jack asked.

Jones shook his head. "I'm surprised she had anything to say. She was Lutheran. They normally stay dead."

"I think she was still dead," I said, remembering her glassy eyes. "She was just talking while dead."

"What did she say, exactly?" Jones asked; he sought my eyes again and seemed to be searching for something. "Think very carefully."

"I'm not likely to forget the details of this morning. It was kind of out of the ordinary."

"Was it?" Jones insisted, like I was intentionally leaving something out.

"Yes," I continued to insist, but it was getting much harder.

"I think maybe you've seen this sort of thing before," Stone said quietly from where she stood to my right. "You shouted at me about something from your past, remember?"

With Jack to my left, Stone on my right, and Jones far too close in front of me, I was starting to feel surrounded.

"My past is off-limits," I snapped at her. My fists scrunched so hard that my fingernails cut into my palm.

"Not if it has to do with magic," Jones said. "Then you'd better tell us all about it."

No way.

"I can't," I struggled to say, my throat tightening. "I'm not supposed to talk about any of that."

"Not supposed to?" Jack looked at the two cops and then to me. "Who told you that you couldn't talk about magic?"

I glared at him. Was he serious? I practically shouted, "Everyone! In case you haven't noticed, spells and necromancer and glowing eyes are not part of normal conversation."

"They are around here," Jack assured me with a patient smile.

Stone nodded encouragingly. "You can tell us. We'll understand. Magic is our job."

Even Jones seemed to have a sympathetic look in his eye. "Please. This is important."

That broke me.

For the second time that day, I told the truth, and, for the first time in a long, long time, I told all of it.

FIVE

The two cops and Jack patiently listened to the whole story. Jack settled into his perch on the nearby desk, and Officer Jones pulled in another chair and resumed taking notes. At some point, Stone fetched me a cup of slightly burnt, industrial coffee and a cookie. The cookie was surprisingly delicious. However, it was the first thing I'd eaten since throwing up, so I probably would have thought cardboard tasted good.

"He mentioned me specifically?" Jones asked.

Around a mouthful of cookie, I said, "Yes. I mean, unless there's another Spenser Jones in town?"

Jones shook his head.

"It's not all that surprising, is it, Spense?" Jack asked. "You are the head magic copper, after all."

"You're bound to be targeted," Stone agreed.

"I'd like to hear exactly what he said," Jones insisted. "Do you still have the tape recorder? The pictures?"

"Oh," I said. Standing up, I emptied my pockets onto the desk. Jones and Stone huddled together flipping through the pictures on my phone. Jack immediately reached for the toe tag.

"You've got good instincts," he said with a bright smile, as he held up the tag. "This might be the big break we've been looking for."

"The toe tag?"

But he didn't answer me, as he was calling over another uniformed cop. If life were a TV show, the cop who approached us would have been typecast as "rookie." His ginger hair was cut in a style last popular in 1952. He even had freckles across the bridge of his nose. "This is Boyd, he's our psychometrist."

I felt like I'd heard that name before.

"Nice to meet you, ma'am," he said, with a nod.

Jack explained, "Psychometry is the ability to read impressions from objects. Since this fell off the necromancer after he awoke, we might be able to get a sense of where he was going or his plans."

Boyd took the tag. I expected him to say something profound the instant he touched it, but instead he said, "I've got a bunch of stuff in front of this, but I should have results for you by morning meeting."

"Brilliant," said Jack. He raised a hand to slap Boyd on the back, but stopped short. "Uh, thanks." As Boyd moved back to a desk filled with an odd assortment of objects, including the wheel from a mountain bike, Jack leaned into me and said quietly, "Not big on touching, that one."

I imagined not. Did he get impressions from everyone and everything he touched? It must be overwhelming.

Officer Jones muscled between Jack and me to hand me

back my phone. Jack flashed him an irritated look before moving aside. To me, Jones said, "I wish you'd gotten more shots of the words. They may be other spells. Something that might be able to help us understand that thing." He pointed, without touching, to the snake coiled around my arm.

"Forensics may have better pictures," I offered. It still seemed very strange to be talking so casually about all this stuff and not having a psychologist taking notes. "I wasn't expecting this to be important. I mean, beyond the whole 'look, I'm not crazy' thing."

Officer Jones nodded distractedly. He was looking at my arm. He noticed I'd caught him staring and his jaw twitched. He glared back defiantly, as if challenging me to call him out on something. When I didn't, he turned to Jack and jerked his chin in my direction. "What about that thing? Any ideas what stopped it?"

"No," Jack said. "We still don't even know why it didn't kill her."

"It wouldn't have killed her," he muttered.

"I don't know how you could be so sure," Jack said.

Jones laid a finger beside his nose. "What's important is how it ended up on her."

They both looked at me.

I shrugged, and sat back down. I looked at the crumbs on the paper napkin, wishing I could ask for another cookie. "Like I told you before, I tried to wash it off, but that didn't work so I dumped some formaldehyde on it."

"That makes no sense," Jones said. "Chemicals shouldn't have bothered it."

"Formaldehyde is used in preserving the dead," Stone offered. "Perhaps . . ."

Jack interrupted. "Before, you said you were swearing. Did *you* curse it?"

"I . . . Maybe? I was a bit freaked out. I might have called it an evil bastard or something."

"A hex," Jack said to his colleagues as if he'd just explained everything. "She's a natural."

"A natural what?" I asked.

"Not a natural what, just a natural. Or maybe you've heard the term 'switch'?" Jack asked.

With his British accent, I wasn't sure I heard him correctly. "Witch?"

"Switch," he repeated, more slowly. "Like the thing you flip to turn on a light."

He mimed with his finger wagging up and down.

"You think I'm a light switch?"

"No, a magical one," he said.

Both Jones and Stone were standing over me, watching the conversation with interest. I looked to them for further explanation. "What's he talking about?"

"A switch is someone who, in the presence of magic, is able to utilize it. It's like magic makes them 'turn on' their own abilities," Jones said. "They can also act like a circuit breaker to enhance the flow of magic, by letting it pass through themselves, or they can, with practice, learn to shut it down, close it off." To Jack, Jones asked, "But are you sure? I never smelled even a whiff of *sensibilitatem* on her."

I fidgeted under their scrutiny, playing with the rim of the disposable coffee cup. I was beginning to think anytime someone started using Latin-sounding words, something I didn't want to know was about to be revealed.

"If she stopped that booby trap with a casual curse, she

might be more than a switch," Jack insisted. "She could be a witch."

Jones frowned sharply. "A witch? If she's a witch, where's the familiar?"

"I don't know," Jack said. "But this was more than some augment gone haywire. Curses are witch purview."

The two men seemed like they might argue over my head for a long time, so I raised my hand, like a kid in class. They stopped and looked down at me.

"Yes?" Jones snapped.

"I already explained this, I can't be magical," I said, setting the still-full coffee cup on the desk. The acrid smell of it threatened to turn my stomach again.

Jones put his hands on his hips and looked smugly at Jack, as if to say: "See."

"Well, why the hell not?" Jack asked me.

"Why not? Well—well, because."

"Because why?" he pushed.

"Because I take very expensive medication not to be, okay?" I snapped, a flood of shame brightening my cheeks.

"Oh." Jack's voice was small, confused, but he seemed unwilling to let my confession stop the conversation. "Okay. Well. Still? Because that could be why Spense can't smell your magic."

"Of course still," I said. "You're very strictly advised not to randomly stop taking the pills just because you feel better." I didn't want to look at any of them. I hated admitting this part of my life, my little "break."

I was always one of those kids who got labeled with an "overactive imagination" because I always thought I saw trolls under bridges, fairies in the garden, gargoyles on the rooftops, and all those fanciful things.

Things started to get rough when my mother died and my father remarried. I was sixteen, going through puberty, still so caught up in grief, and along came this other woman my father loved, it seemed sometimes, more than me.

My father had always tolerated my silliness before. Gayle, the stepmonster, as I came to think of her, convinced everyone that my imagination was a product of hallucinations and pathology. Next came a parade of diagnoses: delusional, bipolar, and schizoaffective disorders . . . even, briefly, schizophrenia. There were drugs, combinations, therapies, and stints in and out of hospitals.

Somehow I survived long enough to graduate high school.

I learned to ignore what I saw and to never, ever talk about it. There were several years that things were mostly okay. I went off to college, even got accepted into medical school. I met Valentine and he made my magic feel like a gift, rather than a curse.

Unfortunately, on a trip home to "meet the folks," I convinced myself that my stepmom was more than just a pain in the butt, but an actual demon from hell. I flushed at the memory. God, what a fairy-tale cliché! You'd think my subconscious could have been cleverer. The worst part was that I talked Valentine into helping me "exorcise" her. He ended up serving eighteen months for aggravated assault. I spent nearly the same amount of time in a locked psych ward.

Jones was watching me with that penetrating gaze again, so I feigned interest in a developing hole in the knee of my jeans in order to break eye contact. "Magic," I continued, my voice a hoarse whisper and my eyes averted, "isn't real. Only crazy people believe in magic. All that stuff I thought I saw, that was my own imagination, paranoia."

"I smell them now," Officer Jones said sadly. "Antipsychotics."

Stone muttered, "Such a tragedy." Her hand covered my shoulder long enough to give me a gentle, sympathetic squeeze. "I'm so sorry you had to go through any of that."

Her kindness was like a punch in the gut. My eyes threatened to fill with tears. I held them back by biting my lip. She could not know what she was apologizing for, but it was a lot: my lover imprisoned, my medical career in ruins, my family—fuck, my family—my dad walking away when I needed him the most. A life full of accusations of being strange, weird . . . insane.

"It's over now," I heard Jones say. "You're not alone anymore."

That did it. The floodgates broke. I sobbed like a baby.

SIX

Stone, who seemed to be the only one able to touch me without triggering a bad reaction from the snake tattoo, put her arms around me and let me cry into her massive, solid shoulder. I have no idea how long I clung there, just letting myself weep.

When I finally calmed to a hiccup, a box of Kleenex had appeared by the desk and the guys were gone. They'd moved off somewhere to give us privacy, apparently.

Stone handed me a tissue. "You and Jack need to talk," she said. "You will benefit from understanding more about who you are."

"What is that?" I croaked, blowing my nose noisily. "What am I?"

Her large brown eyes held a kindness, a softness that belied the rest of her rough-hewn features. "At the very least you are a sensitive. You may be a switch, or, as Jack thinks, a witch—though those are extremely rare."

"I don't understand any of it," I said.

"You will, given time," she said in a patient, matronly voice. "Wait here. You and Jack can go into the interrogation room for some privacy."

I didn't want her to leave, but I knew that was irrational. She had an aura of utter calm that I craved, so with great reluctance, I watched her go. She went over to an office door I hadn't noticed before. It was near the bank of television screens. She rapped once before entering. The name on the door was S. JONES.

While I waited for her return, I looked around the room. The morning's activity seemed to have dissipated. There were still a few uniformed officers at desks, but most of the others seemed to have headed out on whatever assignments they had. Boyd was sitting in front of a pile of oddments. His eyes were closed and he held the bicycle tire in his hand. He blinked suddenly, shook his head, and then, setting the tire to the side, pulled his laptop closer and began to type. At a nearby desk sat a young woman who seemed to be playing solitaire, though the cards she had looked like nothing I'd ever seen before.

Jack came out of Jones's office and stood in front of where I sat, patting my eyes dry. His hands were shoved in his pockets, and he seemed a bit awkward with my tears. "Er, Hannah thinks we should head for the interrogation room. I guess I need to give you a bit of 'the real real-world 101.'"

"Yeah, okay," I said, feeling too drained to ask him to repeat all that in some way that made more sense.

"Spense wants us to meet back in the war room in an hour, though. He wants to get going on the necromancer case as soon as you're up to speed. Oh, right. I hope it's okay, I'm downloading the pictures from your phone."

I didn't think I had anything unseemly on my phone, so I nodded.

"Brilliant. All right, Alex, follow me."

Nothing in Precinct 13 was what I expected. The interrogation room looked nothing like the one in Chicago I had spent significant time in. There was no mirrored window, no scummy, scuffed table, or ghostly white walls that smelled of despair.

Instead, the whole place was bright with sunlight. A huge, nearly floor-to-ceiling window looked out into a snow-spattered courtyard. The walls were exposed brick and beams, and an ivy plant trailed up and around three of the four walls. There was a sunken indoor koi pool in the center of the room, with four golden and one black fish swimming lazily in it. The room smelled fresh and green. The only place to sit was on terraced steps leading down to the pond.

Jack noticed my reaction to the place. "It's as natural as possible. You won't believe how much it freaks out the bad guys." He leaned in conspiratorially and added, "And boosts our abilities."

I gripped my snake tattoo and took a tentative step over the threshold. I expected an angry buzz or a painful constriction, but I felt nothing specific. There was a vague sense of an angry adjustment with an irritated hiss.

Jack's eyebrows raised. "A little persnickety, isn't it?"

"You heard that?"

"Not exactly, more like *felt* it," he said. We were standing by a row of coat hooks. It was warm and moist in the room, and Jack slipped out of his shoes. I saw a mat underneath the hooks, and wondered if I should take off mine, too. I decided my socks were nice enough that I could leave my boots behind.

"Just resist the urge to get naked—not that I would mind—but that's a bit awkward on the first day." He smiled. When I looked ready to call him a pervert, he put up his hands to stop me and added, "It's this place, honest! The room inspires some naturals to go . . . well, au naturel."

I gaped at him for a long moment, and then shook my head. "I can't say that any of this makes sense to me," I said. The room was relaxing, however, and I sighed as I settled onto the cool stone seat. The soft sound of gurgling water reminded me of the little desktop meditation fountain Valentine had.

Jack sat next to me, resting his arms on the step above. "Liar," he said casually.

I was taken aback by his easy accusation. "What?"

"I think after this morning you can finally admit it, eh? This makes much more sense than anything anyone else has ever told you. I imagine you've been harangued all your life to deny what you know is true, and act like you don't see what is clearly there."

"Are you telling me there are monsters under the bridges in Chicago?"

"No, I believe *you're* telling *me*," he said simply. "I'd call them trolls myself. Bridges are a natural gathering place for such creatures. That's why there are stories about them."

I frowned down at the koi, which were turning in circles near our feet. A few of them gulped at the air as if expecting to be fed. The golden ones had interesting patterns on their bodies, reminding me of Chinese dragons. I opened my mouth a couple of times, but didn't have words for all the mixed emotions I was feeling, especially since I'd seen so many dark and twisted things in what I'd considered my unstable, unmedicated times. If that stuff was real, the world was a hell of a lot scarier than most people thought.

"The real mystery," Jack continued when I didn't say anything right away, "isn't whether or not trolls or magic are real—because we both know they are—but why you can see them when others can't. Do you want to know my theory?"

"Sure, why not?"

"That's the spirit," he said gently. I think he could tell that I was beginning to feel very overwhelmed by all this. He stared out at the courtyard through the frost- and steam-covered glass. "I think you might be an actual witch. It's much more likely, of course, that you're a switch. They're as common as dirt. But no switch I know could stop a kill spell in its tracks."

I nodded, my eyes focusing on the snake tattoo. It certainly was an ugly thing. I flexed my arm, trying to feel the malicious presence under my skin, but, for now, it seemed quiet. "So I'm a witch?"

Well, that certainly rhymed with what my stepmother had called me.

"Maybe," he said, hazarding a quick sidelong glance at me. "Thing is, for as many criteria you meet, there's several major ones you don't."

"Like what?"

He stretched his long legs and wiggled his stocking feet. I noticed he wore striped purple and black socks, like the Wicked Witch of the West. "No familiar." His voice dropped and softened. "At least none we've seen. If you had a familiar, you'd have been protected. You wouldn't have . . . Well, he would have introduced you to others a lot sooner."

I was done crying over all that, so I just hugged myself tightly.

Jack seemed to take my silence as an indication to go on. "All children, even those who grow up to be completely *ordinarium*, can see magic. This is one of the reasons we love fairy stories when we're little. We recognize the truth in them."

I nodded, too exhausted from my earlier tears to comment.

"Teenage hormones change everything," Jack said with a crooked smile. "Your brain goes through a massive reorganization at that age, as well. With the mind's remapping, most people lose the ability to perceive magic. They give up their teddy bears at the same time. It's a symbol of an actual transition. *Ordinarium* like to call it 'growing up,' but it's really growing *out* of magic."

That made a lot of sense to me. I'd held on to a lot of "childish" things far into my teenage years.

Jack nodded, as if he could sense my silent understanding. "Those of us who remain sensitive are particularly vulnerable at this time. We don't realize it, but like that other new body odor we're dealing with as teens, we're sending out a kind of chemical signal, a witchy pheromone of sorts— that signals to others of our kind that we're like them."

He turned to look at me, as if hoping for some recognition from me. I had nothing for him. No one had come to this princess's rescue.

"This scent is how our familiars find us. Familiars are like mentors at first, teaching us, keeping us out of mischief, and away from those that would harm us for our power. I wouldn't have survived without Sarah Jane."

"So what's a familiar exactly? You mean like some kind of talking black cat?"

"They don't have to be cats, though familiar animals do tend to be black, black and white, or very rarely albino. There are familiars among all the mammals, some reptiles and amphibians, and the occasional bird." He watched my face carefully, like he expected an aha moment at any time. Only, I didn't have one.

"I never even had a pet goldfish," I said with a nod in the direction of the circling koi. "Our apartments never allowed them."

He frowned at that, clearly disappointed. "Despite the black cat stereotype, most familiars are wild, not pets. They can be anything. Think, Alex, did any animal seem particularly tame around you?"

Having grown up in Chicago, I didn't have a lot of experience with animals, wild or otherwise. We would have squirrels and pigeons in our neighborhood, of course, and I loved going to the zoo and the Shedd Aquarium, but I couldn't remember any special connection to any of the animals I saw. Sure, like every girl at a certain age, I dreamed of growing up and becoming a veterinarian once in a while, but I'd wanted to be a princess more. I shook my head sadly.

Jack didn't seem to want to give up this idea, however. "It's possible if you were . . . uh, medicated early, your scent would have been masked."

I had been on and off drugs all through my teenage years, so I just shrugged noncommittally.

Jack's face reflected the hurt I felt but didn't dare show. "Ironically," he said, "sometimes the more powerful witch you are, the longer it takes your familiar to find you. A very special familiar might have to come a great distance, for instance."

When I still had nothing useful to offer, he sighed.

"It's possible, too," he added cautiously, "that another magical scent blocked yours. Something unnatural, perhaps even otherworldly."

"My stepmom!" But as soon as it was out, my hands flew up to cover my mouth. I didn't want to talk about that embarrassing incident in my life, but it had slipped and I knew I had to say something. "I . . . uh, I thought she was a demon once." Very quickly, I added, "But I got over that."

"A demon would do it," Jack agreed, brightening. "In fact, the presence of a demon would explain a lot of why you weren't able to be located by your familiar." Jack twirled his earring absently. "Certain demons are particularly attracted to witches. They feed on their power. That's part of why the Inquisition was convinced witchcraft involved the 'devil' and his minions." He made the air quotes with his fingers when he said "devil." I was weirdly relieved that that particular creature didn't seem to be a reality. "You could be a witch after all."

"Hooray," I said, because he seemed so happy. "But you know, the doctors told me it was some kind of delusion and paranoid abandonment issues. So, I tried to put it all out of my mind."

"Ah, I see," he said, with deep skepticism. "How did that work out for you?"

Plenty of evenings I still saw my stepmother's snakelike eyes in my dreams, and, considering that she was still in Chicago and I was banished to the hinterlands . . . My heart pounded at the sudden realization. "Oh my God, she's still with my father back home in Chicago. If she's *really* a demon—he's in trouble, isn't he?"

"Hold on." Jack raised his hands to calm me down. I

hadn't noticed myself getting to my feet, but, at his coaxing, I sat back down. "You don't know anything about her, do you? What kind of demon she is?"

"Super-bitch?" I offered, with a little twisted smile.

"That doesn't really narrow it down, I'm afraid," he said, giving me a half smile in return. "I know you're worried, so, after we're done here, we can give all the details you can think of to Spense. He can contact the Chicago Bureau and have someone check out the situation," Jack said, sitting up a little and folding his arms in his lap. "But if the demon was trying to get to you, she'll leave your father now that you're gone. But, er . . ." His eyes jigged away from me uncomfortably for a moment. "It could be true love. Demons and humans have intermarried for hundreds of thousands of years."

I tried not to make the gagging sound that came out of my mouth.

Jack smiled slightly again, but wagged a finger at me exaggeratedly. "Don't be a speciesist. Not all demons are unnatural, and even the unnatural can fall in love. I mean, look at Spenser. He turned out okay, didn't he?"

"What's his deal?"

"Oh, you can't tell? He's half-fairy."

"Fabulous!" I said with a smile. "But don't the kids just call that bisexual these days?"

Jack gave me a frustrated grimace. "You're just being intentionally dense. Spense is half-Scots Seelie fairy. I know you saw it in his eyes and pretended not to notice."

I started to deny it, but gave up. "So what are you?"

He pointed to the Wi-Fi symbol on his chest. "Technomage." At my confused look, he simplified, "A technology-using witch."

"Not a warlock?"

His nose crinkled like I'd insulted him. "'Witch' is a title, not a gender," he said. "You can be either a natural or unnatural witch. Sometimes there are other titles that people use to define their allegiance to magic—unnatural tend to prefer titles like 'necromancer,' 'warlock' . . . that sort of thing."

"So the unnatural are like the 'Evil League of Evil' or something?"

"Oh, no, not at all," he said, sounding startled. "I guess I should've explained all that first. I'm a terrible teacher."

"No, you're not." I reached out and patted him on the leg, and I felt my snake tattoo twinge slightly.

We both stared at my right arm and the ugly black thing that spiraled up my shoulder.

"It's not my usual style," I said. "I mean, if I was going to get something big, it'd be a dragon or something."

"A dragon?" Jack repeated absently. "You can't bind dragons with ink. And a black dragon . . . oak and ash, that'd be a familiar from hell."

"You can have a dragon familiar?" I asked, even though I really wanted to question whether or not he was kidding about dragons being real in the first place.

"I couldn't," he said. "There have been historically, of course, witches who have had, but I don't know if there's a witch alive today powerful enough to attract one, frankly. Holding a dragon's interest for terribly long would be tough as well. You see, the more intelligent an animal is, the more difficult they are to . . . Well, a witch never quite 'tames' their familiar, but there's a certain amount of bonding that happens. Dragons don't bond easily." His voice drifted into a mutter. With a shake of his head, Jack must have decided he'd run the course of that conversation, because he switched tracks. "We need to see if we can get rid of that thing."

"You can do that?" I asked, hopefully.

"Yeah, though I'll need some help," he said. "Let me call Sarah Jane."

Instead of taking a phone out of his pocket or asking to borrow mine, Jack took in a deep breath and closed his eyes. The koi, which had never stopped hopefully nibbling at the air near our toes, suddenly flashed to the other side of the pool with a splash. I jumped. Before I could ask what happened, Jack opened his eyes.

"She's on her way. I think. I mean, well, she does what she likes most of the time, so hopefully she'll come."

I was beginning to think we were talking about a cat rather than a person. Given everything I'd seen today, I thought I'd better ask. "Sarah Jane is . . . ?"

"My familiar, right," he said. "While we wait to see if she comes, I should quickly explain the whole natural/unnatural division."

I kept my eye on the door to the courtyard, watchful for the slinky movements of a cat. I had to admit I was pretty curious to meet Jack's familiar, especially since he seemed so certain I should have one. Would she be like something out of a bad TV show about witches, with a fancy, diamond-studded collar and the ability to talk?

Jack, too, watched the window as he spoke. "About the whole natural and unnatural thing—the distinction is really very straightforward. If you think of power as a river, natural magic uses the existing currents. If you go against the flow, you're tapping into the unnatural."

"So, what, it's like the Force?"

His eyes twinkled at my reference. "I suppose in a way,

in that the energy itself is neutral and what matters is how you use it. But it's actually quite possible for a practitioner to use natural magic for evil purposes, and vice versa. That's why we avoid labels like 'dark' or 'light' or 'chaotic' or 'order.' And, er, why we try not to judge a demon until we meet her, as it were."

The frightened koi returned tentatively, cautiously. I was about to tell Jack that I had no doubt my stepmom was evil when my eyes caught the flap of large, black-and-white wings outside. A magpie hopped onto the frozen fountain and looked at us expectantly.

"Oh, there she is." Jack waved out the window. "Coming, Sarah Jane!"

The bird fluttered to the courtyard door to meet him as he opened it.

"Sarah Jane Smith," he said. "Meet Alex Connor."

I had to guess this beautiful black-and-white bird was his familiar. It had a pearly white vest and silky black wings and a long, graceful tail. In the sunlight, some of the dark feathers shimmered almost metallic blue. I waved in what I hoped was a pleasant manner. I didn't have a lot of experience talking to animals.

"You named your familiar after a Dr. Who character?" I asked Jack, as he closed the door to keep out the cold.

"Well"—he smiled sheepishly—"she is my companion."

The bird made a noise not unlike a rueful laugh, and then took flight. She closed the distance between us in a flash. Perching on the stone step above me, her presence sent the poor koi skittering across the pond again. She cocked her head, first at the snake on my arm, and then catching my eye. Her beady gaze seemed to see right through me, and I had the very distinct impression of being observed by something highly intelligent. I half expected she would just open her beak and say, "Hello." But, instead, she dipped her head in greeting.

"Isn't she brilliant?" Jack asked, proudly, as he sat back down beside me.

The bird hopped down and peered at my arm. I held it out for her. She pecked at it softly, and I resisted the urge to pull away.

"So, what do you think, Sarah Jane?"

The bird very distinctly shook her head.

Jack sat back, obviously irritated with her response. "Well, why did you come, then?"

She made a lot of racket, and the poor fish had apoplexy as she flapped and hopped around.

Jack took all this in stride. "Well, all right, but you know how I feel about you hanging out with that gang. I don't think they're very good for you. The last time I let you talk me into letting them inside, they trashed the place."

The bird didn't respond; instead, she flew back over to the courtyard door and hung on one of the ivy branches overhead. It bobbed under her weight.

Jack sighed. "I suppose we need them," he said to her. Then, to me, he added, "You're about to meet the Outlaws. Prepare yourself."

"Outlaws? That sounds like a biker gang."

"Worse. A gang of magpies," he said. When he opened the door again about ten magpies flew in, all flashing pinfeathers and raucous calls. They swooped and soared around. Two of them dive-bombed my head, making me duck and cower.

"Ah, settle down," Jack yelled. "You're worse than a bunch of footballers."

All the magpies seemed to find this hilarious as the room erupted in a cacophony of barking caws. However, they listened to him . . . eventually. They began to find places around the room to settle. The couple that had been dive-bombing me dropped down near my seat and gave my knee a nudge as if to say, "Just kidding around."

One flapped onto my knee. Even through the fabric of my jeans, I felt the scrabble of its knobby, taloned feet. When I pushed it off lightly, I noticed that it had one of those metal tracking bands wrapped around its ankle. A quick survey revealed they all did, except Sarah Jane. It was, in fact, the only way that I could tell her from the others.

Jack came back with Sarah Jane perched like a hawk on his crooked arm. "Thing is," he said to me, "I might be able to pull the snake out on my own, but Sarah needs her gang to kill it. Normally, magpies aren't much for taking out large prey, see?"

I nodded, still marveling at all the magpies hopping and flapping around the room. A threesome sidled up to the koi pond and seemed to be eyeing up the fish. I waved my foot at them, trying to shoo them off. The look I got was pure wickedness, and I had a very bad feeling that I'd be finding a whole lot of bird shit on my car later, at the very least.

When Jack lowered Sarah Jane to the step, I asked, "So she hasn't passed initiation yet, huh?"

His eyebrow jumped at that. "How do you mean?"

"No anklet yet," I said, gesturing at the leg of a nearby bird.

"Oh right." Jack nodded. "The colors. Apparently, they're

all being tracked by the same ornithologist. He or she must be going mad looking at the places these guys go."

One of the birds dived into the pool, harassing the fish.

"The natives are getting restless," Jack noted. "It's time for magic."

SEVEN

At Jack's words, the magpie gang noticeably shushed. They gathered in a close circle around us with hops and flaps. Their eyes flicked between me and my arm. The room seemed to dim as a cloud passed in front of the sun just outside the window.

"How does this work?" I found myself whispering in anticipation.

"A series of shifts," he said, as though that explained something. "Starting now."

I felt it in my stomach, like a kind of lurch, though nothing had actually moved. There was sudden brightness behind my eyes, a brightness not unlike the flash of a camera. I looked down at the snake on my arm. Its head shifted. The closest magpie—Sarah Jane?—snapped a beak at my hand, nipping skin.

I pulled my hand away protectively. "Ow!"

"Not yet," Jack told the birds. "Watch the tail."

I'd rolled up my sleeve and tucked it over my shoulder in a way that exposed the entire tattoo. Before I could ask Jack what he meant, I felt the shift again. This time my stomach dropped in free fall. I gasped a little when the brightness came, and louder when I saw a black tail protruding from the tip of my shoulder. A magpie cawed in excitement. Another jumped on my head, its talons scraping my scalp as it bobbed for the wiggling bit of snake. Magpies crowded me, nearly pushing me over as they snapped at my shoulder. The room erupted in echoing calls.

One of them must have caught hold because I felt a tug deep under my skin.

"He's got it," Jack said happily, backing up a step to give the gang of birds more room. I could hardly see him through the flopping feathers and feet. I had to put my other arm up to protect my eyes from wings and claws.

Meanwhile, the tugging grew more painful. I could feel the snake resisting, wiggling under my skin. The snake's fangs pressed deeper into the flesh of the back of my hand.

Despite all the noisy pulling, not another inch emerged from my shoulder. After one heroic heave, a beak sliced through the finger's-length of tail, sending the bird tumbling backward with its prize.

The rest of the snake quickly buried itself under my skin and became flat and two-dimensional again.

"We almost had it," Jack said, as the birds awkwardly clambered off me.

"Do that shifting thing again," I suggested, craning my head to inspect the tat. The tip was clearly sliced now, and smears of snake guts formed yellowish stains under my skin. "Maybe more will come."

Jack shook his head. I noticed his face was pale and dotted

with beads of sweat. "Twice was hard enough. Besides, magic isn't free. Shifting, in particular, causes big ripples. Who knows what new deviltry I've unleashed somewhere else?"

"But . . . I thought you said that you used magic to make the precinct seem abandoned," I started. "Are you paying for that?"

"A little," he admitted. "That's why we encourage people to bring in their own natural magic. All the potted plants and such . . ."

"So you drain the energy of the plants?"

"Well, that sounds rather Machiavellian," he said, clearly offended. "It's not like that, not exactly. Plants are renewable sources of natural energy, particularly any that are tended—houseplants, gardens, crops. What the magic takes out, people put back in."

I nodded. "What about all this green?" I lifted my hands to indicate all the plants that covered the room.

"They help," he said. "But the kind of direct magic that I just performed, it's . . . well, bigger."

My hand ached so I flexed it experimentally. I could feel the stab of the snake's fangs like muscle tightness. Meanwhile, the birds had gone back to their mischief. A group was fighting over the severed length of snake tail. The splash of water behind us let me know that one magpie had returned to harassing the fish.

Sarah Jane tucked herself into Jack's lap, as though she were settling on a nest. Jack stroked her head and back lightly. "I think you may be stuck with that for a while," he said, with a jerk of his chin in the direction of my arm. "Hannah was right. It's much deeper than I thought. Also, I got a sense that it . . . well, liked you."

We both looked at the inky blackness spiraling up the length of my arm. My hand twinged painfully again. "Likes me?" I repeated, horrified.

"Remember what I said about not judging? The spell had an original, evil intent, but you changed it when you cursed it. It may be becoming something else. Something a bit more positive."

"You're not suggesting I keep it, are you?"

Jack raked his fingers through his hair, and Sarah Jane fluffed herself in obvious displeasure at the slight displacement his gesture caused. "You may not have much choice. I wonder . . . the quick bonding, the ease with which you stopped its intent . . . Maybe your familiar is a reptile, like a—"

There was a loud splash behind us and a magpie hauled a flopping fish onto the stone lip of the pond. Jack twisted around to see, dumping Sarah Jane. "Hey, put that back!" he admonished the bird.

Sarah Jane scolded the guilty bird as well, and pretty soon there was pandemonium as more birds joined in, picking sides. I noticed a few trying to sneak out another fish during the distraction. When I pointed that out to Jack, he stood up and shouted, "That's it! That's it! Get out!!"

Stumbling over birds and fish, he pulled open the door with a strangled cry. "Go! Get out of here!"

Steam from the cold outside air misted at the entrance as unencumbered birds soared out the door quickly. Those trying to haul off fish or the snake tail, however, hopped along awkwardly. Jack managed to grapple a bright yellow koi from one of the magpies, but two others snuck out with a smaller white-and-black-speckled one slung between them.

Jack waved his fist at the retreating mob as they sailed to

the safety of the rooftops surrounding the courtyard to nibble on their trophies. Only Sarah Jane remained inside. She hopped on the ground near Jack's feet and ducked her head as if embarrassed by the behavior of her friends.

"Well, go on," he said, holding the door for her. "You might as well have a little fish."

She gave his calf a head butt, almost like a cat, but fluttered back to where I sat massaging the back of my hand. Her message was clear. She was staying.

Jack's posture softened. "Aw, Sarah Jane, that's kind, but you're not much of an indoor animal, and Alex and I have to go to a meeting anyway."

She hopped on along the stone steps, and feigned interest in pulling the leaves off a ficus. Her posture made it evident that she wasn't listening to him. I had to smile. The familiars *could* talk, just not in the way I'd imagined.

"Oh, all right," he said, letting the door close. "You win."

I got the sense Jack said that particular phrase a lot around Sarah Jane. For her part, she continued to disassemble the plant. When he got back to his spot, he sighed exasperatedly. "Maybe you're lucky you don't have a familiar, eh?"

Sarah Jane made a sound that distinctly resembled, "Meh."

Jack ignored her and checked his wristwatch again. "I suppose we ought to go join the others in the war room. You should meet the whole team."

Sarah Jane dropped a shiny leaf into the pile she was making and shook herself off. With a powerful flap of her wings, she lifted herself into the air. She flew to the coat hangers near the exit and perched there. She apparently wanted to go to the meeting as well. I looked to Jack to see if he was going to try to argue. He looked ready to say something, but then shook his head.

"Come on," he said to me.

Leaving behind the traumatized koi to return to their mindless circling, we climbed up the step-seats to where Sarah Jane waited. I slipped back into my winter boots. As I bent to fasten them, I noticed a bit of bird poop splattered on Jack's. I wasn't sure if that was meant as some kind of comment, but, if it was, he didn't say anything about it. He just took a Kleenex out from a travel pack in his front pocket and wiped it off.

"Who else is on the team?" I asked.

When he straightened up, Sarah Jane hopped lightly onto his shoulder. She gripped tightly with her talons, and I suspect that was why Jack had kept his leather jacket on all this time. "Well, you've met Boyd already, as well as Hannah. Probably the only new guy will be Devon."

Jokingly, I asked, "So what are his superpowers?"

"Oh, Devon's a vampire and a werewolf."

"Both?"

"Yes." Jack opened the door to the main precinct. I squinted in the harsh fluorescent light, and found myself hesitant to leave behind the comfort of the natural room. We both stood at the threshold for a while, as if working up the courage to go into the noisy, industrial space. "Hey," he noted, "you're making progress. You didn't try to deny vampires were real."

"Woot," I said sarcastically. Holding my breath as if jumping into water, I stepped out into the main room. "So, what do you call a vampire who is also a werewolf? A werepire? A vampwolf?"

"Oh, be sure to ask Devon, he *loves* that question," Jack said in a tone that made it clear Devon would probably bite my head off.

We both let out a sigh when the door to the interrogation room closed. Sarah Jane made a sad, quiet coo. As we threaded our way through the cluster of desks, I held out hope that the war room would be as unexpectedly pleasant as the interrogation room had been. I was disappointed when Jack led me to a perfectly ordinary conference room. At least there seemed to be donuts on the table and a big set of windows that looked out into a different view of the same courtyard we'd been able to see in the other room.

Before we went in, I had to ask a couple of questions, however. "About this Devon guy," I said. "Vampires and werewolves seem like they might be, well, unnatural to me."

Sarah Jane answered before Jack could with a bob of her whole body in a great big "yes."

"To be fair," Jack added, "Devon's a special case. He's an informant."

Sarah Jane nipped Jack's ear.

"Ow!" he said, jerking his head from the range of her sharp beak. "Okay, right, so there's more to it. Devon's not exactly a volunteer. Remember how I told you Spenser is half-fairy? Well, fairies have this thing, right, where if you accept a gift, especially of food, from them, even unknowingly, you end up having to do their bidding. Devon bit Spense, drank a bit of his blood. That's like fairy food times a million."

"So he's a slave to—" I wasn't quite up to calling Officer Jones by his first name, so I trailed off.

"—Spense. Yes," Jack said. "Dev's a bit grumpy about it, but he's been an excellent source on this case. I mean, nobody knows maleficium like a vampire."

"Yeah, I guess," I said. I still hesitated in front of the glass-fronted door, even though I could see Officer Jones waving us inside. "Are you sure I belong here? I mean, what am I going to be able to contribute? I don't know anything about this case. I kind of feel like I should be back at work, you know?"

Sarah Jane cocked her head at me, like she couldn't quite believe I'd just said that. Jack's face had a similar expression. "Do you have a lot of cases to get back to?"

The only other body in the morgue was Mrs. Finnegan, and as long as she didn't have more to say I couldn't imagine her going anywhere until her family showed up. "Uh, I guess not."

"Right, then," he said with a smile. "Come on and meet the team."

Devon didn't look like I thought a vampire should. He was neither tall, nor strikingly handsome. His skin was only as pale as most South Dakotans' after a long winter. There was no cape, brooding expression, or thick foreign accent. He didn't even *sparkle*.

Instead, he looked like the average college student. Wavy brown hair cut in a current style and an easy smile were his most salient features. Otherwise, he wore a navy sweatshirt with the letters SDSU in white block letters. His jeans were worn to the point of being more gray than blue.

Sarah Jane, however, watched him carefully. Her black, beady eyes tracked his every movement.

The only clue I had that there might be something sinister beneath his innocuous appearance was the fact that, when we shook hands, there was no reaction from the snake tattoo at all. On the other hand, Devon seemed drawn to it. "Wow," he said. Still gripping my palm lightly, he turned my wrist to admire my arm. "Nice work. Yours?"

"It is now," I said.

He looked confused at my response and checked with Jack for clarification. "A gift from the necromancer," Jack explained.

Devon's eyebrows rose. "Our little grave robber is still causing problems? The last report I heard, he was dead."

"Dead and walking," I said before I realized that, technically, as a vampire, Devon was in the same state—or, at least I assumed so. "Er, but less . . . together than you."

Jack covered for my gaffe quickly. "Alex was in the middle of the autopsy when she triggered a protection spell. My guess is that woke him up."

Devon scrunched his face as if he found the idea disgusting. "In the middle of the autopsy?"

I nodded.

"Dear God," he said, with a little shiver.

I found it sort of funny that the vampire seemed to be the first one to have the heebie-jeebies about the state of the missing corpse.

Sarah Jane made a noise that sounded like a snort, like she didn't buy Devon's act. Jack gave her a sharp look and put his finger to his lips.

From the front of the room, Jones looked up from a pile of papers he'd been sorting. "What is that damn bird doing here?"

Jack shrugged. "She wanted to come. I assume she has something she wants to add."

"She'd better not shit all over everything," Jones muttered, going back to his pile of paper.

Sarah Jane cawed loudly, clearly protesting the insult.

Devon smirked at both Jack and the bird. "Well," he said to me. "Pleasure meeting you, Alex."

Officer Stone was already sitting at the long, polished wooden table that dominated the room. In front of her neatly folded hands sat a legal pad and coffee mug that had "Got Chutzpah?" printed on it. With her police cap off, her hair was an even bigger disaster. Thick black bangs hung like a clump in front of her face. I really wanted to help her fix it, girl to girl, but I wasn't even sure I remembered what her first name was. Hannah?

Devon took the spot near the head of the table where Jones stood. He reached across and took a large, powdered donut from a box.

As Jack took the seat next to Devon, Sarah Jane flew over to perch on the blinds that covered the window at the far end of the room. She shook out her feathers and began preening.

That left me sitting next to Stone. I settled into an uncomfortable office chair with the sort of dread I usually reserved for the start of a job interview. There was even a whiteboard set up behind Jones. I took the opportunity to study it.

In blue dry-erase marker was the headline "Grave Robbery," underneath which someone had taped the mug shot of the guy who had walked out of my morgue carrying his liver.

Given what Devon had just said, my hunch was that my morning's necromancer must also be responsible for the grave desecrations of the above photos. Why had none of that been in the police reports? Maybe if it had been, I might have—

No, I admonished myself. Even if it had been written in black-and-white, I would never have taken Stone's claims seriously.

But that got me wondering: How did *ordinarium*, as Jack

called regular people, see magic? Was it completely invisible? Did they look past it? Or, did they make up more "plausible" reasons for it? I knew from experience that there were things other people simply saw differently. When I pointed out trolls under the El bridges, my father would pat my head, laugh, and tell me to be serious: They were just homeless people.

But an unearthed grave was something completely different. It was straightforward: a pile of dirt, a broken vault, an open coffin, and a missing corpse. How could you see that any other way?

So what did the police think of the grave robberies? Did they even know about them? They must.

Unless, I supposed, there was some kind of invisibility spell covering each crime scene. I'd have to ask if that was the case.

Regardless, it still bothered me that no one from Precinct 13 had informed the local cops of the possible connection between the grave robbing and the guy they found dead in his apartment this morning.

That seemed like a strange sort of negligence. I thought it must be possible to keep magic out of things, if need be. You just say, "Hey, this guy is someone we've had our eye on;" you don't have to mention necromancy at all.

Maybe the regular cops did know, but kept it out of the official files. After all, the chief had sent me here the instant I mentioned Stone and this morning's body. Maybe he knew this was a case Precinct 13 was already working on.

I liked that thought. Otherwise, it seemed a dangerous game, or, at the very least, that kind of unhelpful rivalry I'd seen the FBI engage in when they took over cases from the locals.

Well, I imagined it wasn't really any of my business how they ran things between the locals and Precinct 13. They must have good reasons for whatever policies and protocols were already in place.

The door opened and Boyd came in looking harried. "Sorry," he said. He had his laptop under his arm. He looked at our seating arrangements for a moment, and then chose the "boy" side of the table, next to Jack. He set his computer on the table and set the toe tag I'd given him earlier beside it. It was encased in a small plastic bag with the word EVIDENCE on it.

"Obviously," Jones said, finally looking up from his papers, "we're now dealing with something a little bigger than grave robbery. The question is: What?" He turned to the white-board and uncapped a red marker. He crossed out the head-line and put a question mark above it. He added the words, *Reanimation spell* and next to it, *Booby trap?*

At that, everyone looked at me.

EIGHT

Shrinking from everyone's attention, I tried to find some spot on the table to focus on. Into my field of vision skittered my iPhone. I grabbed it and glanced up to see Jack giving me the thumbs-up. Officer Jones gave me a nod, as if to say it was time for me to tell my story again.

This time through, however, I couldn't get far before people started asking questions or clarifications. "Why take the pajamas?" Boyd asked.

"Maybe he liked them? Or felt naked without them?" Jack offered.

He was naked, I thought but didn't say. "Does he know about you?" I asked Boyd.

"Me? Why would he know me?" Boyd sounded utterly panicked.

I was so taken aback by his reaction that I had to reconstruct what I'd said. "No," I said. "I meant does he know there's a psycho—um, whatever it is you do—at Precinct Thirteen?"

"Oh!" He sounded deeply relieved by my clarification. Boyd raised his light red eyebrows. "You think it's getting out that there's a secret team of paranormal cops?" He sounded almost excited at the idea.

Jones, who'd stayed at the board taking notes as I spoke, shook his head. "We work really hard to keep this place and the team members hush-hush."

So, everything was super-secret. Interesting. I wondered if there was any special reason for that besides the ones I'd come across in my life: i.e., that people thought you were crazy if you talked about it.

Boyd, meanwhile, looked disappointed.

More and more curious. Was there a contingent in the magical community that wanted to be more out in the open?

When no one else had a comment, I continued my tale. This time I stopped myself. "Why would he take his liver? I had all sorts of bits of him scattered all over the room, ready to be sent to the lab for more analysis. He left all that."

"What's the liver's function in the human body?" Stone wanted to know.

"It does a lot, actually. It makes bile, which is used to help digest food. It processes cholesterol and does a number of detoxification functions—"

"Detox? So maybe he took it to hide the evidence of something," Jack suggested.

"I was looking for poison," I said. "The police report"—my eyes went to Boyd: Was that where I'd heard his name before?—"said they suspected suicide by rat poisoning."

"What?" Jones asked, sounding deeply surprised by this.

I looked at Boyd, but he kept his eyes studiously fixed on something on his laptop screen.

Maybe I was mistaken about the name on the report? "Uh, yeah," I continued. I looked at Jones next. "Weren't you there? I mean, you brought the body in."

"Not really," Jones said. "The place had too-powerful anti-natural wards. We intercepted the body after our guy inside—" He paused as if searching for a name. I gave Boyd a hard look, but he refused to make eye contact. Instead, Jones looked to Stone. "Is it Peterson?"

Next to me Stone shrugged. "One of those guys."

O-kay.

"So, anyway," I continued. "I took a biopsy to send to the lab. If there's something out of the ordinary in their workup, we'll see it." For a second, I forgot just who I was talking to. All the faces around the table were highly skeptical. "Okay, so the report will only show the sorts of chemicals they typically look for. I don't know how to ask them to test for the elixir of resurrection."

"I doubt he has *that*," Devon said. He was slouched back in his chair, doodling on a yellow legal pad. "I'm pretty sure it's a myth, anyway."

"What's a myth?" Jones asked.

Devon set his pen down and seemed a bit surprised to find all of us watching him expectantly. His jaw set and his eyes narrowed. He crossed his arms in front of his chest.

"Don't get like that," Jones said. "Just tell us what you know."

"It has nothing to do with this case, I'm sure of it," he said.

"I'd like all the facts," Jones insisted.

I couldn't be sure of it, but I felt something pass between them as they stared each other down. Eventually, Devon flinched almost imperceptibly and broke eye contact. "It's stupid," he said, sullenly. "There's just this rumor in my community about someone who used alchemy to transform. I don't think it's possible."

I happened to catch Boyd's eye across the table. "Transform?" I mouthed.

"Into a vampire," he whispered behind his cupped hand.

Devon gave us a sharp look.

" 'Bile' *is* a term used in alchemy, now that I think of it," Jack noted. "There's all that 'black bile' and 'yellow bile' stuff, isn't there?"

Officer Jones, who had been scribbling notes like crazy, turned to the table. "You're suggesting that all this"—he gestured at the grave-robbing images—"was to get the ingredients for the philosopher's stone?"

Jack shrugged his shoulders. "People have done pretty insane things to get eternal life."

Boyd coughed like he'd swallowed something suddenly.

Devon looked insulted. "It's not possible to get the dark gift through better fucking chemistry," he said. "This is a dead end."

I hated to be the one to point it out. "He did walk out of my morgue."

Sarah Jane crowed her pleasure as the others joined in poking Devon with "She's got you there," and congratulating me with, "Excellent point."

"Perhaps, if he is a vampire, he's gone somewhere to regenerate," Officer Jones said once the room had calmed down a little. I tried to imagine how long it would take to recover from a nearly completed autopsy. There was a lot that needed to be regrown. Jones continued. "What we need to focus on next is finding this man. Let's break into our usual teams and see what we can find out."

That seemed to be "meeting adjourned." I took my phone and tucked it back into my pocket, wondering what I should do with myself.

I was just about to take a donut from the box and think about heading back to the morgue when Stone stood over me.

"You're with us," Officer Jones said, coming up beside her. "It would be good for you to see the usual suspects."

It was my first time in a police car without handcuffs. I still felt a bit like a criminal since Devon slouched in the seat beside me, looking particularly sullen and trapped.

Our first stop, thankfully, was to drive through the Starbucks.

I tend to judge people by the coffee they drink. Stone got the house blend, black. Plain coffee for a plain Jane: That suited what I'd seen of her personality so far. Devon got a double-shot energy drink, which grossed me out, but didn't seem out of character in the least. Jones, on the other hand, got a skinny, white-chocolate peppermint mocha, surprising me utterly. Admittedly, I considered Starbucks fairly awful as chain coffee went, and, in my opinion, the only way to drink it was with tons of added sugar and milk. Still, peppermint—that was pretty fluffy for a dude. I decided there was more to Jones than met the eye.

I got a regular latte, which probably made me seem a little mundane. It was a feint. The truth is that, given the right circumstances, I could be downright pretentious about my coffee. In Chicago, Valentine and I preferred our local, independently owned coffee shop, which was the sort of place where the baristas routinely won the Midwest Regional Championship. I didn't want these guys to know that about me yet, however. Besides, it was hard to be a coffee snob in Pierre, where my choices were so limited.

Stone had to get out and open our door to pass us our drinks. Once she strapped herself back in, we headed down the street. Jones seemed to be in cruise mode. He drove slowly with one hand on the wheel and the other taking sips of his froufrou drink. Occasionally a pedestrian would give that small-town nod, and he'd reply with the fingers-off-the-wheel salute.

Next to me, Devon chugged his disgusting energy drink.

"Late night?" I asked, and then instantly felt stupid. The guy was supposed to be some kind of vampire after all.

He grimaced as he sucked the last drop from the bottle. "It's my time of the month."

"Yeah, Devon gets really sensitive about a week before the full moon," Jones said in a very ha-ha tone from the front seat. Stone hit him on the arm. He nearly spilled his peppermint mocha. "What was that for?"

"Fifty-one percent of the human race gets a little sensitive once a month, often in tune with the phases of the moon. It's not a joke."

"I guess not." Jones spared his partner a meaningful look, but then returned his attention to the road. He seemed just on the verge of muttering something about females under his breath, but he clamped his mouth shut.

Devon tucked the empty bottle under the seat casually. When he caught me watching him, he put a finger to his lips and mouthed, "Payback."

I wasn't sure if Jones was such a neat freak that finding

litter in his squad car would piss him off sufficiently, or if Devon hoped some criminal would find the container and use it to bludgeon Jones. Considering the empty was about three inches high and plastic, I didn't think it would do much harm. I said nothing.

We continued our slow meander around Pierre's downtown. Just when I wondered whether we were going to spend the rest of the day aimlessly driving, Jones turned the wheel sharply. "There she is," he said.

Devon slid into me as we rounded the corner and pulled up to the curb. With some luck, I managed not to dump my latte on his head. I heard the front door slam as Jones jumped out of the car. I could see him setting a brisk pace, as if hurrying to catch up to someone.

Stone rescued Devon and me from the locked backseat. After the warm stuffiness of the cramped squad car, the crisp air felt good on my cheeks. My breath misted as I arched my back in a stretch.

We were in an industrial part of town. Unadorned business incubators sat in long rows, surrounded by parking lots. A railroad track split the block. Just beyond the intersection, a train car, spattered with bright graffiti, sat abandoned and desolate.

Near a large Dumpster, I saw Jones talking to a woman in a dirty parka with wild gray hair. I thought I recognized her as the homeless woman on the park bench near the capitol from earlier this morning. She had the same duct tape–patched parka and frizzy, matted hair at any rate. "Who's that?" I asked Stone.

"Nana Spider," Stone said. "She's a *civitas veneficus.*"

"What's a *civitas veneficus?*" I asked.

"Anyone who uses city magic," she said. "Most *civitas*

veneficum are soothsayers. They use various methods to fore-see the future or read the signs. They also tend to be her-mits, choosing to live in the urban wild."

"In other words, homeless," Devon piped up from where he leaned against the hood of the car.

"By choice," Stone insisted, quietly.

He arched his eyebrow as if he begged to differ, but he continued, "It's also the only use of power that's been offi-cially designated neutral—neither natural nor unnatural."

Officially? I wondered who decided that sort of thing, the "Ministry of Magic"? I felt far too silly to ask that, however. I looked around at the concrete. There wasn't a tree in sight. A piece of litter, a torn plastic shopping bag, got caught in an updraft and spiraled lazily into the air.

"You see," Devon said, his eyes following the bag's strange, slow-motion dance. "The bag is plastic, the essence of something unnatural, fake. But it's the wind that moves it, plays with it."

The bag dropped suddenly to the ground when the breeze shifted. There was something eerie about it, that was certain. But was it magic? Jack had told me that I'd been seeing magic my whole life, but had been told not to talk about it. In effect, I'd been trained not to see, not to believe.

The bag skittered along the ground. Like some kind of strange, urban animal, it scooted behind the corner of the building, out of sight.

I decided there was definitely something creepy and weird about all this. I would keep an open mind.

The three of us had been hanging back, giving Jones and Nana room to talk. All at once, Jones turned in our direc-tion and beckoned us closer. "Nana's going to read the entrails."

We gathered around the Dumpster expectantly. Nana cut a striking figure in her puffy down coat. Her skinny legs stuck out beneath the filthy gray ball like the stick on cotton candy. She wore clingy, black leggings that accented her knobby knees, and disappeared into mismatched boots: one cowboy-style, the other a fake fur–covered Ugg.

I held the lid of my latte close to my nose to ward off the rather ripe combination of the garbage and Nana. We stood in a loose circle, with the two uniformed cops on either side of the old woman.

Devon, who stood between Stone and me, shoved his hands in his pants pockets. It was the first time I noticed that he was the only one of us without a coat. He only had on his college sweatshirt. I shivered on his behalf and took a warming sip of my drink.

Nana seemed to have commandeered Jones's peppermint mocha, as she was taking large gulps of it as she crouched over her army pack. She was digging through it, looking for something. All the while she was muttering to herself. I only caught the odd word: "maleficium," "water lily," and "highway patrol."

Finally, she pulled out a single tennis shoe. After downing the last of the coffee, she handed the cup back to Jones. He looked at it for a second, as though disappointed to have sacrificed all of it, and then tossed it over his shoulder into the Dumpster.

Nana smoothed a matted lock away from her face and held the shoe out before us with great reverence. It was a large, white running shoe, looked like it might be a man's by the size of it. It looked huge in her thin, bony fingers. It was a Nike; I recognized the black swoosh.

Nana's body started to sway, though somehow she kept

the shoe held out in front of her, perfectly still. The movement was mesmerizing, and I found myself moving unconsciously to the same rhythm. She began to speak. Instead of a spooky, echoing voice, she croaked: "Okay, Great Powers, so where'd the guy go, huh?"

I, for one, was disappointed at the lack of rhyming.

She threw the shoe into the middle of our circle. It hit the asphalt with an unceremonious *thunk.* Everyone's eyes were wide, even Devon's, as we waited for something to happen.

The shoe lay there.

No one said anything for the longest time. The wind hissed around the edges of the building and through the empty parking lot. I started to wonder if I'd missed something. I glanced around the circle. Everyone waited.

Then, apparently responding to some silent cue, Nana shuffled over to look down at the shoe. She circled this way, then that. She bent closely and seemed to study the laces, in particular.

From the squat, she squinted up at Jones and scratched her chin with long, ragged fingernails. "The signs aren't clear," she said. "All I see is that he was close to me this morning."

I accidentally inhaled some latte in my surprise. "It's true," I said excitedly, around hacking the coffee. "I found the toe tag near the capitol. Nana was there on a bench, only I didn't know it was her. I almost went to ask her if she'd seen anyone, but I thought she didn't want to be disturbed."

Nana's pale green-tinged eyes turned to inspect me. They were deep set, but sharp. "Yes, this morning," she agreed. "I was communing with the ghosts." She frowned to herself and dug in her ear. "But to have missed the presence of not one, but two magicals? I must be losing my touch."

Jones cleared his throat. "What about the shoe?"

"I need more than it can give me. Time for the big guns." Nana pulled a fast-food ketchup packet from her coat pocket. She threw it on the ground. In a flash, she lifted her foot and stomped on it. Ketchup spattered explosively.

Devon jumped back as if he was hit. "Jesus, watch where you're splashing that stuff."

Nana paid no attention to Devon, except as she followed the trail of gooey mess to his pants leg. He'd started to shake it off when she grabbed the cuff of his jeans.

"Don't," she hissed. "You'll mess with the signs."

He froze, balanced awkwardly on one foot. She grasped the denim in her clawlike grip. She was hunkered down so tightly, her parka looked like a big gray boulder that had sprouted a frizzled mat of hair.

I thought, by the way he was squirming, Devon was going to fall over onto his butt.

"Okay, okay," she said. "This is better. The bad guy has gone home to roost. With a sibling or other family member or a mouse. And there's something about moons or lovers."

"Oh," Devon said, jerking his foot from her grasp finally. "That's probably for me."

She gave him a squinty inspection. Standing slowly, she glared up into his face. Nana stood only as tall as his sternum, but she had twice the presence. He twitched nervously until she finally demanded: "Werewolf or vampire?"

"Er, both, ma'am," he said.

"Eh, it probably was for you." She shrugged, turning away. The circle began to break up. Jones helped Nana shoulder her army bag. I noticed him slip a twenty into her palm.

Stone, meanwhile, looked like she really wanted to clean up the ketchup packet, but Jones shook his head when she made a move to pick it up. She backed off, and instead came over to offer Devon a wet wipe for the ketchup on his jeans.

He accepted the wipe gratefully. Putting a hand on my shoulder to steady himself, he said, "It's where they come from, you know."

"What?"

"Weird abandoned shoes. You've always wondered, right? How did that get there and why is there only one? Well, now you know."

He let go of me, and walked over to toss the wad into the Dumpster. I looked at the shoe, looking a lot like the other strange, single shoes I'd seen in gutters and lying at the side of the road in Chicago. When he came back over, I had to ask, "What about the pairs strung over wires?"

"Thrown by *civitas veneficus* dowsers," he said. "They mark crossroads or warn of danger. I really don't know how to tell the difference, so if I see some, I usually avoid that part of town entirely."

Nana waved good-bye and hobbled off to wherever she had been headed. I watched her slow progress down the street. When she passed the edge of the building, the plastic bag shot out. It rustled and tumbled along behind her heels like a faithful dog.

"Okay, we have a lead," Jones said, shepherding us back to the squad. "Let's roll, people."

Maybe it was the fact that I'd finished my latte and I finally felt fully caffeinated, but I had a small quibble with Jones's assessment. "What lead is that, exactly?"

He had the car door open and was halfway in. His tight expression made it clear that he wasn't used to someone questioning his decisions or authority. "The necromancer is with a sibling or other family member. Didn't you hear Nana?"

I had, but I'd noticed something else as well. "She also said he could be with a mouse."

"I'm sure it will all make sense in time."

I cleared my throat. "*And* she read Devon's fate in those spatters, so how do we know she's tracking the necromancer?"

Stone, who was opening the back door for Devon, paused to give her partner a meaningful look.

The muscles in Jones's jaw flexed, as he asked, "What do you suggest we do?"

"Can we go back to his apartment? I'd like to take a look around since I missed it this morning. We could look for an address book or something that would give us a clue what family members he's still in touch with. And a mouse? Did she mean a computer one or a furry one? He could have contacts on his laptop, if it's still there."

"It's not a bad idea," Stone said quietly.

Not a bad idea? It sounded like routine police work to me, and I only had a crumby degree in forensic science.

Precinct 13 must have some seriously weird protocols, if this was business as usual. I waited to see how Jones would react.

"Fine," Jones said finally. Dropping into his seat, he shut the car door hard. It wasn't quite a slam, but it had a very similar quality.

When I ducked under Stone's arm to slip into my own seat, she said, "It's a good suggestion. He'll be all right."

Despite Stone's assurances, it was a tense ride to the necromancer's apartment building. In particular, Devon seemed to revel in Jones's discomfort. He leaned right up against the bulletproof Plexiglas and said, "Real police work . . . are you sure you remember how to do this sort of thing, Spense?"

My ears pricked up. So I wasn't the only one who thought maybe Jones had gotten sloppy.

At Jones's growled response, Devon tipped his head back and laughed wickedly. At that angle, his canines were noticeably pronounced.

Stone turned around and pointed a finger at Devon. With a deliberate motion, she tapped the glass. It cracked with a pop, like a bullet. Both Devon and I flattened ourselves against the backrest in surprise. "Holy crap!" Devon shouted.

I stared in horror at the spot where a finger-sized dent bowed out the safety glass. A spiderweb of cracks spread out around it.

What kind of strength would you need to be able to do something like that? And she'd done it so casually.

Jones, whose lips twitched with a suppressed smile, said, "Damn it, Stone. That's the third one I'm going to have to get replaced."

"Sorry, boss," she said, though clearly without any remorse.

"Someday, Golem, someone's going to wipe that word right off your forehead," Devon sneered.

She just smiled at him and said, "I'd like to see you try, *noshech kariot.*"

Devon's eyes narrowed. It was clear he'd been insulted, but the confusion about what exactly she'd called him rippled across his face. "Oh yeah? Well, same to you."

Stone laughed and turned her back to him. The mark her finger left in the glass remained, hanging there ominously.

I looked at Stone with renewed interest. What the hell was a "golem?" The only Gollum I knew was a creepy, cave-dwelling hobbit with an invisibility ring. Stone certainly didn't look like that creature from *The Lord of the Rings*, and he always seemed sort of scrawny and weak. Stone was clearly as powerful as her name.

No one had much to say after that. I desperately wanted to know more about Stone, but it was clear that this was not the time to ask. Pulling my phone out, I Googled "gollum," but all I got were pictures and articles about the movie version. Perhaps I was spelling it wrong?

I didn't have a chance to try alternate spellings because we'd arrived.

Before getting out, Jones turned around to admonish Devon. "You kids need to play nice now. Or I'll have to separate you."

"She started it," Devon muttered.

Stone opened the door for me. I watched her carefully as I stepped out into the parking lot. She smiled at me as I moved to let Devon out. Stone did a little fake-out of slamming the door on him, and he pulled his feet back with lightning-fast speed. When he looked horrified, she gave him a halfhearted apologetic look. "Truce?" she asked.

"Yeah, okay, sure," he said nervously.

The place the necromancer lived was a duplex. The house was constructed of white stucco and broad wooden beams— sort of Tudor, but an uninspired version that was little more than a square with a pointed roof. If I had to guess, I would have said it was built in the thirties or early forties. The sidewalk looked as though it hadn't been shoveled all winter. The only pathway was a narrow melted footpath, a mess of sand and salt. We walked, single file, to the cracked and uneven steps.

There were piles of yellowing newspapers in front of one

door, and a mailbox crammed to overflowing with mail. Yellow tape had been placed in an X over the door; it was covered with the words CRIME SCENE and NO TRESPASSING.

Stone pulled a key from her pocket and fitted it into the lock. She pushed the door open with a jerk. The air that escaped smelled stale, with the tinge of cat urine.

Inside, going off to the left, was a set of stairs. They were fashioned of wood, but like the exterior, not terribly fancy or ornate. We headed up to the landing, single file, with Stone and Jones in the lead.

Devon trailed behind me, keeping as much distance between himself and Stone as possible.

At the top of the stairs, I expected everyone to go in and start checking the place out. Instead, Jones stood in front of the unlocked door staring at it. He took a number of deep breaths, as if steeling himself for something. I wondered what on earth was on the other side that would cause him to need to prepare like that. He took the doorknob in his hand and flinched. After only a second, he jerked his hand away, as though it had burned him. As he shook out his hand, Jones looked to Devon.

"Damn anti-natural wards. Would you?" he asked.

Devon crossed his arms in front of his chest. "You asking or telling?"

"Asking," Jones said, in a tone that made it clear that that could change depending on Devon's response.

Devon's usual petulance deflated with a shrug. When Jones stepped aside, Devon took his place in front of the door. He twisted the knob and pushed the door open a crack. I craned to see what all the fuss was about. I only saw shadow. It might have been my imagination, but the snake on my arm seemed to sigh happily and relaxed its hold.

Meanwhile, Jones had backed up so far that he was pressed against the wall. His face was hard and tense. Devon looked over his shoulder at him and sneered.

"Looks like the fairy is out for the count." Devon cast his gaze first at Stone and then at me. "So which of you two lovely ladies will be able to accompany me into this den of unnaturalness?"

Stone pushed the door open farther with her hand. "I can go."

She pushed past him, giving him a very slight nudge that nearly brought him to his knees. He straightened quickly and looked ready to strike, but she'd turned to face him already. She stood straight, tall, and solid. "Before you say *anything*," she said, "kabbalah is *not* maleficium, understood?"

Her finger was raised and pointed at his chest. Devon stared at it, no doubt remembering, like I was, the hole she'd put in the bulletproof glass with no effort at all.

"Understood?" she repeated, her finger still pointed like a loaded gun.

"Devon Fletcher," Jones said, slowly, and I got the sense that the use of Devon's full name was significant.

I could see Devon's eyes narrow, though he never took them from Stone's finger. "All right," he said.

Though I thought his response sounded hollow and insincere, Stone seemed to find it acceptable. She deliberately turned her back on him, and went inside.

"Unless she asks for your help, you'll stay here where I can keep an eye on you," Jones told Devon.

"I rue the day we met, fairy. Would that I had ripped out your throat and not paused to sup," he snarled.

"I bet," replied Jones flatly.

With the door pushed wider, I could make out more of

the interior. Heavy curtains were closed to the daylight, but just enough eked through to reveal a very sparsely furnished efficiency apartment. The view from the hallway afforded a good look at a wall leading to the kitchenette. At first I thought it was painted black, but then it became clear that the same gibberish I'd seen on the necromancer's body had been scribbled all over the walls.

I'd moved inside for a closer look before realizing the significance of it. I was staring at a doodle of a chicken-headed man defiling a sheep when I heard Devon's voice saying, "That must be a disappointment for you."

I glanced back at the doorway. Should I be worried that I crossed the threshold so easily?

Stone had put on surgical gloves and was thumbing through a notebook. When she noticed my stricken expression, she said, "I wouldn't worry, if I were you. From what I can tell, you've cast exactly one spell your whole life. It was a curse." She nodded in the direction of where the tattoo was under my coat sleeve. "You are only unnatural for lack of experience."

"So you can change? Someone natural could become unnatural and vice versa?"

"Magic users, yes," she said.

From the doorway, Devon said, "Magical creatures, however, are whatever their masters made them, aren't they, Hannah?"

"Shut up," she snapped.

"You won't speak again until I tell you to," Jones said.

Could Jones really control Devon so completely? Not letting him talk at all seemed kind of harsh. When Stone handed me a pair of gloves for my hands, I noted, "Nobody likes Devon much."

"That's because he's a first-class jerk."

I nodded, but I wasn't sure I agreed. He seemed to provoke Jones and Stone easily, but I hadn't found him particularly loathsome or especially deserving of the intensity of their reaction. In fact, they seemed most upset when he said things that appeared to be true. Stone was the one who'd been defensive about her ability to tolerate entering the necromancer's apartment. I pulled the gloves on with a snap.

I wandered over to the window and pulled the curtain back to let in some light. The instant the sun hit the writing on the walls, it vanished.

I closed the curtain again and the writing reappeared . . . changed. I could see that the chicken-headed guy was now getting it on with a tiger, for instance. "Sorry," I said to Stone, who had paused in her perusal of another book, to watch me. "I kind of forgot that would happen."

"What?" asked Jones from outside the door.

"I let some light in," I said. "The words changed."

"Get out!" he shouted, just as the spiders started dropping from the ceiling.

NINE

The dozens of spiders descended on thin lines. Their abdomens were the size of my fist. Hairy legs stretched out nearly twelve inches. Five bulging eyes glowed red. Mandibles clicked and chattered. Directly above me, one twitched its legs, lifting them to reveal hideous fangs.

Reflexively my hands went up to protect my face. The snake's head nestled between my thumb and pointer finger twitched. The ink began to lift itself from my skin. I felt a thin slip of tongue flicker. It raised its head up out of my flesh. The snake hissed at the spider, showing its larger fangs.

But before the snake's head could defend me, Stone batted away the spider. One-handed, she scooped me up and threw me over her shoulder. I bounced against her shoulder and back. Webs snagged at my hair. Squealing, I covered my face with my hands. The snake struck and spit.

In three pounding strides, Stone had carried me out the

door. The moment we crossed the threshold, the snake collapsed back into my flesh. This time, the head rested across the back of my hand. Its nose curled along the ridge of my knuckles. Its tongue extended slightly. From my awkward position, I took a moment to stroke its head. "Thank you," I whispered and made a solemn vow to myself never to let Jack's bird gang try to eat it again.

I felt hands swatting at my back and legs. After a few moments of that, Stone let me slide down to a standing position.

Jones stomped on something that tried to scurry back under the door. "Fuck. That was a disaster."

"Not entirely," Stone said, holding out the book she'd been looking at when I triggered the spell. "I got this. It's a diary of some kind. Besides"—she nodded in my direction—"we learned something valuable."

"That the new girl has a nose for booby traps?" Jones snarled.

"Well, yes," Stone said. With the toe of her boot, she nudged a smudged spot on the stairs that seemed to be smoldering slightly. "But also, sunlight will wipe everything clean."

Jones scratched his jawline, staring at the same smoldering spot on the carpet. "He's using *aethra*-magic?"

I had no idea what that meant, but the semantic nerd in me felt a need to point out the misused verb form. "Used," I said.

"Excellent point," Stone said. "Perhaps the spells have devolved to the point where they're affected by natural light."

"So we could go back in there if we had UV lights or something?" I wondered. I thought I'd spotted an iPad on the kitchen counter that I was certain would be even more helpful than his journal. "Or maybe just break the window on a sunny day?"

"We're going to have to do something," Jones said. "We can't leave those things in there for some normal to find."

Devon leaned both shoulders against the wall of the landing, listening to all of this with a "serves you right" smirk on his face.

Jones turned on him. "Go to my house and fetch my light therapy box right away. It's in my office on the desk." He dug keys from his pocket and thrust them at Devon. "Bring it back here as fast as possible."

Devon took the keys. His fist curled around them so hard that I thought he might crush them. His face was barely controlled rage, but he obediently turned on his heels and took off down the stairs. He moved fast, like a wild cat, in leaps and bounds.

In a matter of seconds the door slammed behind him, and he was gone.

That left the three of us standing on the steps. Stone had gone back to flipping through the book. Jones began to pace around the small square landing. I thought he could be a handsome man, if his face wasn't so constantly pinched. He had the kind of right angles and sharpness that could suit an actor or teen idol. In fact, if he let his hair grow, he could look like one of those guys who were one square jaw away from being prettier than their female costars. I wondered if that was why he spent so much time frowning. It disguised his beauty thoroughly.

As did his personality, frankly.

But, then again, perhaps he was depressed. "You have a glow light?" I asked. "Do you have seasonal affective disorder?"

He stopped abruptly. I could see a blush creeping up his neck. He looked ready to deny it, though he clearly couldn't.

Without looking up from the book, Stone said on his behalf, "Fairy are outdoors creatures. Humans seem to prefer dank, dark caves."

"Like office cubicles," I said. "And morgues. I guess I'd have to agree."

A spider leg made a tentative wiggle under the door frame. Spotting it, I stomped, but it scuttled back too quickly. I watched the gap below the door for more legs, considering. Absently, I continued to stroke the snake's head on the back of my palm. The camera flash had been some kind of trigger for the necromancer's tattoos. This morning the place must have been crawling with CSI agents and cameras. "Why didn't the locals get jumped on by these spiders?"

Not having followed my internal thoughts, Stone and Jones shot me confused looks.

I considered laying it all out, but instead I went sideways. "How quickly do spells degrade after someone dies?"

"Depends if the user is natural or unnatural."

"Natural lasts longer," I guessed. "Because it draws on the energy of living things, right?"

Jones nodded. "I suppose for an extremely unnatural mage, the spells could begin to devolve almost instantly."

I hazarded a glance at my new tattoo. That didn't quite fit the necromancer, did it? His spells clearly lasted until triggered. In the case of the spiders, they'd lasted long after the necromancer died. Unless, it was his unnatural state of being walking-around-dead that kept them active?

There were too many things I didn't understand about magic. I looked to Jones and Stone. Jones had resumed pacing and Stone's nose was buried in the journal. Neither of them seemed interested in unraveling what I considered a rather critical puzzle. I cleared my throat.

Jones's eyes flicked in my direction. His face crumbled in irritation. "What?"

"Aren't you wondering the same thing I am?"

He scowled at me for a long moment. Eventually, he managed a snide: "Enlighten us."

"Why did the spider spell trigger now?"

"Because *you* let in the light," Jones said simply.

"Well, yeah, but I mean, why didn't it also trigger earlier, when he was first discovered? I mean, don't you presume the necromancer must have set it up before he committed suicide or whatever happened to him this morning? I can't have been the first person to push aside the curtains. And, anyway, photo flash worked on the other spells. Moving the tattoos around . . . and all that. Even if no one opened the curtains before, shouldn't all the picture-taking have set something off?"

Jones's lip curled. It was an oddly threatening look.

Stone, who was still paging through the book and was oblivious to the expression on her partner's face, said, "Maybe the spell only works in the presence of a magical."

Oh. I hadn't considered that. I supposed that could be true for the tattoos as well. "But . . . wasn't Boyd here this morning?"

"Boyd?" Stone said. "I thought it was Peterson."

"Swanson?" Jones offered.

"Whoever," I said. "The point is: Wasn't someone on the team here?"

"Peterson is *sensibilitatem*," Jones said. "So is Swanson.

Neither one is really magical, they've just grown sensitive to it. They've been exposed enough to sometimes see. That's why they work for us."

That could happen? Was that why the precinct worked so hard to stay hidden?

"But you were on the scene," I insisted.

"Obviously I couldn't go inside," he said. "We came as soon as we heard Dispatch read the address. I had to stay in close proximity to the EMT guys." He saw the confusion in my face, and added, "I used glamour to convince them to let us take possession of the body once we got back to HQ. It works sort of like blarney; I have to keep them actively engaged."

Not that I knew how either glamour or blarney worked, but I nodded anyway. "What about you, Stone?"

She had put the book aside at some point and was listening quite intently. "I went in, Spense," she admitted. "The curtains were open. I do remember the sun was really bright, now that I think of it. The only thing I saw that seemed magical at all was the altar that the lab crew was dismantling. Our guy on the inside, Peterson, pulled me aside and told me it was a decoy. The real magic was somewhere else but he didn't know where, though he thought it was in the body. I came right down to tell Spense, and we brought the body to you."

"So this Peterson guy or whoever was left behind?" I asked.

"Are you suggesting Peterson set up this spell?" Jones asked brusquely.

Honestly, I was still convinced it was Boyd. I made a note to check my e-mail as soon as possible.

Jones was shaking his head vigorously. "There's no way.

Not only do I trust him implicitly, but he's only a sensitive. He couldn't set a spell of this magnitude."

"What if all he had to do was shut a curtain?" I asked.

Jones didn't like the implication, but he considered it. He absently chewed the edge of his thumb for a moment. "Why would Peterson be in league with the necromancer?"

I shrugged. *How should I know?* I still thought it was Boyd who'd been here earlier. "Jack said people do stupid things for eternal life. The necromancer was clearly on to something, or he wouldn't have been able to walk out of the morgue. Maybe Peterson wanted a piece of it."

Jones and Stone exchanged a couple of glances.

I waited and wondered what they silently communicated about. What I wanted to know was why Jones was so hostile to anything I suggested? Was he one of those cops who'd grown soft in a cushy job? Devon's comment seemed to imply that could be the case.

And what was up with all that business between Devon and Stone? This precinct seemed rife with infighting about who was natural and who was not. Maybe they no longer worked as a functioning team.

I shook my head sadly. I thought the Chicago cops were messed up.

"Okay," Jones said finally. "I'll entertain the possibility we have a traitor on the team. I don't like it, but I think you might be right that someone set up this trap after the locals left. It makes sense that someone from our unit would be the next one in the door. I'm not willing to put Peterson entirely in the frame just yet. He's been with us a long time, and this is a serious accusation. It's possible there was some-one else, someone we don't know about among the *ordina-rium*. But we'll watch Peterson extra closely."

I nodded, pleased to hear Jones sounding like a real cop. Maybe there was hope for him, after all.

We fell back into silence. Jones returned to pacing and chewing on his cuticles. Just when I started to wonder how long we would wait for Devon, we heard a pounding on the door.

Jones, who was already halfway down the stairs, walked the rest of the way and opened the door for him. Devon stumbled in to where I could see him. Steam rose in heat waves from Devon's head. His breath was a cloud in the colder air. His arm trembled as he handed over the lamp. Once relieved of it, he clung to the door frame, panting. I wondered if the order "as fast as you can" had brought him to this state of near exhaustion.

Muttering a quick word of thanks, Jones leaned in close to say something else. With a quick nod, Devon limped back outside. The door swung closed. I hoped whatever Jones had ordered him to do next, it involved rest. I reminded myself to never eat or drink anything a fairy offered. Ever.

Jones handed the full-spectrum light to Stone. "You're going to have to find an outlet, I'm afraid."

"Wait," I said, thinking of all those horrible spiders, "She can't go in there alone. The only outlet I saw was in the kitchenette. She'll die before she gets there."

"All I need to do is clear a path to the curtains with the light," she said. "I'll open them wide and the sun will do the rest of the work."

"But . . ."

Stone cut me off with a small smile, and her hand came down heavily on my shoulder. "Thank you for your concern, but I'll be fine."

She handed me the book and took a moment to straighten

her police cap. Her bangs shifted slightly and I saw strange indentations on her forehead. They weren't scars; they were a smooth series of dents, like someone pressed a finger into wet concrete and wrote something. Jones and I stepped back as she pulled open the door. The flip side was covered in spiders, crawling all over each other. Several scurried away from the light, back into the room. I had to bite back a scream as I saw one leap and attach itself to her back.

Fighting my instincts to pull her back out, I pushed the door shut quickly.

Jones stomped after one that was making a brave run at him. He missed. When it scuttled over my boot on its way back under the door, I felt my snake shift. Quickly, I covered it with my other hand. For some reason, I was convinced that Jones wouldn't approve if he saw the way it seemed to want to protect me.

We stood together outside the door, straining to hear what was happening inside with Stone. I hoped she was right that the spiders couldn't hurt her. I held my breath until she called the all clear.

Cautiously, I pushed open the door. Stone stood near the windows. The glow light was on the kitchen counter. The curtains were wide open, and the place looked entirely empty. There was no sign of the creepy scrawl on the walls, or any trace that the place had been overrun by arachnids with gigantism.

In the light, all was hidden.

With the sun streaming in, Jones seemed to have less trouble tolerating the unnaturalness of the space. He was able to lean into the room and look around. I grabbed the iPad, while Stone stuffed a few more books under her arm. We both still wore our gloves. I'd forgotten to take mine off earlier, and my hands were slick with sweat underneath the latex.

Before leaving, I took a quick look under the sink. I found no sign of rat poison, though I no longer really expected to.

In fact, I was beginning to suspect that whoever wrote the report—Boyd or the mysterious Peterson—may have intentionally lied. Now, why they would, I didn't know. It was possible, of course, that "poison" was the cover story to satisfy the *ordinarium.*

I didn't think it was a purposeful attack on me. How could it be? No one knew I was magical before this morning, not even me, but what had Jones said? Something about being convinced the spell he'd sensed in the body would knock me out? What if incapacitating the coroner had been part of a plan hatched between co-conspirators? And, what if that meant that I was now in the crosshairs, for having evaded that part of their scheme?

I decided it behooved me to become the detective here if no one else would.

I checked the room thoroughly.

There was one closet, and Stone met me in front of it. Neither of us reached for the knob. Instead, we stared at the door nervously. "Inside is where they found the altar," Stone said.

"The decoy."

"If Peterson was telling the truth," Stone said. She seemed a lot more at ease with the idea of his possible betrayal. Before I could say something about it, she asked, "Do you feel anything? Any magic?"

I had no idea what magic was supposed to feel like. I held my snake-covered hand up in front of the cheap plywood. There was nothing from the snake, though it hadn't warned me about the spiders either.

"I don't know," I admitted. "But we should look."

Stone stepped in front of me and pulled the door open. The interior was larger than a standard closet, big enough to walk inside several steps: a perfect place for a hidden altar. Clothes hung on a bar along the left side and a pile of laundry was heaped underneath. Our necromancer seemed to have an interest in vintage cartoon characters. He had a lot of T-shirts sporting Warner Brothers images. He also had an apparent fondness for leather and buckles. I was kind of half-surprised not to find any fetish wear or obvious bondage equipment.

The other side was completely bare. The only evidence that an altar had been there were the black wax spots spattered on the carpeting. I thought it might be a dead end, after all, but, on a whim, I knelt down to feel the floor. I found a loose section of carpeting. "Here," I said.

Stone pushed me gently aside. I let her. I wanted to see what, if anything, I'd found, but I also didn't need a blast of black magic in the face, especially if it involved more spiders. The carpeting pulled up with a rending sound. "Sometimes I don't know my own strength," she admitted, holding the carpet shred.

"He's probably not too worried about his security deposit, anyway, being dead and all," I noted.

I looked around her shoulders and saw that we'd found a trapdoor.

"What's going on?" Jones yelled from the doorway. The closet was on the wall opposite the kitchenette.

"There's a trapdoor," I told him. "It's got some kind of latch. Do you think we should try to open it?"

"I think we'd better get Jack," Jones said. He pulled out his cell phone and punched in a few numbers. After a brief conversation, Jones snapped the cell shut and slid it back into the holster on his belt. "Let's sit tight. He can be here in ten."

While we waited for Jack to arrive, I finished my survey of the apartment. Something felt very off to me, and not just in the "there might be spiders lurking in the shadows" way. "Does this guy own any other property?" I asked Jones, who'd taken to leaning a hip on the door frame and thumbing through one of the books Stone had identified as important.

"I don't know. Why?"

I ignored the continued hostility in his responses. Maybe he didn't care if the corpse was after him, but I did. "No beakers. No test tubes. No hoses dripping neon green goo."

"What are you talking about?"

"One of the theories is that this guy was trying to create the Philosopher's Stone, right? A formula for eternal life? Well, where's all his lab equipment? I don't even see a home-brewing kit. You'd think he'd at least have jars of eyes of newt or whatever, right? Where is all that?"

"Maybe it's behind door number one," Jones said with a nod in the direction of the closet.

Maybe.

I went back to flipping through the necromancer's iPad. Luckily, he hadn't bothered to install a lock code. But a quick perusal of the apps made it clear why not: There was nothing much on it. He played a lot of Angry Birds and bought a bunch of erotic romances that involved M/M/F pairings and light BDSM via the Kindle store, but otherwise I didn't learn that much about him. Even his e-mail was fairly mundane. He had a few friends, but they seemed to correspond about their shared enthusiasm for various rock bands while mangling the English language. Unless there was some hidden code among all the "dude, srsly!"s, I didn't see anything magical being discussed. His Twitter account was slightly more cryptic, but that was mostly due to his atrocious spelling and the fact that most of the tweets were out of context.

I did notice that one name came up a lot, someone going by the Twitter handle @skull_lady. She—or he, since there was no way to verify the gender, really—had a Gmail account under the same user name. A lover? A possible accomplice?

I showed Jones my findings. As he was copying down the information in his trusty notepad, there was a knock on the door. It was probably Jack. I handed Jones the iPad, and told him I'd get it.

Jack wore a lime green stocking hat with large, floppy pointed ears hanging off the sides. When he saw me staring at it, he smiled. "Yoda ears. Do you like them?"

Honestly, on him, it sort of worked, even with the straggles of black hair that stuck out from underneath the edges and hung down to his shoulders, ruining the illusion. "Yeah," I said, stepping aside to let him in.

He stomped his boots on the welcome mat, knocking off the bits of slush that clung to the treads. He'd exchanged his leather for a long wool coat.

I'd left my own coat slung over the back of the necromancer's couch. We walked back up to the apartment, and I noticed Jack staring at my arm. "It's changed," he said before I could hide it. He was looking at the snake's head.

He stopped abruptly, causing me to pause with him. We were just outside the door. Jones looked up expectantly. "It's bonding to you," Jack said, worried.

"We can talk about that later. We've got a trapdoor to open." I turned away so he couldn't see the mixed emotions I was sure were visible on my face.

Turned out Jack couldn't enter the room any more than Jones could. Instead, he shouted orders to me from the doorway. Unfortunately, I had no idea how to do half the things he asked of me.

"Open your mind," he said.

I rolled my eyes. I'd never understood how to do that even when the hypnotist asked as part of my therapy. "Okay," I said, though my brain felt no more open than it had a moment before.

"Tell me what you see."

A ripped piece of carpet and an obviously handmade trapdoor cut into the floorboards. The latch was an eye and hook. But, as I was staring uselessly at it, wondering what the hell I was supposed to be noticing, my eyes slipped out of focus. All of a sudden, words appeared. They looked like they'd been carved onto the surface with a wood-burning pen. But the moment I tried to focus on them they disappeared. "Words!" I shouted. "I saw words."

"Good, they're probably a spell guarding the lock." Jack couldn't quite disguise the relief in his voice. "What did they say?"

"Um." I let my focus blur again. I stared just above where I'd seen them appear, and after several attempts, they reappeared. "It's Latin, I think. *Mal*—"

"Stop!" Jack shouted. "Spell it. Don't speak it."

Oh, duh. I felt stupid. I almost fell for the oldest trick in horror movies: Never read the spell out loud. Instead, I slowly listed each letter, which was actually probably easier since I wouldn't have known how to pronounce the words anyway.

Jack let out a low whistle when I'd finished. Beside me, I heard Stone sigh, as if deflated. "It's a tough one, huh?" I guessed.

"It's okay," Jack said. "We can counter this. I just need to think for a minute."

My knees were getting sore from kneeling in front of the trap. I put my hand down to steady myself as I shifted position. I hadn't considered which hand I was using, until I felt the snake's head moving. It slithered out of my skin and over my fingers. The scales were warm and soft, though I could feel their shape. A tongue flicked out once, twice, and by the third time, I knew something was different.

The lock spell was broken. I sensed, rather than heard, a kind of click of release. When the snake slowly returned to its new position on the back of my hand and seemed to nod its head once, I was certain.

Even so, my fingers hovered over the hook. I let my focus blur again, and was satisfied to see that the words had disappeared. "I got this," I said, as I undid the latch.

"You do? How?"

I lifted the lid slowly, cautiously. I knew whatever the necromancer had hidden here was sure to be a doozy. But even so, I wasn't quite prepared for a severed head.

TEN

A moldering severed human head stared back at me from beneath the floorboards. Its shriveled skin stretched over bone and teeth, giving it a skull-like grin. Eyelids flattened over liquefied eyeballs. The hair had been carefully arranged at some point, probably for a funeral, and clung, lacquered, to the forehead.

I guess we knew why the necromancer had been robbing graves now.

It was clearly bespelled because it neither smelled nor attracted any vermin. Also, silver wires crossed the forehead and throat, holding it in place. The wires were nailed to the subflooring, and continued around a series of nails arranged in a perfect circle. They'd clearly been woven in a specific pattern of loops and knots.

Something glimmered inside the corpse head's mouth. I had to resist my scientific urge to pry the jaws open to see what it was. So, I could only guess that it was either a large,

polished stone of some kind, like hematite, or a piece of sil-
vered mirror.

I felt Stone peering over my shoulder. I was about to ask
her what the hell this thing was supposed to be when its
ruined sockets seemed to blink and its mouth moved. The
sound that came out rattled like death, even as it quoted
scripture, "Ask and it shall be given, seek and ye shall find."

"Where is the necromancer?" I asked it, because I thought
I might as well give it a try.

A dry, spooky laugh full of dust filled my ears. "Look in
the mirror."

I hate riddles almost as much as I hate trying to "clear
my mind," and this one stumped me utterly. Did the head
want me to see the answer in the polished surface inside its
mouth, or was it trying to imply that I need to do some self-
reflection?

"Well, that was cryptic," I told Stone.

Though I normally found her expression hard to read,
she seemed to be looking at me especially strangely.

"What?"

"Did the head talk to you?" she asked.

"Of course, not that it made much—wait, didn't you
hear it?"

She shook her head. "I only heard you ask it a question."

I returned my attention to the severed head. I half
expected it to give me a grotesque wink or something, but it
just lay there, suddenly appearing very dead, indeed. "Well,"
I said. "It told me that if I want to find the necromancer, I
need to look in the mirror."

"It thinks you're a necromancer?"

"Maybe," I agreed reluctantly. I pointed at the papery
skin pulled taut over the slightly opened jaw. "There's also

something shiny in there." Pitching my voice loud enough for Jack to hear, I asked, "Can I touch it, do you think?"

"I wouldn't," Stone murmured.

"I don't know," Jack shouted back. "Frankly, I'm surprised you got around the lock. I guess you should trust your instincts. They haven't failed you so far."

Except, I thought with a quick glance at the snake, *I didn't see that one coming.* My ignorance also caused the spiders to, quite literally, jump out of the woodwork.

I hesitated for several heartbeats. I stared at the snake curled on the back of my hand. It had helped me twice now. I wish I knew how to control it, how to ask its advice.

A big part of me rebelled at the mere idea of leaving evidence of this magnitude behind. I wanted that object badly. The severed head had told me the answer to my question was in the mirror. But had I asked the right one? Did its answer mean I needed to do it literally, figuratively, or what?

I decided to try the indirect approach.

Pulling myself up to a kneel, I fished my iPhone out of my pocket. After making absolutely sure there was no way there would be any kind of flash, I took several pictures of the head in situ. Then, moving in as close as possible without actually disturbing the head or breaking the magical circle, I took a picture of the inside of the mouth. If the answer was reflected there, maybe I could take a photo of it.

Examining the image on the screen, I saw that the object was a metallic stone, very likely hematite as I'd first thought. A reflection was barely visible. I used my fingers to expand that section of the photo. The image still wasn't terribly clear, thanks to the irregular curvature of the stone, but I saw the back of my own hand holding the camera. The back of my hand—where I could just make out the tattoo of the black snake.

The severed head had answered my question both literally *and* metaphorically. I was carrying a part of the necromancer with me. If I was going to find him, I'd have to use the snake in some way.

I wasn't sure I liked that answer at all.

I pulled myself to my feet, slowly, conscious of cramped muscles.

Stone stood as well. Her eyes watched me as I stretched out, my joints creaking and popping. "You found something," she said.

Likewise, Jack and Jones seemed to be waiting to hear what I might say. I wanted to fall back on old habits, to shrug and say I'd seen nothing. Ironically, they'd never believe me.

I took in a deep breath. "Why don't I explain it all in the car?"

We put the iPad and the books Stone had grabbed into the truck of the squad. She kept the journal, however, and continued to glance through it in the front seat. Jones had turned the engine on for the heat. Devon was passed out, snoring, in the seat beside me, looking like some drunk college kid. Jack nestled up against my other side. At first, he'd been hesitant to touch me, but when our knees accidentally bumped, it was clear he wasn't going to get a shock from the tattoo.

I wasn't sure if that comforted me or not.

"So what happened?" Jones wanted to know. He twisted in his seat, looking back through the cracked Plexiglas shield. Since Jack had come in his own car, we idled in the parking lot. The Radio Dispatch crackled with the usual cop chatter, but Jones had turned the volume down low. I caught a bit of a discussion about an unauthorized flyover.

After taking a steadying breath, I repeated the conversation with the severed head verbatim. Then I showed them the picture of the reflection. I even pulled the image wide enough for everyone to see my hand holding the camera phone.

Jack did not come to the same conclusion I had. Instead, he asked, "So you think the necromancer is going to call you?"

Stone, too, took a completely different tack. "No," she said. "The answer is in the pictures she took of his body that are stored on her phone."

Jones was the only one giving me a dark, suspicious glare. Even though his expression wasn't too far from his "normal" look, I found I couldn't meet his eyes. I also wasn't in a hurry to spell out my own theory. After all, despite what Jack had said, it was clear that unnatural magic was judged pretty harshly by this team.

Jack and Stone continued to argue their points. I sat quietly, idly stroking the head of the snake on the back of my hand. In the end, though, Jack asked a question I'd been dreading. "How did you end up opening the lock?"

"I didn't," I told my hands, clasped in my lap. My unmarked one covered up the other, as if I could protect the snake from what was to come. "The tattoo did."

Silence.

The only noise in the car was the sound of the voices on the police radio. Everyone seemed to be holding their breaths. I felt Jack pull his body tighter, away from me.

On my other side, Devon stirred, shifting slightly. Jones must have released him from the prohibition from speaking, because he said, "Sounds like I'm no longer the only unnatural on the team."

I tore my gaze away from my lap. My mouth opened, but I didn't deny it. I'd been thinking the same thing. What if the snake tattoo had not killed me because of my accidental curse? What if it had sunk into my skin because it had found a new home—a place similar to the necromancer? Maybe the severed head's mirror was metaphorical, as well. Maybe to find the dark, I just had to look inside.

All this talk of being a natural was nice, but my life before this . . . It was hardly unicorns and princesses, was it? It was trolls and demons and fucked-up nightmare shit.

Unnatural.

Devon opened his eyes and smiled slightly, gently. "It's not such a terrible thing, you know."

I couldn't stop the snort that came out. In his collegiate sweatshirt and easy smile, Devon did not look like someone who'd experienced much that was hard and painful, nothing like months in a psych ward. "It's been pretty terrible so far," I said, thinking of all the days that had led up to this one.

"Your past doesn't necessarily mean anything," Jack said, his voice soft and full of concern.

Not necessarily, but maybe it did.

I kept my eyes focused on Devon because I was afraid of what I might see in the others' faces. It was a strange thing. This morning I discovered magic was real and I was a part of it. All the shame I'd ever felt about being different had been erased, lifted.

Yet, in the same day, I found out I was very possibly something *not* natural, and all those old, dark feelings threatened to return. I wanted to go back into hiding, return to being invisible.

Jack patted my thigh lightly, awkwardly. "I still think the jury is out," he said, clearly pitching his voice to be heard by those in the front seat. "The tattoo was a trap, maybe it's still acting on orders. Perhaps the necromancer wanted us to find the head."

Seemed like a stretch to me.

Jones nodded, though. "The tattoo is clearly maleficium. It's influencing Alex's polarity."

"Exactly," Jack agreed. "Until it's removed or completely neutralized, we won't know her true nature."

"Should we worry that it will have undue influence at this early stage in her development?" Stone wondered, looking up from the book.

"It is pretty deeply bonded to her," Jack agreed with a deep frown, which was oddly juxtaposed with the silliness of the Yoda ears flopping as he shook his head.

"I think we can just keep watch," Jones said. "We'll reserve judgment."

Devon sighed and closed his eyes again.

I said nothing, happy to be talked about as though I wasn't there.

"Well," Jones said, his eyes skimming off me before turning around in his seat. "I think we've done what we can here. Let's head back to the precinct office."

Jack made his good-byes. He made a point of touching my leg again and saying, "Maybe we could talk later? Call me?"

"Sure. That would be nice," I said by rote.

Instead of going with the rest of them, I had Jones drop me off back at the morgue. I told them that I wanted to follow up with the lab rats to see what came of all of the tests I'd ordered. Plus, I'd left the morgue in a terrible state. I needed to do some cleanup. However, I agreed to join the team for the morning meeting the next day at eight. Jones reminded me that I needed to give him the details I could remember about my demon stepmom, so I should come in a bit earlier. I nodded in agreement, and made a note of it in my reminder app: "Tell cop about demon bitch."

I stood on the curb as the squad pulled away. Devon gave me a little wave from the backseat, and our eyes held each other until the taillights disappeared around the corner.

When they were completely out of sight, I shuffled off to my basement refuge.

I was pleased to find it still devoid of my assistant. I checked on Mrs. Finnegan, but she had nothing new to say.

Finding my supplies, I began to clean and organize. It had been a strange day. I let the routine of work wash over me. Pulling up music on my iPhone, I let my mind go blank as I scrubbed and labeled and organized.

I pulled up the e-mailed report. The name on it *was* Boyd. I was right. I made a mental note to tell Jones about it the next time we met.

When I finished all that, I called my contact at the hospital about the toxicology report. I knew there was no way they'd have even preliminary results yet, but I had to let them know that there had been a problem with collecting all the samples from the liver, and that the body had . . . er, been *moved* before I could get tissue from the brain. They were not happy, but said they'd do what they could with what they had.

I spent the next several hours composing drafts of two autopsy reports—one for Jones and his crew, the other for the folks upstairs, the *ordinarium*, as I was beginning to think of them.

I'd left my tape recorder at the precinct office, but I remembered most of the pertinent information. It bothered me that there was so much unfinished in the usual procedures before the necromancer had walked away. I ended up concluding both reports with "cause of death: uncertain." I saved the files on the desktop computer with a frustrated sigh.

The clock on the wall told me I'd missed lunch by a mile and, if I didn't go home soon, dinner as well. I locked up the office, the lights switching off with an electric crackle.

I spent the drive home considering all the unnatural things in my life, and in life in general. Roads had to be unnatural, what with all the asphalt and concrete. Houses, cities, they were all man-made and artificial . . . though Devon had said that city magic was neutral, because cities had equal parts of both. I supposed that roads could have been laid on old wagon tracks that had been driven over deer trails, or maybe aligned with grids that followed the natural rising and setting of the sun.

I shook my head.

I didn't want to think about this stuff anymore. I just wanted to sink into a nice, hot bath and go to bed.

When I pulled up in front of my place, I was surprised to see the lights on. I shared the house with my roommate, Robert, but he normally worked the second shift at the hospital. I was disappointed because I wanted time alone to wallow in my increasingly melancholy mood. On the flip side, Robert was a fabulous cook and I might be able to mooch some of whatever he was making himself for dinner.

Robert's house was a typical 1950s, one-story, ranch-style place with white aluminum siding. We had scrubby yews on either side of the steps that would be in need of trimming once the last of the snow melted. The yard was small, but Robert kept the sidewalks tidy and clear of snow. Actually, I insisted that he did since despite having a two-stall garage I was expected to park on the street. To be fair, his car was much fancier than my beater. In my keep-it-to-myself opinion, however, that meant that *my* car needed the heated garage more in the winter, when my ancient battery was likely to die.

I didn't fight over those sorts of details with Robert, though. I let the homeowner win. Besides, he'd taken me in when I was fairly desperate. He'd even helped pay some of my moving costs. Considering we met playing an online game, he'd turned out to be an amazing friend.

He could have his heated garage. It was a small price in the great scheme.

I followed the path around the house to the back.

The smell of curry met me at the door. Inside the mud-room, I hung my coat up on the peg and kicked my boots onto the rug. "Smells great, Robert," I told the creaking linoleum floors and the sound of sizzling coming from the kitchen. "Did you get a day off or something?"

At the same moment, I happened to look through to the living room and recognized the battered duffel bag slung over the arm of the couch.

Valentine stepped into the archway. "No," he said. "You called and I came."

ELEVEN

I probably should have asked him how the hell he got to South Dakota so fast, or what part of his brain thought it was sexy to break into my house—not to mention ferreting out my street address somehow—but I didn't. Instead, I ran straight into his open arms.

Burying my face into the fabric of his cotton tee, I smelled his familiar scent: a combination of wood smoke and leather.

I tilted my head to look up at him. He had a long and graceful neck, and such proud features. Dark hair cropped short, though just beginning to curl at the edges. His fathomless black eyes searched mine, but I wasn't quite ready to talk.

Laying my head back down, I cuddled close to his heart. His chest was solid, massive, and strong—though not hard like stone, more like supple sinew and muscled armor, but cold, too.

I was about to tell him that he shouldn't have come,

when his hand, which had been gently massaging my back, strayed down my shoulder. He stepped away with a hissing breath. Holding my arm out, away from my body, he frowned as he examined the snake tattoo. "What's this?"

Where to even start?

He'd begun chuckling darkly before I could respond. "This is what you do to yourself when I leave you? Go all death-metal Goth chick on me?" Dropping my arm, he gave me a sly smile. "A dragon would have been more your style."

"Funny. I was just saying the same thing to Jack this morning."

"Jack?" His voice was full of teasing jealousy, but I sensed a tremor of the real thing as well.

"Just this guy from work," I said.

He turned back to the stove, and stirred whatever he had cooking here. I pulled a stool from the island and sat facing him. "Work, yes," he said. He pulled an onion from the bowl and sliced it on our cutting board. "Did your dead guy ever come back?"

"No," I said. I got up and fetched two beers from the fridge. I twisted the tops off the bottles and set one on the counter for Valentine. I took mine back to my seat.

He chopped with the speed and precision of a professional chef. "You're a lot less upset about it now, I see."

"They believed me," I said, peeling the label on the bottle. "Every single person in this town believed every word I said."

Valentine added the onions and then turned the gas down to low. He leaned against the counter and took a long pull of beer. He was wearing a shirt I'd bought him at the Navy Pier in Chicago. "No wonder you moved here."

Of course, the truth was that I'd moved here to get away

from all the things I thought were driving me crazy, including Valentine. Only now it turned out those things were real and I had never needed to run out on him.

I should find a way to apologize, but, instead, I said, "I met a half dozen people today who believe in magic. They think *I'm* magical."

"I have always said so. And so you are." He set his beer down. Standing in front of me, he lifted my chin. His kisses tasted of hops and memories.

The curry smoldered into sludge while we rekindled our romance. The fire alarm went off while we were in the throes of passion. Valentine rushed out and doused the smoking pan in the sink. I ran to the windows and opened sash and storm, and then waved my arms around frantically trying to fan the smoke outside.

When the beeping finally subsided, I fell back onto the couch laughing. I was sure the neighbors got quite the sight of us running around in various states of undress trying to air out the place.

"Robert is going to kill me," I said.

Valentine moved aside his duffel bag and sat down beside where I sprawled. He tugged at the spikes of my hair playfully. "We should order a pizza. I'm starving."

I pointed a finger at him and shook it halfheartedly. "You're supposed to say something gallant, you know, like how you'd never let Robert hurt me."

He grabbed my fingers and kissed them. "It's a given," he said. After kissing my knuckle near the snake's outstretched tongue, he let my hand drop. "I don't need to say things you already know."

Except that was always one of our problems. He would never say what I most needed to hear. He returned to absently playing with my hair, massaging my scalp. I looked up the long expanse of his body, wondering if I should destroy the moment and tell him my feelings. As I considered, I was struck by how much more like a vampire he looked than Devon. His skin was pearly white, almost alabaster, and unusually hairless for someone who clearly possessed plenty of testosterone. He was strikingly handsome, or at least I always thought so, but some of my girlfriends back in Chicago used words like "wicked" or "cruel" when describing his features. As much as I loved him, I had to admit his eyes were cold. I have no doubt that the jury of his peers took one look into those black eyes and made the decision that sent him away. The biggest argument had probably been, "How long of a sentence are we allowed to give him?" Of course, they hadn't misread his character or his guilt. I'd had to beg him not to *kill* my stepmother.

He chose that moment to ask, "What are you thinking?"

"I met a vampire today," I said, because I *had* been thinking of Devon in a roundabout way.

"During the daylight? That's unusual," he remarked dryly, smoothing the frown lines from my forehead.

"He's also a werewolf."

"We should lock the door on Wednesday. It's a full moon."

His complete lack of shock made me realize that talking to Valentine had prepared me for Precinct 13 in a way. Following the advice of my therapist, I'd cast him as an "enabler," but now I asked, "Have you met any vampires?"

"Russia is lousy with them," he said.

Yesterday, I would have laughed at this point, sat up,

socked him in the arm, and told him how much I loved his sense of humor. We would have kissed, fallen back into bed, and I would have thought no more of it.

Now, when I pulled myself into a sitting position, I anxiously searched his face. "Are you shitting me?"

"No. They're everywhere back home. One of the first recorded uses of the word 'vampire' was in a Russian book in the ninth century or thereabouts. Many people believed Rasputin was a vampire, as well." He was very casual when he answered, very conversational, but my stomach began to knot.

"So, you're saying you've met vampires before," I said, and, though it was a statement, my words hung in the air like a question.

"There are a lot of bloodsuckers out there. Some people say they're running the government." There was a tiny bit of a mock in the smile that played on the edges of his lips.

Now I did sock him in the arm. I hated the way I always lost control of the conversation whenever I tried to talk to him about something important. I could never pin him down and get a straight answer from him. "God, you frustrate the hell out of me. I don't want to play this game with you because you always win. Forget it. I don't even know what we were talking about anymore."

He leaned in and kissed my pouting lips. Then he got up and ordered pizza.

We'd eaten, finished what we'd started earlier, and were lying spooned in my bed when Valentine surprised me by saying, "I think this place is good for you."

We'd heard Robert come in about an hour ago, and we'd had trouble keeping from giggling. It seemed we were destined for interruptions tonight. I smiled and hugged Valentine's arms encircling my waist. "Yeah, I like Robert's house a lot. It's very comfortable. He can be kind of a June Cleaver, but I'm really thankful he offered it to me when I suddenly . . ."

I had to stop or I'd have to find a way to apologize for running out on Valentine.

"I didn't mean this house, I meant Pierre."

"Oh?"

"It's an unusual city. It seems just large enough. Or maybe just small enough that less is hidden."

"You mean things like vampires and necromancers?"

"Yes."

His breath was in my ear, soft and steady. I felt him drift easily to sleep in a moment. Meanwhile, I lay awake for a long time. He'd *told* me, after all. He'd answered the question I'd been so desperately trying to ask earlier, even though I hadn't figured out quite how to formulate it. With that simple idea that there were things hiding in plain sight, extraordinary bits that people might pass by, unthinking, in a larger city, he told me everything I needed to know.

Valentine *understood* magic.

He had known the truth all along.

A phone call woke me up at five fifty-six the next morning. I fumbled around until I managed to get the receiver in proximity of my face. "Mmm?"

The sharp, succinct voice on the other end could only be Jones. "Jack is picking you up. We've had a new development out at Jerry Olson's ranch."

"Nnnn?" I asked, but Jones had already hung up.

I pulled my feet over the side of the bed and sat there for

a long moment, working up the energy to find some clothes. I considered the pile at the end of the bed. It was a mix of mine and Valentine's, but I was pretty sure my underwear was still somewhere in the living room. I should probably wear fresh, at any rate. Luckily, the closet was less than a step away. I pulled something on in the dark, and stumbled out of the room, careful not to wake Valentine.

In the kitchen, I started the coffee as quietly as my morning clumsiness allowed. While that brewed, I scrawled a note on the Post-it pad on the fridge. "At work. Explain later."

Looking at it, I wasn't sure who the note was even intended for—was I planning on explaining Valentine to Robert, or Precinct 13 to Valentine?

I decided it worked either way and left it.

The loudness of the knock at the door made me jump. Thank God Jack hadn't thought to ring the bell. I ran to open it. It was still dark outside, but the corner streetlight illuminated his broad smile. The Yoda ear hat flopped as he bounced up and down on the balls of his feet. "Crop circles," he said without preamble. "Cow mutilations."

"Coffee," I said continuing the list of random words beginning with "c."

I was turning back toward the kitchen when he stopped me with, "No, your coat. Get it. We've got to go now while the readings are fresh."

I did as he asked with a grumble. As I jammed my boots onto my feet, I wondered, "Can't we at least drive through some place?"

Jack, it turned out, was a tea drinker, and he told me all about his favorite "monkey picked" oolong tea while I ordered a super-duper venti mocha to go. The barista seemed as bleary-eyed and annoyed by Jack's chipperness as I was. Though I had to admit I was happy not to have to carry much of the conversation. I just let his monologue roll over me as we got back into his car.

A dusting of snow covered everything. The highway was almost invisible, just pale tracks of the wheels of whatever vehicles had come this way before. The air was hazy, causing halos around the lights ahead. I held the coffee in my gloved hands, close to my face, to keep warm. Jack's car was a bright yellow VW bug, one of the old ones from the sixties. It had flower decals all over it, a peace sign on the door, and no heater.

"I hate you," I said.

Jack had been telling me something about winter mornings in Beverley, East Yorkshire. "What?"

"Why am I up at this ungodly hour again?" which was really what I'd meant to say the first time, but hadn't ingested nearly enough caffeine to be civil.

"Didn't Jones tell you?"

"I was sleeping."

"Right, well, this rancher, Jerry Olson, called downtown this morning in a state of hysteria. He's got crop circles and dead cows."

I nodded, but I still felt I was missing something. "Who died?"

"About six cows," Jack repeated.

"But no people?"

"Right," he said.

"Take me home," I said. When he shot me a confused look, I explained. "Cows and humans are completely different species. I think they have six stomachs. I'm not a veterinarian."

Jack shrugged and didn't turn the wheel even the slightest. "You're all we've got."

I had intended to make my case to Jones the moment we pulled into the ranch. Instead, I found myself standing in a frosty field staring down at a mauled animal. It was hard to even tell what it had been. My boots scrunched on the stiff clover as I bent closer to examine the haunch. "Looks like something chewed on it, here." I gestured with the lip of the coffee cup.

The rancher, Jerry Olson, a beefy guy in a cowboy hat and parka, nodded. "Coyotes. I had to chase them off with my shotgun."

I could still see the pale moon hanging in the morning sky overhead. It was nearly full. I exchanged a look with Jones, because I'd noticed Devon's conspicuous absence. Jones shook his head slightly, and I took that to mean that Devon's alibi for last night was solid. So, *real* wolf-type animals, not the were-vamp kind.

I returned to my examination.

Underneath my coat, I felt the tattoo constrict suddenly and I looked down at it. I glanced up just in time to see the mangled head of the cow lift off the frozen ground.

TWELVE

The meat of its skinless flesh steamed in the cold. Its exposed, lidless eyeball hung loosely in its socket, but somehow seemed to look directly at me. It lowed pitifully. Then it dropped its head with a wet, sticky sound.

"Holy shit!" I fell back on my ass in shock. The remains of my coffee spilled on my shoes. I scrambled to my feet and pointed frantically. "It . . . it . . . it . . ." I was about to tell them that the cow was clearly not dead and needed to be shot in the head, when I looked again.

The light in its eye had gone out.

"Are you okay?" Jack asked. He bent to pick up the coffee container and brushed the grit from the side. He handed it to me. There was a little mocha left inside. I took it and tried to communicate with my eyes that we needed to talk somewhere without Olson.

"Sorry," I said. "I slipped. I guess it just freaked me out

a bit." My excuse sounded stupid even to my own ears. I hid my face as I brushed the snow from the butt of my coat.

"Why don't you show Alex the other thing?" Jones suggested.

Jack led me through the pasture. We threaded along the uneven ground, careful to avoid the lumps of icy cow pies. It was the third time, or maybe fourth if I counted the necromancer, that something dead had spoken to me. My stomach shivered and threatened to revolt.

Once we'd gotten to the far side of the stables, Jack asked, "What happened?"

"You didn't see?"

He shook his head. I wasn't surprised, but I was still disappointed. Despite everything that I knew about magic now, it still bothered me when I experienced things that no one else did. I had a hard time trusting what was real.

Bits of hay covered the gravel near the entrance to a long, brick building. Inside, the few remaining cattle huddled near the grain bin. Their glossy black hides tensed and shivered, as their brush-tipped tails flicked like an irritated cat's. Waves of heat from their bodies were visible in the chill.

" 'I see dead cows' is the dumbest superpower ever," I said. I took a swig from the mocha before I remembered I'd dropped it. The drink was cold and slightly crunchy.

"It tried to communicate with you?" Jack asked, shoving his hands deeply into the pockets of his wool trench coat. "What did it say?"

" 'Moo,' " I explained.

"Oh. Right," he said, looking at the clump of cows. They stomped their hooves and bellowed lowly amongst themselves. After a moment, he asked, "Do you suppose that's a sign it was killed by magic?"

I looked around for a place to dispose of my cup while I considered. Not all the dead things that had talked to me thus far were killed by magical means. Though both the necromancer and the severed head were clearly under some spell, I wasn't so sure about Mrs. Finnegan. From all accounts, she'd died quite naturally. I spotted a metal garbage can just inside the door. "I don't know what it means," I admitted, tossing the cup and putting the circular cover back in place. "I wish it would stop, though."

He gave me a sympathetic nod. "The crop circle is over here."

I followed Jack around the side of the barn. Rolls of hay, taller than our heads, dotted the field. Nubby remains of the harvest threatened to trip my clumsy feet. I tried to walk, tightrope style, along the narrow tire treads. The sun broke on the horizon, throwing pink and orange onto the cloud cover.

Under my coat, I could feel my tattoo shift and squirm the closer we got to the circle.

Given that the hay had all been baled last season, I wondered how the circle had been formed. I was about to ask Jack, when the answer became obvious. Just ahead I could see green tendrils of plants, growing up from the frost-sheathed ground. Knee-high, they stood out in sharp relief to the mowed field.

My tattoo buzzed angrily.

"Wow," I said, because it was strangely beautiful, with the sun glinting off the straight, stiff stalks. Though there were no visible seed heads or blossoms, I swore I could smell a spring freshness coming from the circle. I edged as close as my arm would allow. "So aliens are real, too?"

"What? No," Jack said. He was kneeling in front of the grass, his hand brushing the tips. He withdrew his fingers quickly and rubbed them together, as if checking for residue of some kind. "Don't be ridiculous."

"Oh," I said, shoving my gloved hands into the pockets of my coat. The tattoo ached so much that it felt like someone was twisting my skin. "It's just that I heard something on the police radio yesterday about an unidentified flying object. Or maybe it had been a plane that hadn't registered a flight plan?"

"That's something else entirely," Jack said. He stood up and took a digital camera from the inside of his coat and started taking pictures. "We're tracking that."

Was it morning grogginess, or did Jack seem a little distant and snappish suddenly? Could he feel my tattoo's response to the green circle? Did it remind him that I might be one of the unnatural ones? Maybe that accidental "I hate you" hurt his feelings?

I shook my head and let my gaze drift toward the windbreak of trees on the horizon. The sun's light made the frost on the long expanse of mowed field sparkle—blue, white, and pink.

"So if it's not aliens, what makes crop circles?" I wondered aloud.

"Zombies," he said, walking along the edge of the green, snapping images from all angles. "That's why we wanted you out here. Zombies could be related to the necromancer."

I nodded, wishing I had more coffee. Zombies made crop circles. *Of course.* How many magical things happened in this town, anyway? Maybe Valentine was wrong. Pierre seemed almost too small this morning, because *too much* was visible. I could see my breath and my cheeks stung in the wind. "Do zombies usually make things sprout like that? That seems kind of"—I rubbed my aching arm—"natural, doesn't it?"

Jack paused to scratch the whiskers on his unshaved chin. "It does," he agreed. He shoved the camera deep into the pocket of his coat and shook his head. He glanced in the direction of the pasture just beyond the barn. "Spenser is going to be pissed off."

I thought that defined Jones's usual disposition, but I didn't say so. Instead, I asked, "Why?"

"It's obviously a fairy ring, isn't it?"

By the time we left the farm, the sun had warmed the interior of Jack's car. I cracked a window to get a bit of fresh air.

Jones had, in fact, been quite mad about a number of things, it turned out. He wasn't happy that I had no veterinarian training and could not positively identify the cause of death of the cows. I mollified him a bit when I told him it looked as if something massive had staved in their heads, and that the coyotes had probably tried to drag the bodies off at a later time. But we'd argued again when Jones made arrangements with the rancher to send a carcass back to my morgue. I told him that unless he planned to also send along a butcher, I had no use for a bunch of cow meat. At that point, Jones played the boss card and ended the discussion.

I was currently chewing Jack's ear off about the whole situation. "He's not even my boss, you know. I work for the county. I was elected. Why did I let him push me around like that?"

Jack had no comment. I didn't blame him. I'd been saying the same thing over and over for the last few miles, getting increasingly angry at myself.

I sighed. "The dumbest part? I don't even have a freezer big enough for the stupid thing."

"At least it's not likely to walk off," he said with a smile.

"With my luck, it probably will. Or moo through the entire autopsy." I pushed at the manual lock button angrily, clicking it closed and then pulling it open. "And, anyway, what am I supposed to do? It's like the necromancer all over again. I don't know what the signs of a bloodthirsty fairy attack should look like."

"You don't have to. That's our job. Just tell us what you find, like you would in any case."

Except no one seems that interested in doing detective work besides me, I thought but didn't say. Besides, I liked Jack and didn't want to insult him any more than I probably already had between my casual slight and the snake's reaction to the circle.

"Fine," I muttered, but I conceded his point by allowing a change in subject. "So, speaking of the necromancer, any new developments? Did Boyd get a reading on the toe tag?"

Jack shrugged. "I don't think so. I guess he's doing other work for the Lyman County sheriff about a missing girl or something."

I remembered the bicycle tire and nodded. I understood that missing persons cases were time sensitive, but I wondered exactly how long it took to pick up vibes or whatever from an object. Jack didn't seem overly bothered by the delay, however, so it must be business as usual.

"How'd it go last night?" he asked.

At first, I thought Jack knew about Valentine's return. I blushed remembering the fantastic, if often interrupted, sex. "Uh . . . What do you mean?"

"At the morgue?" he prompted. "When we dropped you off? Did you get a lot accomplished?"

"Oh, oh . . . yeah, sure," I started. Then I remembered the truth. "No, not really. I filed paperwork and all that sort of thing, but I don't really feel like I got much done. I don't know what killed the necromancer. In fact, from what I can tell, nothing did."

"You think he faked his death?"

"If magic weren't a factor, I'd say no without hesitation," I said. "When I cut into him, he was definitely dead." When Jack gave me a quick look, I added, "Trust me, when you cut a living person, it's a very different experience. Blood flies everywhere."

"Oh. Er, I'll take your word for it."

Oops. I guess that was the wrong thing to say. God, I needed more coffee. From the paleness of Jack's face it occurred to me that I probably shouldn't have mentioned that I *did* have experience seeing a living body slashed. Jack couldn't know details of what had happened with my stepmom, at least. I shook my head. I didn't want to remember that right now, anyway, especially with Valentine at home in bed.

Jack drove a short distance without speaking. I wished his car had a working radio, but there was a hole in the dash where the stereo would normally be housed. Instead, I watched the fields pass outside the window.

"You never called me," he said, a few miles down the road. "I left my number on your phone. Didn't you find it? I was hoping to take you out to dinner."

Wow, that had to be the most passive-aggressive way to ask me out in recorded history. "Oh, um . . ." The truth was I hadn't even really looked at my phone since he handed it back to me at the meeting. "A friend of mine came into town last night unexpectedly. I was . . . distracted. Sorry."

Even though I'd been careful about how I said that, Jack looked disappointed. "Maybe after your friend leaves, we could go out."

I wondered if Valentine had plans to leave anytime soon. A better person would've confessed right then that my friend was more than that, and let Jack down easy and early. But, if the past was any indication, Valentine *would* get restless eventually. He might be here for the moment, but I could never hold him in one place for very long.

Not without trouble, anyway.

Selfishly, I told Jack: "Yeah, maybe we could go out sometime."

Jack rewarded me with a genuine smile and happy chatter for the rest of the drive back.

Even though it was held in the war room, the morning meeting was very different from yesterday's more intimate one. Everyone was there—tons of people I didn't know, in uniform and out—milling around, drinking bad coffee from disposable cups, and talking and laughing about last night's reality shows.

I stuck to the edge, near the door, trying to look like I belonged.

The whiteboard with all the information about the necromancer was off to one side. I was pleased to see that Jones had updated it with information about the mysterious Twitter correspondent and the severed head. Another whiteboard had been set beside it, with only a few words written on it: *cow mutilation, crop circle,* and, most curiously of all, *dragon*. There were no pictures or any notes under those yet, though.

Stone stood against the side wall, a hand wrapped around her chutzpah cup. The other played with a bit of her hair, which was as loose and disorganized as ever this morning. A young detective, the sort who wore his golden badge clipped to his belt and his sleeves rolled up, seemed to be telling her a very earnest story. He was half her height, though tightly muscled. She listened shyly, flirtatiously. It was sweet, if a little strange, to see such a massive woman so demure.

Jack pressed a cup into my hand. I looked down at muddy brown burnt-smelling stuff, but thanked him anyway. He noticed my interest in the guy talking to Stone. "That's Vito," he explained. "We've got an office pool going for when he finally asks her out."

I was curious to know what held Vito back, but Jones called the morning meeting to order. Everyone hushed, as he spoke. "As you all know this is an unusually busy time for us. We've got three active cases at the moment, and I want updates on all of them."

Stone pushed herself from the wall and, with a little fond smile at Vito, made her way to the front of the room. She gave a neat, precise rundown of everything we knew about the necromancer so far. I learned that he'd come to the precinct's attention three months ago, when the first grave had been robbed. I was extraordinarily disturbed to discover that, besides the head, he'd taken a hand and three toes. None of the other body parts had been found so far.

I sipped my coffee accidentally and burned my tongue on the rancid liquid. My arm, at least, had stopped hurting on the drive back to headquarters. I rubbed it now, absently, through the fabric of my sweater. Thanks to dressing in the dark, I'd ended up in the garish Christmas sweater with the jingle bells attached to the reindeer's reins that my stepmother had bought me the first year she'd moved in with us. I hated it about as much as I hated her. I had no idea why I still had this thing, much less why I'd dragged it all the way to Pierre.

Guilt, maybe.

Stone wrapped up her briefing, and Jones took over again. "We got a call this morning about a crop circle and cow mutilation out at the Olson ranch. Preliminary investigation does not indicate a connection to the necromancer case."

This revelation seemed to shock everyone in the room.

Jones pointed to two guys in uniform standing near the front. "I want Peterson and Hanson to cover the *ordinarium* procedures. Interview all the neighboring ranchers. Find out if the rancher, Olson, has any enemies. Use words like 'cattle rustling' and 'property damage;' we don't need 'cow mutilation' getting around."

The two cops nodded.

I remembered Peterson was the poor guy who everyone assumed was Boyd. Honestly, I couldn't tell who was who at this distance. They were both white guys with short hair . . . in uniform. Absolutely no distinguishing features at all.

"Jack, you're on damage control. Make sure the Internet stays quiet about this one."

"Yes, sir," Jack said, saluting Jones with his coffee.

"Alex, since you're new here, you can come with me while I touch base with my local fairy connections."

I was surprised by this, but I gave a little wave of acknowledgment when everyone craned around to see who Jones referred to. I really wished I hadn't dressed in the dark. I must have looked like a complete idiot wearing a Christmas sweater in April. No one seemed bothered, however. I didn't get more than the usual curious looks. After Jones went back to assigning various tasks, Jack leaned in and whispered, "Lucky you."

Considering that the only other job I had for the day was trying to figure out what the hell I was going to do with a dead animal carcass, I didn't mind tagging along. The thought of spending alone time in close quarters with Jones didn't particularly thrill me, however.

The meeting wrapped up quickly after that. Nothing was said about that last item on the board, so I asked Jack as we filed out of the room. "What's with the dragon?"

He shrugged. "No one knows. It could have just been a flyover."

A uniform I didn't recognize added, "The ID was shaky, but it's the right time of year for migration. I think the boss is just being cautious, since cattle got mauled."

I stared at him blankly.

He had the slightest hint of a paunch and a cherubic face the color of windswept sandstone. His hair was slickly black, and I thought he might be either Latino or Native American. "Dragons are responsible for ten percent of all unsolved cattle-rustling cases. The number is especially high during peak migration times."

"Oh," I said, because what else could I say?

"This is Denis. He's our George," Jack explained, with a nod at the uniform, who instantly offered his hand.

"Our George?"

"As in saint," Jack added, as if that made things clearer.

"Oh, as in Saint George and the Dragon?" I asked, as a dim connection formed in my brain. Denis smiled in acknowledgment. The hand I shook was calloused, but the grip lighter than I'd expected. "You slay dragons?"

He started. I let his hand go, uncertain if he'd been shocked by my question or my tattoo. "Ah, no," he said quickly. "I'm actually not sure that's possible. Technically, I've been trained to combat them—just hold my own, really—and to speak their language, but it'd be a dark day if I had to go up against one of those bastards."

Jack added, "Think of Denis's job like a hostage negotiator. Every unit is required to have someone trained in it, but you hope like hell you never have to use it, you know?"

"Sure," I said in response. Though I really wanted to know from Denis: "Have you ever seen a dragon?"

"Only in books, I'm afraid," he said, tucking his hands behind his back. He dropped his eyes a bit, as though he was embarrassed by the fact.

"They're extraordinarily rare," Jack said, as though in Denis's defense. "There's probably less than a half dozen known to still exist."

"And one just flew over Pierre, South Dakota," I said.

"Exactly," Denis agreed.

Jack and I were literally standing by the watercooler when I heard Jones's approach. He continued to bark out orders. I turned around in time to watch him stop by the desk of the woman I'd seen playing the strange game of solitaire yesterday. "Beth," he said. "Cast every chart, bone, and tea leaf you can think of. I want to know what the hell cosmic convergence is causing all this activity right now."

She got to it as Jones barreled toward us.

I'd barely put my water down when he said, "Alex, let's go."

I swallowed back a "Yes, sir!" but found myself snapping

to attention, despite myself. Jack cupped his hand in front of his mouth and whispered, "Good luck," as I hustled after Jones.

This time I got to sit in the front of the squad car, like a big girl. I buckled myself in. The dash was an array of fascinating buttons and screens, along with all the usual controls for heat and such. I wondered which switch controlled the siren and the flashing lights. Out of the corner of my eye, I noticed the Refocus had not been replaced yet. I ran my fingers over the spot where Stone had poked her finger through the bulletproof glass. When Jones climbed in, I turned around quickly.

"How are you settling in with the team?" he asked, after starting up the engine.

"I'm not really sure," I admitted. *Especially considering how much you seem to hate all my suggestions.*

The police radio crackled with noises from Dispatch. Apparently, somewhere in the normal world there had been a dispute between two truckers at the Dunkin' Donuts.

"I should be in the morgue, not the field," I said in all honesty.

Jones nodded thoughtfully. I glanced over at him. He drove casually, with one arm resting on the window, the other draped over the wheel. He'd set his cap in the space between us, and the sun shone reddish through brown hair. I thought he looked tired, but it may just have been the way the light brought out every line on his weathered face. "We need a lab rat among those in the know, the magical community."

"So I'm it, huh?"

"You can go back to your basement once we catch the bad guy. For now, it will be good for you to get a feel for how our operation works."

I shrugged. So far I wasn't sure it was working at all. I didn't think I could tell him that, though, so I sat back and looked out the window. At least the patrol car had a functioning heater.

We rolled past a corner grocery store. The light flashed OPEN in red neon. A hand-lettered sign advertised that they specialized in preparing pheasant meat. Bison was also on sale, apparently.

"You might want to tell me about that demon you met," he said, as we passed under the bright lights of a gas station. "Jack said you're worried about someone you left behind. Your father? That you need me to contact the Chicago Bureau?"

How strange to think there'd been a shadow magical organization in my hometown all the while I'd been force-fed antipsychotics and mandatory therapy sessions to transform real demons into inner ones. "My dad," I said, feeling like I was giving him the title of some bad teenage horror movie, "married a demon."

"Sumerian, Egyptian, or Judeo-Christian?"

"I have no idea," I said. I wasn't used to being taken seriously on this subject, and it was hard not to default to my usual self-deprecating, deflecting jokes or comments. Normally, I'd start talking now about *why* the doctors said I'd had the break—about my mother's lingering illness and untimely death and how Father's marriage had come too soon in my grieving process.

Jones spared me a look. He was frowning, as usual, but I thought it held a slight edge of concern. "It would help any extraction team if they knew what they were up against.

There are a few easy tells. Wings, for instance. Do you remember wings?"

So much of those days had become an indistinct fog. "Reptilian eyes. I think they were my stepmother's, anyway."

That clearly stumped him. "Are you sure she was a demon?"

"Of course not," I snapped. I hadn't meant for that to come out so hard, so I added, "I mean, that's how I ended up in a psych ward."

Jones rubbed his forehead, and gave me a sympathetic grimace. "It's not necessary that we know. Anything you can remember would help, though."

I chewed on my lip. I'd worked so long and so hard trying to forget all of this, it was hard to remember how it had all started. What *had* I seen? I had a dim memory of walking in on them, in the middle of sex, which would have been traumatic enough at my tender age, but she'd looked at me, smiled with such a possessive, wicked expression . . . "A forked tongue," I said. "Horns?"

"But no wings?"

I shook my head. I couldn't remember.

"She might be an ifrit," Jones said.

He turned the wheel as we pulled into the driveway of an average-looking house. He turned off the engine, and shifted in his seat to look me in the eye.

"I assume your father never turned into an animal," he continued.

I shook my head. My dad had been a jackass, in my opinion, but I was sure that wasn't what Jones meant.

He said, "That rules out an Egyptian ifrit, which is good news. Ifrit, generally, are pretty minor as these things go. Shoot me an e-mail with his address and any other details you can remember. We'll get a team to make sure he's in no trouble. I assume Jack told you that it could just be . . . uh, interspecies romance."

I just nodded, because I didn't trust myself to speak without spitting or making inappropriate noises.

Jones looked out at the house. It was a two-story built of yellow brick. By far the tallest of those on the block, it had the feeling of having been an original farmhouse that the city had built around. Despite that, it was cheerful. Painted wooden flower boxes, though still empty from the previous winter, looked well cared for, as did the burlap-covered shrubbery. The trim around the windows and roofline had been painted green, and I could see white lace curtains through the glass.

Though it was impossible through the closed windows and the distance, I swore I smelled freshly baking bread.

"Homey," I noted, as we got out of the car.

"Watch yourself," Jones said, putting on his cap and adjusting his gun belt. "Don't take anything offered, not even her hand."

"Seriously? I can't even shake hands?"

"Just don't. It could be considered accepting an offer of friendship. I'm not even going to introduce you. The less attention you attract from the fairy folk, the better." He pulled a small vial from a snap pocket on his belt and handed it to me. It had white crystals inside that looked a lot like—"Salt," he said. "If she invites us in be sure to sprinkle it over the threshold. If we don't break the circle, the next time we step outside it might be a hundred years gone."

"Christ," I muttered, following him up the curved cobblestone walk to the front steps. The place looked innocent enough, but I gripped the vial inside my fist. As we got closer, I suddenly noticed how odd it was that the door was bright purple. It was the only part of the house painted so garishly. How I hadn't noticed it instantly was a mystery. Jones rang the bell.

A kindly-looking older woman opened the door after the third buzz. She wore a green and blue plaid shawl over her bent shoulders, and white curls cascaded loosely down her back. Her eyes were rheumy and her irises were such a pale color that I thought she was blind at first. She had a large nose, and I half expected a stereotypical hairy wart at the tip. But her smile was warm and gentle, and when she saw Jones, she said, "Ah, Spenser, *mo bhilis*. To what do I owe this pleasure?"

Jones doffed his hat, and gave a short bow. "Not pleasure, I'm afraid, ma'am, but business."

"Bah," she said, batting her hand at him. "That's always been your problem, son. Not nearly enough pleasure." She toddled away, back into the interior of the house, leaving the door open in invitation.

Jones jerked his head at the threshold, and I sprinkled a clear line of salt. At least I hoped it was clear. There wasn't a lot of salt in the tiny container, and it came out faster than I expected. He seemed satisfied, at any rate, and entered.

I shoved the empty vial into my jeans pocket. Then I followed, taking one step through.

Suddenly, I was surrounded by a circle of ancient, gnarled oak trees. Fern fronds brushed my calf, and my boot crunched on freshly fallen leaves. The air smelled of forest in late autumn. I looked up to blue sky. A check behind showed a sliver of . . . space, through which I could see the concrete steps and the patrol car parked in the drive.

As if of its own accord, my hand, the tattooed one,

reached back and gripped the door frame. One foot was inside, but my other heel seemed stuck as though the salt were glue instead.

Acorns were thick on the ground; I could hear them popping under Jones's boots as he walked toward a giant, moss-covered boulder in the center of the grove. A shaft of light seemed to fall on the woman perched on its rounded peak. She was breathtakingly gorgeous, with a riot of inky black curls and a formfitting green dress trimmed with the same plaid as the old woman's shawl. She lounged seductively, her head resting against one hand, the other toying with some bit of greenery. Through thick lashes, she gazed down at us from her vantage point.

Jones couldn't have looked more out of place in his police uniform, but he stood erect and at attention at the foot of the standing rock. He held his hat in one hand, and the other rested casually on the holster of his gun. I thought, though, that in this verdant setting, the frown lines of his face smoothed and he seemed more handsome.

"State your business with fairy, half-breed." Though full of insult, the woman's voice was like some familiar music from my childhood, and I felt a strange compulsion to step closer to hear it better. I started forward, but my hand wouldn't release its death grip, and I jerked to a stop.

"I beg your indulgence, my lady, but I must know if any of your people were in my territory last night?"

She sneered most delicately. "Only one."

"May I know for what purpose?"

"You may," she said. She lay back and stretched with a supple, feline grace in the sun.

Jones waited for a long moment as she stared at the sky

saying nothing. I thought she may have fallen asleep. Finally, he asked, "What was it?"

"Surely you know your own mind, Spenser, *mo bhilis*."

"Me? Are you saying I was the only fairy in Pierre?"

She never turned to look at him, just spoke up at the sky. "Be grateful, half-breed, that I count you among my people at all."

Spenser's lips grew thin, and his body tensed. The muscle of his jaw worked furiously. Stiffly, he sketched a bow and backed toward me slowly. "My lady," he said through gritted teeth.

She waved a casual dismissal, gracefully rude.

I would have stood in the door gaping at her beauty for the rest of my life, but Jones pushed past me angrily. He knocked me back into the bleak chill of Pierre. I blinked in the gray ugliness on the step, breathing hard, as if all the air had been pushed from my lungs. When he slammed the door shut, I could have cried out in pain.

"Wha—Why?" was all I could manage.

He was stomping down the crooked path toward the waiting squad car. "Fucking goddamn fairy."

My hand reached for the doorknob of the house, but somehow I knew if I opened it, it would be to doilies and rag rugs and old-fashioned furniture. The forest and all its splendor would be gone. With a heavy sigh, I joined Jones in the car.

His hands were curled around the steering wheel so tightly that his knuckles showed white. "It's got to be a lie or some tricky riddle," he was saying. "That's a fairy ring out at Olson's place, I'd stake my life on it."

"She was so beautiful," I said wistfully, looking longingly at the purple door. "Who was she?"

"My mother," Jones said. "Maeve, Queen of Fairy."

And I thought my family had problems. "Oh."

I would have said more, but at that moment my cell phone buzzed in my pocket. The number was local, but not one I recognized. I answered it anyway. "Hello?"

"Connor? Alex Connor? This is Genevieve, your assistant. There's a dead fucking cow in the morgue."

"It should just be dead," I said casually. "If it's doing something rude to the dead, I think you should send it back to the rancher and remove Mrs. Finnegan to somewhere safer."

"What?"

"I'll be right there."

THIRTEEN

My assistant was a lot more frazzled than the last time I saw her. Gone were the Isabel Toledo shoes, the Vera Wang dress, and the matching high-class attitude. She met me at the door with a horrified, "Help me!" expression. Her polished nails dug into my sweater painfully as she dragged me into the room. "They had to put it on the floor! With a forklift! It has no goddamn *face*, for fucksake."

"I know," I said. To her credit, my assistant seemed to have had the presence of mind to spread a tarp out on the floor upon which the cow now rested. She had also piled heaps of ice around the carcass. "This is good." I indicated all she'd done—or, more likely, gotten someone else to do. "Thank you. But what were you doing here?"

"I work here," she said, her voice confused, but clearly affronted.

"All of a sudden? You couldn't be bothered when I checked in Mrs. Finnegan and . . ." I'd gotten out of the habit of referring to the other body as anything other than the necromancer. ". . . everything else. Why did you come in today?"

She tried to keep up the offended look, but it faltered around the edges as she groped for an answer. "It's . . . the second Tuesday of the month. I always come in then."

"Even when we're not expecting anybody?"

"I . . . come in to do routine paperwork," she said.

"The main office is upstairs," I noted.

"Yes, that's where I was, until the call about the delivery came in," she said. I might have been convinced she was telling the truth, except for her nervous glance at my corner desk. Following her gaze, I noticed the computer was on and opened to my autopsy report on the necromancer.

I stalked over to the desk. With a punch of my fingers, I closed down the document. Thank God it had been the one for the upstairs office, not Precinct 13. "You were spying on me!"

She drew herself up and glared at me over the body of the cow. "So what if I was. I'd heard they brought a guy in who had poisoned himself, but I can't find his body anywhere. What did you do with it?"

"Me? I—" I started to sputter out a defensive response, but stopped myself. I didn't need to explain myself to her. The chief of police himself was the one who'd sent me to Precinct 13. He knew we had a missing body. If she was snooping, it wasn't for him. "Are you still working for my predecessor?"

Her face turned bright red, but she said, "I'm employed by the county."

"Officially. What about unofficially?" I asked, though I didn't really need to hear her answer to know the truth. It seemed pretty clear. Still, she'd taken good care of the carcass. I pulled a pair of gloves from the box on my desk. "Listen, I'm ready to fire you on the spot. If you want to work for me, you could do me one more favor. Find me the name of a good veterinarian."

Her mouth opened and closed, reminding me of the koi in Precinct 13's interrogation room.

Maybe it was all the time I'd recently been spending in much scarier and stranger situations than this that gave me the wherewithal to say, "I need help figuring out what killed this thing. Either *assist*, or get out of my way."

I didn't really expect an answer, so I turned away to get into my lab coat and splatter apron. I was surprised to hear her deflated, "My cousin is a vet. I'll call him."

Genevieve's cousin was a guy named Mark, and her exact opposite. He was down-to-earth, friendly, and extraordinarily helpful. He was also schlubby and hopelessly disorganized. Still, he was able to confirm that the claw and teeth markings on the cow's haunches belonged to average-sized coyotes, and had been inflicted postmortem. We both puzzled over the head wounds, however.

"The skull is crushed," he noted. "*Totally* crushed."

Whatever had smashed the cow's head had exerted enough force to pulverize teeth. "Do you know anything that can hit this hard?" I asked him.

"No animal," he said, stepping back and pulling on the short hairs of his soul patch. "If it weren't a downward blow like that, I'd say a car or a tractor. Something massive."

We talked cow physiology for a while, and I took copious notes. I thanked him for his time and offered to buy him lunch at the city hall cafeteria. He blushed, clearly flattered, but declined. "I have to get back to my own practice, I'm afraid."

His pager had been going off constantly. He'd apparently left a lot of kittens who needed to be spayed and such. Thanking him again, I told him I owed him one as he rushed out the door.

That left Genevieve and me staring at the dead cow and each other. She gave me a weak smile. "I found the vet. You find the butcher."

I was about to tell her that she was by no means off my shit list when there was a gentle rap on the door. I thought maybe Mark the vet had forgotten something, so I shouted, "Come on in."

Valentine stuck his head through the door. He glanced at the cow and then up at me. "I thought I'd invite you out to lunch, but if you're already eating . . ."

"Funny," I told him. "Just give me a minute."

As I passed her on the way to hang up my coat and apron, Genevieve whispered, wide-eyed, "Who's the hottie?"

I took a great deal of satisfaction saying, as I tossed my gloves into the biohazard bin, "My boyfriend."

Valentine insisted we go home so that I could change out of the awful sweater. I was about to protest that I hadn't driven my car to work, when he walked us to it. My mouth hung open, stupidly staring at my own Toyota.

"I borrowed it," he said. My key ring was on his finger and he jangled it playfully. He'd parked my Toyota in the spot reserved for the mayor.

I stood beside the passenger door and Valentine casually

walked around to the driver's seat. Planting my hands on my hips, I said, "If I didn't give you permission, technically, it's stealing."

"All right. I stole it. Get in."

I noticed something else as I took my seat. "You washed it."

"I like my things shiny. This is why you're going home to change."

Robert was just finishing up breakfast as we walked in the door. He stared grumpily at the milk left in his otherwise empty cereal bowl. The smell of scorched coffee and curry hung in the air.

As usual, Robert looked like a high-powered executive in his tailored shirt, silk tie, and crisply ironed slacks. His blond hair was parted neatly, and his chin perfectly shaven. No one would guess by looking at him that he was a computer programmer with a penchant for MMOGS. He was a pretty scary orc online. In real life, he was just pretty.

He brightened at the sight of Valentine. I had to say that my Russian-born lover certainly knew how to dress for the winter. He wore a Soviet-era wool great coat, heavy leather gloves, and matching boots. No fur hat, however. In fact, he went hatless, despite the chill.

"Oh my God," Robert said, when his eyes finally left Valentine to glance at me. "What are you wearing, girl? Did you dress in the dark?"

"I did, actually," I admitted. My coat's zipper had snagged on one of the jingle bells of my sweater and I was teasing it out.

"Let me find something better," Robert said, which,

given the tight glance at Valentine that accompanied it, was clearly code for "we need to talk."

So I left Valentine in the kitchen and followed Robert into my bedroom. The bed was exactly as we'd left it, and the room smelled of sex and man. "Uh," I said, a blush creeping up my neck, "I'm sorry."

"Don't be, he's beautiful. Anyway, we don't have an overnight-guest notification clause in our roommate agreement." Robert dug through my closet, clearly searching for something specific. I lingered in the doorway, feeling awkward, like a stranger in my own room. Though his head was deep in the recesses of my wardrobe, Robert continued, "I just had quite the shock this morning: him, sitting there, bare-chested in the kitchen! You have no idea how long I sat and prayed that I'd been much drunker than I thought last night and somehow forgot bringing him home." He pulled out a lovely, sapphire-blue cashmere sweater I barely remembered owning and threw it at me. "There. That's your best look. I've got to go. I'm late for work."

As Robert squeezed past me out the door, I asked, "Is it okay if he stays awhile?"

That stopped him. "Longer than a few days?"

"I don't know," I admitted guiltily.

"Depends on how crazy you drive me," Robert said, as he grabbed his briefcase off the dining room table.

"Fair enough," I said, as he hurried out the door.

Valentine and I were sitting in a Chinese restaurant fifteen minutes later. The staff was strangely solicitous to us, showing us to a large, cloth-covered table on a slightly raised dais. Behind us on the wall was a relief image of a classic red and gold Chinese dragon and a lavishly plumed phoenix. A golden spotlight shone on the artwork, giving it a strange dimension in the darkened restaurant.

The waitress bowed twice before rushing off to fill our water glasses.

"Uh," I said, watching as the waitress whispered something into the ear of an older gentleman sitting at a stool. Seeing me, he dipped his head respectfully as well. "Must be a slow day at the buffet."

The place *was* fairly empty, but my theory was ruined when the waitress returned with a plate of freshly cooked appetizers and a heavily accented, "On the house."

Valentine took all this attention in stride, like he was used to being the rock star at the local Asian buffet. "We'll leave a big tip." He shrugged.

He deftly used chopsticks in a way I never quite mastered. I tried not to be jealous as a huge chunk of noodle slid back onto my plate before I could catch it in my mouth.

After I'd finished chewing, I asked him, "Do you remember if stepmonster had wings?"

"She did not," he said, sounding vaguely offended by the suggestion. He picked up the teapot and refilled my cup before tending to his own. "Why?"

We were alone in a corner of the darkened restaurant. A family of four was gathered near the buffet, but they had taken a table closer to the door. Even so, I leaned in under the pool of light shed by the paper lantern over our booth. "Jones is talking about sending a team to check on my dad. He wants me to try to remember everything I can."

He sat back against the red vinyl booth. The cup was balanced in his steepled fingers. "A team? Of what?"

I shrugged. "Highly trained magic users, I suppose."

"Humans?"

It was a strange question coming from Valentine, and my chopsticks hovered halfway to my mouth. "I don't know. I mean, I suppose they might have someone like Devon or Stone on their team, too."

"Mmm," he said, his eyes shrouded in the dark of the restaurant. "You should tell your friend not to underestimate Gayle. I made that mistake, remember."

That wasn't the way I remembered things. The noodles I'd swallowed earlier stuck in my throat. "Underestimate?" I repeated. "You nearly killed her."

"Nearly," he said darkly. "Yes, *nearly*. More than that, I was captured, imprisoned—outmaneuvered, out-tricked. She successfully separated us for eighteen months."

I put my chopsticks down. "She?" I might believe in magic nowadays, but I also remembered the arrest and everything that came after. "Gayle didn't put you in prison, the American justice system did."

He didn't say anything for a long moment. Then he lifted his shoulder in a shrug. "Yes," he said flatly. "Of course."

The doctors had told me, time and again, that Valentine was my real problem. They'd said he never took responsibility for his own actions, and that he used my paranoid psychosis as an excuse for his own homicidal tendencies. I'd denied and denied, but listening to Val now, the old doubts crept back. Did he really believe that my stepmother had that kind of influence? That she could somehow control circumstances like his arrest and trial?

It worried me, too, the violent arrogance in his voice. The way he seemed offended that she'd somehow avoided being killed by him, like it was an affront to his abilities.

He set the teacup down and pushed the remains of his lunch around with the tip of his chopstick. Like me, he seemed to have lost his appetite. "I should take you back," he said quietly.

"Yes, that would be a good idea."

I asked Valentine to drop me off at the precinct headquarters. Though it was only a few blocks, the ride was quiet and tense. I turned on the radio to fill the silence. He pulled up into a space next to the storefront and frowned at the empty shop. "This is it?"

By chance, Jack opened the door. His back was to us, but I recognized his Yoda hat and the colorful scarf. He held the door open, talking to someone inside. For a moment the illusion was broken, and the flickering image of the busy interior of the precinct was visible through the windows.

"Interesting." Valentine turned off the engine. He unbuckled and got out of the car. Leaving the car door open, he leaned on the vehicle's roof to watch the stuttering spell.

Finished with whatever conversation had held him up, Jack turned, smiling toward the street. His grin wavered when he noticed us watching him. His eyes seemed locked on Valentine, and color drained from Jack's face.

I got out quickly. "Hey, Jack," I said, smiling warmly.

Jack blinked, and seemed to see me for the first time. A weaker version of the smile returned to his face. "Oh, hello, Alex."

The car door slammed, as Valentine joined us on the sidewalk. "Jack," he repeated slowly, thoughtfully, as if committing his name to memory. I was sure I wasn't the only one who found it sort of sinister.

I tried to make things better with an introduction. "Jack, this is Valentine. Uh, my friend who's visiting."

Neither offered each other a hand to shake. In fact, Jack kept looking at Valentine with wide eyes, not saying anything.

"Jack," Valentine said. "You were going somewhere. Run along."

Jack blinked. "Oh. Right. Well, nice meeting you." He hurried off then, but kept sneaking backward glances at the two of us as he did. At the corner he nearly ran into the lamppost. We watched as he shook himself off and then quickly dashed out of sight.

Okay. That was weird.

Still focused in the direction of Jack's hasty retreat, Valentine smiled thinly, with a smug satisfaction. Suddenly, his focus shifted, and he glanced upward sharply. A magpie settled on an overhead wire. It cawed belligerently before dropping into a swoop. I ducked, wary of talon and beak, but Valentine stood, unflinching, as the bird dive-bombed.

"Sarah Jane!" I shouted; it had to be her. "Stop!"

He was unfazed as she struck at him, time and time again. Just as I was ready to shout that he should run for cover or something, he raised his hand and gestured slightly, as if brushing dust from his shoulder.

The magpie, which had been coming around for another attack, rolled tail over beak in the opposite direction, as if blasted by some invisible wind. She disappeared over the roof of the headquarters.

"Oh no," I said, standing up and searching the sky frantically. "Sarah Jane? Are you okay?"

I thought I heard a weak caw in response.

The door to the precinct flew open with a bang. Jones

and several other officers came rushing out, looking ready for trouble. They stopped dead, staring past me to Valentine.

"Holy shit," I heard someone say.

"Get the George! Get Denis. Pronto!" Jones snapped. He pulled his gun from his holster and pointed it at Valentine's chest. "There's a goddamn dragon at the door."

FOURTEEN

Dragon. The word jiggered through my mind. Even as clues fell into place, my mind refused to accept them.

Valentine pulled himself to his full height, which suddenly seemed much larger than his already impressive six foot two. He took in a sharp breath that sounded like a hiss. His eyes narrowed to slits, and focused on the gun.

There was a commotion at the back of the crowded doorway as Denis began to elbow his way to the front.

"Run, Valentine!" I shouted. "Denis is their George."

My feet, which had felt rooted to the spot earlier, began to move. I was determined to put myself between Valentine and whatever danger Denis represented.

I only made a few steps before Valentine dropped to a crouch and then sprang up into a powerful jump. His feet leaped from the ground, easily as high as the top of the car. Instead of coming back down, however, he was suddenly airborne. I watched as he snapped out his arms, and gigantic batlike wings unfolded from his back. His body elongated and shifted. Yet somehow he was still recognizable to me with a slender, elegant neck and massively powerful chest. Scales, as white as snow, sparkled like diamonds in the sun. A snakelike tail curled and twisted, whipping back and forth in fury. Coal black reptilian eyes seemed to find me despite the speed of his ascent. What did I see there? Sorrow? Regret? I wasn't certain, but it was a decidedly human expression despite the proud, cruelly handsome snout.

He cocked his head, showing spikes of an icy crest, and roared.

The sound shook the ground.

Many of the officers crowded on the sidewalk flinched and ducked in the icy blast of air that followed. Like the wind of a blizzard, it sent sharp pricks of sleet into my skin.

Jones came up from his hunched position faster than the others. I watched in horror as he raised his gun, tracking Valentine's flight. I could see his intention in his closed, hard expression. I was nearly in front of him so I grabbed for his arm. I pulled it downward with all my strength.

The shot went wild. A hot casing smacked me in the cheek, but I held on tight. My eyes riveted to the strokes of Valentine's powerful wings as he continued his upward climb.

Denis made his way to the sidewalk just in time to watch with the rest of us as Valentine disappeared into the clouds.

I wasn't in handcuffs, but I might as well have been for the suspicion with which everyone treated me. I don't even remember quite how, but I'd been hustled off to the conference room. The door was closed. The window drapes had been pulled. I sat on one side of the table and Denis on the other. Jones paced behind him, wearing thin the linoleum and shooting me dark, angry looks.

Someone had given me a damp washcloth for my face. The casing had not only bruised my cheekbone, but had given me a nasty burn as well. I leaned against the cool cloth, feeling worn out, even though they hadn't even asked me more than the obligatory, "Are you okay?"

I'd murmured, "Yes," but I was in shock.

Valentine was a dragon.

I'd known him for all these years, but I never suspected . . . No, that wasn't true. I knew he was something special, magical, even. But I guess I always thought he was human.

Maybe he still was. After all, I had no idea if he was a human who transformed into a dragon or a dragon that turned into a man. Or if there was a difference.

The ice, now, that hadn't surprised me at all. I'd always sensed *that*. If Valentine was going to be a dragon, it would be one of snow and cold. That suited him perfectly.

Denis cleared his throat. His clasped hands rested in front of him on the table. He'd brought in a leather-bound notebook or journal of some kind. It looked old and musty, but he'd put those little colored tape flags on various yellowed pages. He watched me calmly. He was clearly supposed to be the good cop to Jones's bad.

"Jack tells us you introduced him as 'Valentine,'" Denis said. "Do you know what he uses as a surname?"

I did, but I wasn't feeling particularly cooperative. I may have just discovered that my lover was some kind of dragon, but I wasn't entirely ready to tell all to the slayers and the cops just yet. Despite this incredible secret Valentine had kept from me, we had a history together. Granted, it wasn't always a good one; even so, the one thing I knew for certain about Valentine was that he'd never betray *me*. He'd had plenty of opportunities to throw me under the bus, tell everyone that what happened with my stepmom was all my fault, but he didn't. He stood by me, even in the craziest times. I would do him the same courtesy. My mouth stayed firm and shut.

"This is very important," Denis insisted. "If he is a Russian or Slavic dragon, we need to know if he is an *azdaja* or a *zmaj*."

My surprise betrayed me. I couldn't help but start at the last word, since I'd always known him as Valentine Zmajov. "*Zmaj?* You mean that's a type of dragon?"

Denis let out a relieved breath, and turned to Jones. "It's the better of the two—for us, at any rate. At least he's not complete evil, or might not be. Some *zmaj* have even been known to protect cities. Probably for their gold, but . . ."

"Still a goddamn dragon," Jones muttered, his eyes on me. "What were you doing with a dragon?"

I almost laughed. *Like I knew?* "Is it some kind of crime?"

Jones stopped pacing to rest his hands on the tabletop. He leaned in menacingly. "Do you know what dragons are capable of?"

Oh, I think I did. I'd just been remembering that night—the blood, the viciousness. Strangely, now I think I understood what Valentine had been implying at the Chinese restaurant a moment ago. If my stepmother could stop a dragon from killing her, she must be something pretty powerful.

I ignored Jones and turned to Denis. "Is there a demon strong enough to stop a dragon?"

"Maybe," Denis said thoughtfully. "Mostly the successful opponents are angels or saints. I suppose if the demon is a fallen angel he could."

"A fallen angel? You mean like a biblical angel?"

"There's a lot of debate about that," Denis said. "I tend to think not. But, talking to an angel is about as rare as surviving an encounter with a dragon."

Jones's face had grown redder and redder during our discussion. "I want to know what your relationship is with that dragon!"

"He's my boyfriend," I said. "Has been for years now."

I figured that the stuttering breath that escaped Jones's mouth was the sound of his brain exploding.

Denis, however, kept his cool. "How did you meet him?"

I opened my mouth to respond and realized that I didn't actually know. I remembered the first moment I saw him: our eyes meeting on a crowded El platform, how amazing he'd looked, the temperature of the air, everything. But, had we really met like that? Like strangers? I was certain I'd known him before that moment, as if someone must have introduced us at a party at college or somewhere. We fell in together so naturally, talking like old friends meeting under new circumstances.

And, though I could picture that scene so clearly in my mind, I struggled to remember when it had been, exactly. Two years ago? Three? More?

Finally, I shrugged. "He just showed up when I needed him."

Jones's face had lost all its earlier color and his posture continued to deflate until he pulled out a chair and sank into it. If Denis noticed, it didn't bother him. Denis continued,

"Were you traveling? Like through Ukraine or Serbia or Macedonia or Russia or somewhere in that area?"

The only time I'd been out of the country was a high school trip to Spain. "We met in Chicago, when I lived there."

Denis shook his head in disbelief. "You met a Russian ice dragon in Chicago by chance?"

"No," Jones said, his voice coming out as a choke. "You heard her. The dragon found her. She's a witch, damn it. He's her familiar."

FIFTEEN

Apparently, that revelation was enough to take both Valentine and me off the Most Wanted list, because Jones got up and erased "dragon" from the list of cases. Denis made a note and stuck it in his journal, shook my hand, and told me how much he'd love to have a chat with Valentine sometime.

I smiled and nodded pleasantly enough, but thought, *Fat chance.*

Because, despite how quickly Jones and Denis accepted this verdict, I had my doubts. "Familiar" seemed a much closer thing than Val and I had ever been, even on our best days. If I were Jones, I wouldn't be so quick to write him off as something "tame" or anything that I had a chance of controlling. For people who were so informed about dragons, they knew jackshit about Valentine. And they were just plain stupid if they no longer considered him dangerous.

"Well," Denis said, standing in the open office doorway.

A broad smile graced his round face. "This is one for the history books. I've never even heard of a natural with a dragon familiar."

"That's because most witches with dragon familiars aren't natural at all," Jones said from where he stood, studying the whiteboards, his back to me. "The only previous one was also half-fairy, and became the legend that is Morgan Le Fey."

Denis's eyes widened when he looked back at me. "Oh," was all he said before suddenly finding somewhere else to be.

I glared at Jones's back. If I were the evil hag he seemed to think I was I would have cursed him on the spot. Instead, I said through thin lips, "I think you're a prejudiced bigot. I was told unnatural is just how the magic comes to you, not some kind of moral statement."

"Tell me truthfully, Alex," Jones said, turning around slowly to face me. "Is this Valentine of yours a model citizen? Have you stayed clear of trouble since he's been in your life?"

I didn't give Jones the satisfaction. Turning on my heels, I stalked off.

It was a lovely, dramatic exit. Unfortunately, it stalled out somewhere in the vicinity of the watercooler. I took the opportunity to wring out the washcloth and refresh it. When a flutter of black-and-white landed on top of the plastic jug, I nearly fell over in surprise.

"Sarah Jane," I said happily. "You're okay!"

Her talons skittered noisily on the slippery surface, but she nodded proudly. She took a few moments to preen her feathers.

"Yes," I told her, and despite myself I smiled. "You were incredibly brave to take on a dragon."

She fluffed her wings as if to say that it was no big deal.

Though I wondered why she had attacked him. Did she think Valentine a threat to me . . . or to Jack? My little white lie about my "friend in town" flitted through my memory. Maybe she thought Valentine was a rival for Jack?

"Is your partner hiding from me?" I asked her.

She shrugged both wings, but turned her sleek head in the direction of Jack's desk. He had that deer-in-the-headlights look again when I spotted him, a large bite of a Subway sandwich half in his mouth.

I supposed I owed him a bit of an explanation. Not that I entirely understood the situation myself. Sarah Jane must have sensed my plan, because she soared across the room and landed on the back of his swivel chair. It took me a few extra minutes to cross the distance, but I took the opportunity to snag an empty chair and pull it across from Jack.

He hadn't swallowed his mouthful, and his eyes bugged.

This wasn't going to be an easy conversation, then. I decided I might as well lay it all out for him. "Jones thinks Valentine is my familiar."

He choked a bit, but seemed to get control of himself after a sip from a plastic soda bottle.

"I don't quite buy it, though," I continued. "He was white, right? I mean, I saw Valentine turn into a giant white dragon, didn't you?" Jack nodded, so I continued, "I thought you said familiars were usually black."

After clearing his throat with another sip, he said, "Usually black." He nodded at Sarah Jane, who had hopped onto his desk and was pulling shiny paper clips out of a bowl and dropping them into a pile. "And black *and* white. But white happens."

"White happens," I repeated, with a little frustrated laugh. "Kind of like: 'Shit happens.'"

Jack looked shocked for a second, but then, seeing the smile on my face, broke into a light laugh as well. "Yeah, I guess so. Holy crap, huh? I mean, I take it you didn't know. Otherwise you were an awfully cool customer when you asked about dragons before."

"I had no idea," I admitted.

"Dragons are like that," he said. "I mean, at least by reputation. Tricks and disguises and riddles. They like games and mystery. But, you'd know more than me."

"Are you kidding? I didn't even know magic was real until yesterday." Had it really only been twenty-four hours since all this started? No wonder I had a headache.

Jack gave me an understanding look as he chewed on his sandwich. I could smell onions and banana peppers.

Jack offered a sly smile. "You're a witch. With a dragon familiar, no less."

Sarah Jane lifted her tail and deposited her opinion of dragons in the middle of Jack's desk.

"I guess so," I said, trying to share Jack's enthusiasm for the revelation.

Taking a Kleenex from his desk, he scooped up Sarah Jane's gift. "It's cool," he assured me. "Once you figure out what kind of magic you have, you're going to kick some serious butt."

"What kind of magic I have?"

Jack nodded, and pointed to himself. "Technomagic."

Sarah Jane found a binder among the pile of paper clips

she'd assembled. It was colored metallic pink. She dropped it on the desk, and turned it around with her foot, as if admiring it.

"Jones thinks I'm the next Morgan Le Fey."

Jack started. "That's so rude!"

I was glad to hear him think so, but I didn't want to talk dragons or magic anymore. In fact, my mind felt overwhelmed, unable to process all the mixed emotions tumbling through it. When that happened, I tended to focus on work.

I cleared my throat. "So, uh, I came back to the office to give Jones my notes about the cow. My assistant found a vet who helped me confirm a few things, but now I need an expert in the supernatural to help me figure out what would have the kind of strength needed to crush a cow's head." I glanced over my shoulder at Jones's office door. I could see him through the glass, filing some papers into a metal cabinet. "I'd talk to Jones about it, but, honestly, I'm kind of mad at him right now. Do you know who I could ask?"

"Well, what about me?"

Jack had never been in a morgue before, and seemed a little spooked at the prospect. He kept noticing all the drains and commenting on them. "I suppose that's for blood, eh?"

Just to be a little mean, I said, "And other bodily fluids."

He shuddered.

My assistant had disappeared without even so much as a note. Not that I had really expected Genevieve to hang around, but it disturbed me that she was so untrustworthy. God only knew what she'd run off to tell my predecessor. I probably should have fired her right away, but I was torn. It wasn't like I didn't need help with the mundane aspects of this job.

The cow was exactly where we'd left it. As predicted, it had not reanimated and walked away. I was strangely disappointed, since the ice was in dire need of refreshing. The tarp had contained a lot of the melt, but areas of the floor had become slick with water and cow "runoff." It was going to become unsanitary really quickly, if it wasn't already.

Jack summed up the situation quite nicely. "Uh, disgusting!"

I shook my head. I needed to get rid of this thing. I wished I'd been more adamant with Jones this morning. The cow's body belonged with the rancher, Olson, not me. "I really just need to keep the head at this point." I sighed at the mess. "I suppose I'd better call the ranch and see if they can retrieve the body."

"A dragon could carry it," Jack said with a mischievous smile.

"And what? Drop it from the sky? In this state, it would go splat."

"He could eat it."

I made a face. "Are you trying to turn me off him? Because that is the grossest thing I've ever heard."

Jack shrugged. "I was just thinking it would be expedient."

It probably would. Olson must have written the meat off as a loss the moment he agreed to send it to the autopsy. Of course, knowing what I did about Jones's ability to convince people with blarney or glamour or whatever it was, Olson might not even remember sending the cow our way. I gave Jack a sidelong look. "I don't know."

"You doubt he's your familiar, right?"

I nodded. "What's that got to do with anything?"

"If he's your familiar, he'll come. Or, at least, he's more likely to."

I thought about all the times Valentine had been there when I needed him most. Was it true? According to Jack, all I had to do to find out was call. It was tempting because I also hated the way we parted. If he left for good, I'd never get a chance to ask him everything I wanted to know. Maybe I could catch him before he got too far away. "If I call Valentine, will you promise not to get all starry-eyed?"

"Starry—?" he started, and then pursed his lips petulantly. "I was just surprised to see a dragon, that's all."

"No asking him weird, awkward questions, either."

Jack nodded vigorously. "Do you think he'll really come?"

"I have no idea."

I really didn't. For all I knew Valentine headed back to Chicago the moment he was found out. He might be angry at me, or feel embarrassed for having been exposed like that. Maybe he thought I wouldn't still love him.

Did I?

I turned away from Jack and the dead cow, ostensibly to fetch my phone from the pocket of my coat. I'd hung it up on the peg near the front doors. As I searched for the phone, I considered. Did I still love Valentine? He was a dragon—something possibly inhuman, something everyone seemed to imply was dark and unnatural.

Of course, Jones thought I was unnatural, too.

I pushed the numbers and listened to the ringing. It went on long enough that I started to think he wouldn't pick up. I almost pressed END when I heard the click. "Alex."

"Will you come back? I need you."

There was a moment of silence. I heard the rush of air

through the speaker. Then, "I will always come when you need me."

While we waited for Valentine, I separated the cow's head from its body. Jack, most helpfully, retched into the sink. He kept his back to me while I found an empty storage freezer and placed the remains inside it.

I thought, for a second, I heard Mrs. Finnegan mutter, "Oooooh, company!"

Unless she spoke "cow," I suspected she was going to be disappointed with her new bunkmate. Jack was still gripping the edge of the sink as I stripped off my gloves and dropped them into the biohazard bin. "How can you do this job?" he asked.

"I don't know," I said. "Maybe I have necromancer tendencies just like Jones thinks, but dead things don't bother me. They never have. I found a mummified cat in my grandmother's barn one year when we were visiting and spent weeks just watching it decay. Is it morbid or scientific curiosity?"

Jack looked a little green again, so I changed the subject.

"So tell me what supernatural creature has the kind of strength to smash a cow's head so hard that it pulverizes teeth?"

He toyed with his earring as he thought. "Vampire, maybe. A golem, certainly. An angel. A god? All the beasts like gryphons and dragons, but I don't think they'd crush a cow, so much as eat it."

I keyed all the options into my notes app. "I'd like to do this scientifically. I think I could get a supply of cow heads from a butcher. Do you think Devon and Stone would agree to come in and show off their strength?"

Jack smiled at the idea. "If you make it a competition, certainly."

"What about these other things on your list? Can I get access to those?"

He pulled himself up to sit on the counter next to the sink. His feet swung off the edge. "I heard a rumor that they have an angel in the New York Bureau. Maybe we could set up a videoconference. Of course, you'll have to get him to admit his true nature."

"I seem to have a knack with that lately."

The doors opened and Valentine stuck his head in. "Talking about me?"

Despite his promise, Jack looked utterly stricken at the sight of Valentine. I had no idea what Jack saw, but to me Valentine looked the same as I always remembered: steady, strong, and . . . predatory. The only difference was that now I knew why there was always that bit of scary around the edges. Tension that I hadn't realized I carried in my shoulders dropped. I smiled and took the hand he offered.

He brought my knuckles to his lips and smiled toothily. "What does my princess require?" The romance of the gesture was ruined slightly when he smacked his lips noisily and wiped them on the back of his hand. "Gah," he said. "Antiseptic soap!"

"You should be used to that with me," I teased. I leaned in to give him a kiss on the lips, but stopped short, remembering that we weren't alone. "Uh," I said, stepping back, "you remember Jack?"

Valentine glanced sidelong at Jack. "Ah, yes, the jack-rabbit."

I poked him in the ribs with my elbow. "Be nice."

Jack didn't help Valentine's opinion of him by stumbling as he made his way around the exam table. He brushed himself off in a way that reminded me of Sarah Jane's preening, and he watched Valentine surreptitiously while trying to gather his dignity.

Valentine, meanwhile, had spotted the now headless cow melting on the floor. "You ate the least interesting part first," he noted.

Jack sputtered.

I had to laugh. "The head is in the freezer, and actually, that's what we wanted to talk to you about . . ."

It took me a while to convince Valentine that getting rid of the cow carcass wasn't beneath him. Eventually, however, he impressed Jack and me by gathering up the edges of the tarp and hauling the cow out the door.

In the hallway, he paused. "To take it much farther, I'll need all four limbs."

I wondered if Valentine the dragon would even fit in the narrow passage of the city hall basement. "Oh," I said, hating how small and timid I sounded at the thought.

He frowned down at me, a formidable look. "Are we okay?"

The strange thing was that we were. In many ways, we were better than ever. So much of what I didn't understand about him before made a kind of sense now. But, there were still so many questions—questions that were fundamental to our relationship, like whether or not he was even human.

I looked up into his face, so *familiar* with its noble ruthlessness, and said, "Will you come home tonight?"

"If you'll have me." His voice was a husky growl that

made the hairs on the back of my neck stand up and a delicious shiver run down the length of my body, all at once.

"Always," I said.

I considered hanging around to watch his transformation again, but Valentine shooed us out, telling us it was bad enough that he was taking out my garbage. He did not need gawkers.

Thus, Jack and I spent the rest of the day setting up my experiments. The first butcher I called surprised me by being very willing to donate a few heads to the cause of science if I would put in a good word for him with the chief of police. I said I would, though I wondered how much weight I actually carried with the *ordinarium*.

Meanwhile, Jack used my computer to make inquiries to New York and elsewhere. He found a woman in Ohio who had a gryphon familiar who was more than happy to participate. We worked out a way for her to send me all the specifics I needed, and she even thought she might know someone with access to a Sasquatch.

When we hung up the videocall, I had to ask, "Really? Sasquatch?"

Jack just smiled. I went back to carefully measuring and documenting the damaged cow with a shake of my head.

The angel, as predicted, turned out to be extremely reticent. When I realized who Jack had on the line, I couldn't resist peering over his shoulder at the Skyped image. The man on the computer screen was extraordinarily beautiful, but so androgynous as to be somewhat unsettling. He was mixed race with dark skin, and had the kind of loose-flowing wavy hair that I associated with Indian women. No trace of stubble dotted his chin, and its smooth flawlessness might have made him seem a bit soft, but for his eyes. In them there was a hollow mercilessness that frightened me more deeply than anything I'd ever seen reflected in Valentine's.

"No," was all he said.

With that, the conversation was over.

Jack let out a breath as we both stared at the static image of his Skype icon: the Los Angeles Angels' halo-encircled "A." "I suppose that went pretty well," Jack said. "He didn't tear us asunder."

By the time we finished that evening, I had several cow head trauma experiments ready to go. According to Jack, Devon would be incapacitated for another night, so we'd plan to start some time tomorrow. That having been decided, I looked around the morgue for something else to do and found nothing. It was just as well. Thanks to the early morning and all the day's excitement, my eyes were getting blurry and my muscles ached.

I was ready to go home.

I offered Jack a ride back to the precinct headquarters, but he declined. He made some noises about needing fresh air after having been cooped up in a basement all afternoon, but I thought, perhaps, he didn't want the intimacy of even such a short drive.

That made me a little sad, but I could hardly blame him. He'd basically asked me out this morning, and I'd agreed under false pretenses. Jack had every right to want to inject a bit of professional distance back into our relationship.

Even though I was tired, I found myself dawdling before

closing up the morgue. I wasn't sure what things were going to be like at home with Valentine waiting there. I'd told him we were okay, but now that I faced the prospect of "us" time, I was less sure. I locked the door and made my way to my car.

The air outside finally felt like spring, heavy with the wetness of melting snow. Stars sprinkled across the immense blackness of the sky. I paused for a moment before getting into my car, and stared up at the cloudless night. What must it feel like to fly?

I drove the rest of the way home trying to wrap my mind around the fact that Valentine *knew*.

SIXTEEN

There was no dinner on the stove when I walked in the door this time. In fact, the house was dark. I left my coat and boots in the mudroom with a sigh. Valentine must have found somewhere more interesting to be, though I did notice that his duffel was still on the couch at least.

I picked it up, thinking I'd put it in my room. The last thing I wanted was for Robert to get annoyed with the way Val left his things strewn around. The duffel was much heavier than I expected. Since the zipper was open, I peered inside to see if he was carrying the anvil. Instead, I found something that looked a bit like a bowling ball, except it had no fingerholds. I picked it up to inspect it. It was some kind of black stone, polished to a shine, with flecks of white crystals in fernlike patterns scattered throughout.

"Snowflake obsidian." Valentine stood in the archway between the living room and the small dining room. The lights were off and he was entirely in shadow. For a moment, all I could see was the glow of his ghostly pale skin.

I jumped and nearly dropped the massive stone. "What is it?" I asked. Then, realizing he'd just answered that question in a way, I rephrased. "What does it do? Why do you have it?"

When Valentine stepped into the light, he looked as if I'd woken him from a nap, wearing warm-looking, heavy cotton navy sweatpants and not much else. His short hair was slightly mussed.

All in all, he seemed very . . . human.

"I have it for the same reason I have anything. It's beautiful." Then, almost as an afterthought, he added with a little self-satisfied smile, "And I stole it."

A very dragonlike answer.

Carefully, I returned the stone to his duffel and set both back on the couch. I'd ask him if it bothered him to carry something so heavy around, but I had seen him pick up a dead cow like it was nothing. I knew him too well to expect much more of an answer as to why have it at all. I collapsed onto the cushions with a sigh. "You're not human, are you?"

Instead of joining me, he came up behind the couch. His hands massaged the knots in my neck. The pressure was just right: hard enough to pop and stretch, but never quite hurting. "Depends, I suppose, how narrowly you define 'human.'"

The hands that caressed me were calloused and dry and, as I closed my eyes, I could almost imagine the silken hardness of scales. But not quite. This afternoon's transformation seemed far away. Right now, I let myself relax into his touch. "Jones is convinced you're evil incarnate, you know."

"Jones . . ." Valentine considered as he worked my shoulder blades, ". . . is the one who tried to shoot me?"

In between happy noises, I managed to say, "Yes."

"I didn't like him," Valentine said, and I could hear the disgusted crinkle of his nose in his voice. "He smelled of fairy silver."

"Yeah," I said, remembering the other strange visit of the day. "He would. His mother is the queen of fairies."

"With a mother like that, your friend may easily mistake indifference for maliciousness. Being evil requires that you care enough about the outcome to actively thwart the efforts of another."

I twisted around to look Valentine in the eyes. As usual, I saw that cool detachment there. "So you're not evil, you just don't care?"

"I care a great deal about many things," he said. His thumb traced the thin welt that the casing's heat had left on my cheek. "One of the most precious is you."

Valentine had never said anything like that before, and it hung between us, profoundly. I'd turned all the way around in the couch, so I was kneeling on the seat.

He kissed me. I wrapped my arms around him, drawing him closer. My dragon-hearted lover might never say he loved me, but at least he'd told me that I mattered to him. A single tear streaked down my cheek.

When we pulled apart, I asked, "Why didn't you tell me what you were?"

"You never asked," he said.

"That's no answer," I insisted. "We were talking about demons and crazy things. Things I *thought* I saw, but that you *believed* in. Why wouldn't you tell me something so important about yourself?"

"You know you weren't ready. For every second we spent talking about bridge trolls, you would spend hundreds of hours rationalizing and denying them. You were tying yourself into knots, making yourself sick. If I had told you, it would have scared you to ground. You would have bolted just like your jackrabbit friend."

Though he was unnecessarily unkind to Jack, I knew what he said was true. Even so, all the hurt of those times roiled up. I pulled away, and crossed my arms in front of my chest defensively. "Jack said familiars are supposed to protect a witch, introduce us to our own kind, and make sure we don't have to go through shit like that."

My angry accusations didn't even faze him. "And I would have, if it weren't for the immediate threat that Gayle represented."

The stepmonster.

Of course.

Turning, I slumped back down onto the couch. This time, Valentine came around to perch on the end table in order to face me. "She masked your signal very effectively for many years," Valentine said. "I only began to hear the call after you left home for college."

I'd been planning on medical school from the beginning and, in order to save money, had stayed close to home for undergraduate work. I had lived with my dad a lot on and off during those years, despite the atmosphere there. "You 'heard' me? I thought it was a smell."

He cocked his head slightly. "Smell, yes, but more than that. I'm not sure I can describe the feeling to a creature with no sense of instinct. Sometimes, there are simply things I *must* do. Finding you was one of those."

I felt weirdly flattered, but there was still so much I didn't understand. Other than seeing things that no one else did,

I'd never felt especially magical. In fact, that'd just made me feel weird and out of place. Everyone else's life seemed cooler. I couldn't conjure things from my mind. I'd never been able to cast a spell in my life, at least none I ever knew about. I was even terrible at those card tricks and other phony illusions you could buy in magic shops. "Why? Why me?"

"I don't know," he said. "All that was certain to me was that you were something I had to have, own, possess— *guard*, like the finest jewel in the hoard."

Well, at least now I knew why he never told me he loved me. I wasn't sure I liked this particular revelation, though. I pushed my back against the couch. "I'm your very best possession, huh?"

He surprised me by laughing. "You, my dear, have proven a surprisingly difficult gem to acquire. I don't believe I have managed that feat just yet. You are far too wild, too . . . willful a thing to be owned in any decent fashion. I have had to satisfy myself with continual pursuit."

My defensive posture melted slightly at that. After all, I thought of him the exact same way.

The mischievous glint in his eyes inspired me to duck under his arm. I dashed across the room.

"Okay, then," I teased from around the archway. I enjoyed his stunned expression. With a laugh, I dashed into the dining room in the direction of the bedroom. "See if you can catch me!"

Though we played that game for a long time, I have to admit that at several points during the night, Valentine completely and quite thoroughly possessed me.

* * *

I woke up to an empty bed, however. When I reached over to give Valentine a morning cuddle, I found the big black stone ball instead. He'd stuck a Post-it note to the top of it. With blinking morning eyes, I read his scrawling, old-fashioned cursive: "Had to fly. (Ha. Ha.) Will be back."

Of course, I had no idea if he meant tonight or sometime next year. I crumpled up the yellow paper and tossed it onto the floor. I should know by now that the easiest way to get rid of a dragon is to give him what he wants. I'd bored him by giving in last night.

At least I had his promise that he'd come back around eventually.

I was beginning to think that was a fairly big commitment from someone like Valentine. Despite myself, I smiled as I got up and dressed for work.

When I went in for the morning meeting, the precinct office was buzzing with excitement. Two zombies had been spotted at Big Tom's diner. Stone and Jones were on their way out to collect them if they could. Everyone thought the reanimation was likely the work of the necromancer, and it could be the big break we were looking for in this case.

Devon stood next to the watercooler with an empty cup listing in his hand. He looked completely hungover. He wore the same college sweatshirt he'd had on days ago, but now it was rumpled and stained with dust and grime. A hole had been ripped in the knee of his jeans. Deep bags hung under his eyes and there was a bruise on his stubbled chin.

I decided not to ask the obvious question. Instead, after

he muttered a "morning" in my general direction, I asked, "Does Big Tom's have brains on the breakfast menu or something?"

He stared at me blankly.

"Zombies," I said. "Don't they eat brains?"

Devon yawned and rubbed his neck, as if he had a sore muscle, and said, "Not in my experience." He gave me a quick appraisal and added, "Rumor has it you're shtupping a dragon. I told Margot I didn't believe it for a minute." He coughed out a laugh like he thought that was the most ridiculous thing he'd ever heard.

Because he was so smug about the impossibility, I said, very proudly, "It's true."

"Well, then, welcome to the unnatural club." He gave me a salute with his paper cup. "I'm glad I won't be the only one in the office everyone hates."

"Oh no, Devon, don't worry. I'm sure that will still be the case."

His mouth hung open as I sauntered away.

Over my shoulder, I added, "Don't forget your appointment at the morgue this afternoon. You and Stone have some cow heads to smash."

He smiled a bit. "I wouldn't miss it for the world. Finally a chance to show her which of us is strongest."

"Good," I said.

Without the morning meeting to attend, I wasn't quite sure what to do with myself. I wished Jones had assigned me a desk. When he came back, I would ask him about it. Meanwhile, I found myself drifting over to where Jack sat reading the *Capitol Times*. Leaning against the edge of his wooden desk to peer over his shoulder, I asked, "Does it mention Olson's cows?"

"Yes," he said, pointing to the piece. "And some neighbor mentioned seeing 'dancing lights' and space aliens."

The article was buried in the community section, under the fold on a middle page. Still, I couldn't imagine Jones would be very happy with this. "At least there's no picture."

"Small miracles," Jack muttered, taking a sip from a mug at his desk. Whatever he was drinking smelled very green. "The interviewing officers said a lot of people mentioned lights. I wonder if they're fairy?"

I shook my head. "The queen was very clear that the only fairy in Hughes County is Jones."

"You should really learn to call him Spenser. Everyone does."

It was the first time Jack pulled himself from the newspaper long enough to look me in the eye. I smiled at him sheepishly. "That'll take some doing," I admitted. "It's a lot easier for me to believe in magic than call a cop by his first name."

"Is it a respect thing?"

"Sort of," I said. "And fear. Cops scare me."

He didn't ask me why; instead, he shrugged and returned his focus to the paper. "You, of all people, should have nothing to fear. Call him *Spense*, for oak's sake."

"Me, of all people? What does that mean?"

"You're the one with the dragon," he said stiffly.

Everyone seemed obsessed with that fact this morning and rather pissy about it as well. I'd thought Jack was cool with the fact I had a dragon familiar. Or was he feeling hurt about the other rumor Devon had heard? I'd told Jones that Valentine was my boyfriend. Had Jack not figured that out?

How ironic that Valentine had left me—with nothing but a note and a giant black ball. It made me wonder, though. Talk was clearly circulating. What did people think of me now? Where did I fit in the office politics hierarchy with my tendency toward the unnatural and a dragon on call?

I wasn't sure I wanted the aggravation. I'd never asked for this gig. The only office mates I'd wanted to have to deal with were dead people—ones who didn't talk back!

"I'll be at the morgue if anyone needs me," I told the back of Jack's head as I walked out the door.

Unfortunately, Mrs. Finnegan was in an especially chatty mood today. She told me all about her daughter who was coming to pick up her body. I tried to make polite, interested comments for a while, but when I realized that only encouraged her, I gave up and put on my headphones.

My mind wandered as I listened to the music. Jack was jealous, that much was clear. It made no sense to me, however. In my mind, he'd gotten the better familiar. Sarah Jane was charming. She might come with a bullyish band of magpies, but I doubted she'd ever done time for grievous bodily harm. As far as familiars went, she seemed perfect. Mine was violent and temperamental, and even on his best days he could be crafty and deceitful. Our entire relationship was founded on a lie, or at least a dishonest disguise. Sarah Jane was exactly as advertised.

Of course, he might just be old-fashioned jealous, too. Maybe I was right and Jack hadn't realized Valentine was my lover as well as my familiar until someone in the office told him.

I wished I could explain to Jack that, even with Valentine

in my life, there was room for more affection. Valentine was many wonderful things to me, but he'd always have the emotional distance . . . of a *dragon*.

That was such a relief to be able to say, because the coldness I got from Valentine used to eat me up. I thought there was something wrong with me, some part of my personality that wasn't fulfilling him. But, now I knew. It was just his nature. He loved me in his own way; it just wasn't the human way.

Jack had nothing to be jealous of.

Hell, Jack actually knew magic and how to perform it intentionally. The only thing I'd ever done, magically speaking, was accidentally graft someone else's weapon to my arm. I couldn't even hope to get rid of it without Jack's help.

I glanced at the snake's head on the back of my hand. It had moved again. The tip of its nose was tucked slightly under its scaly neck, almost like a sleeping cat, except its lidless black eye stared out at me.

It looked content and comfortable.

I should have been repulsed, but instead I had to resist the urge to give it a gentle, loving stroke.

What was wrong with me? Was Devon right? Had I gone over to the dark side finally?

I let out a frustrated snort. *Maybe I'd never left it.*

The music switched to something that always reminded me of Valentine, Mariah Carey's song "My All." "If it's wrong to love you," I sang along, "then my heart just won't let me be right."

My emotions were a complete tangle. I made some headway on both cases, however.

The lab at the hospital came back with some preliminary results of the tox screen on the necromancer. They found trace amounts of sorbitol and paradichlorobenzene on the skin samples I'd taken during the autopsy. Both were chemicals used in embalming. Sorbitol was used to return moisture to the body and the paradicholorobenzene was a mold inhibitor. I supposed he could have picked both up while handling the bodies he'd robbed from the graves, but there was another chemical present that made me wonder—borax. It was a common enough household chemical, but it was also used to adjust the pH of embalming fluids. That seemed more like the kind of thing you'd have on your skin if you were actively mixing those chemicals, like a mortician would.

Checking the department's database, the necromancer's last job was listed as a stocker at the local grocery. Unless embalming was a hobby of his—which, given his tendency to have body parts in his closet, it might be—he hung out at mortuaries a lot.

Maybe that was the sort of thing that was a "duh" for Precinct 13. I supposed that "necromancer = mortuaries" wasn't a big stretch, but I thought it might be a clue as to where he'd gone off to. Given the state he'd left in, he may have wanted his body stitched back together. A mortician could certainly do a good job of it.

What had Nana Spider said? Something about a relative? Maybe our necromancer had family in the funerary business. I took a few notes and stored them in my phone.

I came across my previous notation to myself about Boyd. I needed to remember to tell Jones that it wasn't Peterson who had been at the scene—or, at least if he had been there, Boyd had been, too.

Next, I spent some time really examining the cow's head trauma, thinking about what Genevieve's veterinarian cousin had said about the force of a car. The shape of the wound had me thinking about every forensic scientist's best friend, "the blunt instrument." I'd have to wait to see the kind of shape that a supernaturally strong fist might make, but I should probably have a few more experiments ready for different kinds of shovels or tools.

I was on the office's phone making arrangements with the butcher when my phone buzzed. I put the butcher on hold while I answered. The number was unidentified, but I didn't know many people in town.

"We have a dead body for you." The matter-of-fact no-introduction could only be Jones.

"Where?"

"In the interrogation room. The zombie stopped being cooperative and died. For real."

SEVENTEEN

For some reason, downtown was busy today. I found a parking spot several blocks away. As I rounded the corner, I saw the chief of police pacing back and forth in front of the storefront illusion. He wore a heavy leather police jacket and his breath came out in steamy huffs. "I know you're in there," he shouted.

I hesitated, wondering what I should do. I knew we had a camera pointed at the front door. Someone must know he was out here. Why weren't they letting him in? I wondered if I should try to find a backdoor. Though, given how camouflaged the front was, I doubted I'd ever discover the back by accident.

The chief must have seen me out of the corner of his eye. "Hey, Connor," he said, waving me over. "Tell these yahoos to let me in."

Part of me still wanted to run, but I steeled myself and

approached him. The belt buckle today was a golden eagle. It glinted in the sunlight. "What's going on, sir?"

"That's what I want to know. Why were there zombies at the damn diner? And the newspaper is reporting aliens! You people are supposed to keep all that stuff under wraps."

I could use a rescue about now. I stared bitterly at the front door, which remained closed. It was obvious no one wanted to deal with this. "I don't know," I said firmly. "I'm just the coroner."

The chief poked a meaty finger at my chest. "You tell Jones that I want answers. He'd better have them for me by lunchtime, or I'm busting the battering ram out of storage and I'll break this goddamn door down, you hear?"

Because there wasn't a better answer, I said, "Yes, sir."

His black-and-white was parked out front. In special lettering on the door were the words: CHIEF OF POLICE. He grumbled to himself as he made his way to the car and then slammed the door shut before driving off. I watched him go, but he never spared me a second glance.

The door stood resolutely closed. I put my hand on the knob, expecting to find it locked. It twisted open easily. Had he never actually tried the door?

Inside, the room was hushed, as if everyone were holding their breath so as not to be overheard by the police chief. When they noticed it was me instead, noise began to slowly return. I shook my head at all of them: bunch of cowards.

I hung my coat up on the peg and went in search of zombies.

It seemed to be the day for arguments. Jones and Stone were at it in front of the interrogation room.

"When I said be 'bad cop,' I didn't mean that bad," Jones snarled. He looked more tired and worn-out than usual. He had a long scratch on one cheek, and his usually neatly combed hair was disheveled.

Stone slowly crossed her arms in front of her chest. "I have told you a thousand times. Though the rabbi who created me is dead, I am still oath-bound never to kill. I had nothing to do with it."

"Well, something happened. He was plenty reanimated when I last talked to him."

"Maybe he's allergic to fairy dust."

As curious as I was about what "fairy dust" might actually be, I might have let them continue to fight. But, they were blocking the entrance. I interrupted with a wave of my hand. "You called?"

Jones's rage had been so focused on his partner that he looked startled to find me standing there. "Oh, Alex, good. The zombie corpse is inside."

He stepped out of the way to let me past. Before I went through, I told him, "The chief is pretty mad. He wants to talk to you."

Jones spat some swearword I couldn't quite catch, though it sounded foreign, and added, "He's just pissed because we got called before his guys did. He hates it when the chain of command gets broken."

I didn't tell him that I thought it might be more than that this time. Stone, however, used the opportunity to defuse the conflict. "You should go play politics," she said. "Lay on some more glamour. I'll drive."

That seemed to be the right thing to say, because he agreed with a brisk nod. They took off purposefully, leaving me on my own with the dead zombie.

* * *

I had never seen a zombie before, but I discovered I had a lot of preconceived ideas about what one should look like. I thought it would be bug-eyed, rotted, and possibly still muttering something inane like, "Braaaaains!"

Instead, the zombie's body sprawled at the lip of the koi pond. One bare foot dangled in the pool, and curious fish nibbled at the flesh of the big toe. Despite the missing shoe, the corpse had been dressed for a funeral. He was facedown. The suit was split up the back, exposing graying shoulder blades and spine.

I knelt beside the zombie's head, which was twisted to the side. He looked to be in his late eighties, and exposure to the air had made his skin extra saggy.

His face surprised me the most. He hadn't just been dressed for a funeral; he'd been prepared for one. The makeup that the mortuary had applied gave his face a plastic sheen. In the natural light of the interrogation room, the rouge made his cheeks and lips a bit gaudy. He had a nearly full head of silver-white hair. I brushed stiffly sprayed stray hairs that had come undone aside to look at his sunken eyes. They were open, glassy, but a faint remnant of humanity remained in the deer-brown depths. I thought he looked nice, like the sort to keep a hard candy in his pocket.

He could be someone's grandfather.

No wonder the chief was mad. Animating bodies from a cemetery in a small town was bad business. The necromancer or whoever had done this had apparently chosen bodies that weren't too far decomposed. That meant this man had died recently, maybe even less than a week ago. His family and friends had said good-bye to this man, grieved his passing, and now he'd wandered into the town's popular diner.

Not cool.

I pulled the edges of the coat so that they covered more of his body and patted his shoulder gently. We needed to stop whoever was doing this.

Similarly, I could understand Jones's impulse to be angry at Stone. If I didn't know better, it would appear as though he'd been pushed. But she would have had to shove him from behind and that was atypical of an angry blow in a fight. No, from the angle of the body, it was clear he'd been walking forward when his legs gave out.

He'd collapsed, plain and simple. His arms splayed in a way that indicated that he had *not* tried to break his fall, either. He'd simply gone down limp, like a rag doll.

I wondered if there was some sort of limit to the edges of magical influence. Perhaps, like a radio-controlled toy, he simply walked out of range and stopped getting the signal.

Or someone had turned it off, like a switch.

Sitting back on my heels, I looked for other clues. I checked the side of his neck near the carotid artery for a puncture wound. I found it, small and neat, and the corresponding drainage hole on the right jugular. The mortician who'd done the embalming was careful and precise.

Somehow, I didn't quite picture the long-haired, tattooed necromancer being this exact, but I could be wrong. I shouldn't judge someone by the image they presented to the world. After all, the doctors had been so very wrong about Valentine.

After massaging the skin along the side of the corpse's abdomen, I placed the time of death sometime after the necromancer had left my morgue—possibly even as recent as yesterday. This man might not have even had his funeral yet.

Oh, now, *that* was evil.

How upsetting would it be to find out that your dearly departed was seen eating breakfast at Big Tom's the morning before the funeral?

Pulling myself upright, I hit REDIAL on the last incoming call. I didn't expect Jones to answer, but he did. "This better be good news, Connor."

"I think whoever animated this corpse is a mortician at a local funeral parlor, or is the friend of one," I said, and then I explained that I thought there was a strong possibility that this body hadn't been dead longer than forty-eight hours. I also told him about the findings of the chemicals present on the necromancer's skin. "I'm no cop, but my instinct is that there's an accomplice, some relative who works with bodies."

"Do you think it's 'skull girl' from Twitter?"

I had forgotten about her. "That seems a little casual for a mortician," I said. Though maybe not if she and the necromancer shared the same worldview, as it were. I reconsidered. "Could be."

"Well, keep me informed."

I started to say good-bye, but Jones had already hung up. I'd never get used to how no-nonsense cops could be. Putting my phone away, I sat down on the concrete step in front of where the body sprawled over the lip of the pond.

Water had seeped up the zombie's pant leg. Crouching on the lip precariously, I lifted his foot up out of the water. I set it gently on the edge. I didn't know what else I could learn from him, and an autopsy seemed cruel. I was sure his cause of death was already known.

I should probably take him back to the morgue anyway,

to check for signs of zombification. Of course, I had no idea what those might be. For all I knew it was just a spell and a wave of a wand.

Just when I was thinking that I should fetch a sheet or something to cover him with, the tattoo on my arm started to itch and tickle. It started as a tingling in my shoulder and ran all the way to the back of my palm. I braced myself. This had happened right before the dead cow had mooed. I had a very bad feeling that the corpse was about to talk to me.

"M a med merring . . ."

"What?" I asked.

He said the same thing again only louder, and I suddenly remembered that the mortician would either have glued or sutured the mouth closed. I listened very carefully the third time I asked him to repeat his statement. "You're a red herring?" I finally asked.

Though I thought there was no way I'd gotten that right, he nodded. "Mmes mis taunting moo."

"He is taunting moo . . . I mean, you, or us?"

More nodding and then, "Me mates Menser."

"He hates Spenser?"

That was all he seemed able to give me. He put his head back down and resumed being dead.

"Thanks," I said. I scratched at the skin over the snake tattoo absently. It was strange that it didn't ache as badly as it usually did when the dead started talking. The corpse had been extremely helpful, too, not like Mrs. Finnegan's odd ramblings or the cow's undecipherable moo. How often did something just sit up and actually tell you it was a red herring? It was mighty suspicious.

"Are you lying to me?" I asked the body.

Of course, now he had nothing to say.

I told the corpse I'd be right back with a modesty cloth and someone to help move him to the morgue where he could wait safely for his family to pick him up. I had no idea if he could hear me, but Mrs. Finnegan seemed to appreciate it yesterday. Maybe, like her, he'd become more talkative the more time we spent together.

Egads, there was a thought.

At least the cow hadn't mooed since I separated its head from its body.

I wandered back into the main precinct office, looking for a couple of able bodies. It must have been closer to lunch than I realized because the office was surprisingly empty. I found two uniforms loitering near the conference doorway. I recognized them as the guys Jones had picked to interview the neighbors of Olson. Their heads were together and they seemed to be strategizing about how to deal with Jones's inevitable reaction to the newspaper's space alien story.

The taller of the two seemed to be the brains of the operation. His flattop was a mousy-brown that matched his eyes. "Listen, Peterson, we've got to strike first. We need to storm into Spenser's office and demand to know why the techno-wizard didn't cover our tracks better."

"Throw Jack under the bus?" Peterson asked. He had sandy hair and a similarly washed-out complexion. "That doesn't seem cool, Hanson. Besides, it wasn't his fault. The meme was too strong. I don't even think an army of glamour-using witches could have stopped that one from getting out; *everyone* reported seeing lights."

"Did you see the chief this morning? Jones is going to be looking for scapegoats on this one. Neither of us is magical."

Peterson pursed his lips at the idea. He pointed two fingers at both his eyes. "But we *see*. We're sensitive, that counts for something."

"When cuts come to this department, it's not going to matter much."

Peterson shook his head. "We should stick to the truth. The fact that we're ordinary isn't why the 'don't see me' failed."

"What's a 'don't see me?'" I asked, forgetting that I was supposed to be eavesdropping.

Hanson started guiltily, but Peterson turned to me and explained, "It's a spell powder we carry on fact-finding missions. It helps people do what comes naturally—look the other way when weird things are happening."

Aha! I wondered how things were kept hush-hush when dragons flew overhead and such. "So it's like that pen they used in *Men in Black*?"

"Well, yeah, except not as dramatic," he said. He cleared his throat before adding, perhaps for his partner's benefit, "Obviously, it doesn't work when there's buy-in." Using his thumb, he indicated himself and his partner. "That's why we're not affected."

Hanson added, "The spell can't make someone forget what they saw, it only heightens the instinct not to get involved."

"Speaking of getting involved . . ."

I managed to rope both Peterson and Hanson into helping me arrange transport for the zombie's corpse, and in the process I learned more about what they'd found out from the rancher's neighbors.

Because of the sunken auditorium design of the interrogation room, the cops had to haul the zombie's body all the way up the stairs to the door. Though he'd re-died, the body refused to stiffen, so they hauled him by the arms and legs in a two-person carry.

"You said all the rancher's neighbors hated him?" I asked from where I held the door open, as they grunted up the incline.

"Yeah, I guess Olson's organic in a crazy way," said Peterson.

"And free range," added the other, as they made it to the top step. "That's the real problem. His cows routinely wandered into the neighbors' pastures and caused all sorts of damage. Instead of making nice, he'd get all up in their faces and demand restitution for all the nonorganic feed they'd ingested."

"Sounds like a pain," I said.

They settled the corpse into the wheelchair I'd found in a back closet. I wasn't quite sure why the precinct had it, though Hanson said that sometimes the precog on the team would bring in random things like that. "Yeah," said Peterson. "She gave me the business card for a tree removal service three days before that big tornado last year."

"Too bad you removed the wrong tree, huh?" His partner laughed, taking the arms of the chair to wheel the corpse toward the door. The body flopped around disconcertingly, lolling off the arms of the wheelchair like a human-sized sock monkey.

I stopped them for a moment to tuck the modesty sheet around the zombie's shoulders and thighs. The cutaway clothes the funeral home had given him were worse than a hospital gown for random exposure. The cops watched my ministrations curiously.

I had no comment. After all, I had a lot of respect for the dead. They were my job.

We'd decided that since the zombie's body was so pliable, the two cops would simply set him into their backseat and drive him to the morgue with the wheelchair in the trunk. I'd head over separately and get a freezer ready.

Both Stone and Devon were waiting for me outside the doors. With the excitement of the zombie, I'd forgotten that I'd made an appointment with them to smash cow heads. I checked my watch. Miraculously, I was only a few minutes late.

It looked like whatever argument they might have hadn't quite started yet. Devon slouched against the wall, his arms crossed defensively in front of his chest. His gaze focused on his shoes.

Meanwhile, Stone watched him. Her face was alert, but otherwise completely expressionless. She could be a statue. She hardly blinked or even seemed to breathe.

"Hiya," I said cheerfully.

Devon pushed off the wall and cracked his knuckles noisily. "I'm looking forward to really letting loose," he said.

"Good," I said, opening up and showing them both inside. "I want to see what you've got."

If the morning hadn't been so interrupted, I would have had coffee and donuts ready for them both. I tended to really enjoy these sorts of things. I opened the curtain in front of the first splatter booth with a "Ta-da!"

I hoped they were as impressed as I was with my work. I had the experiment set up to as closely approximate the experience of walking up to a cow and bashing it over the head as I could. That meant, in Devon's case, he'd be just slightly taller than eye to eye with the beast. Also, to punch it down, they'd have to displace the weight of an upright cow. I had a bunch of heads ready to attach to my cow contraption.

"Okay," I said, after handing each protective clothing. "Let her rip."

I let Devon do whatever came naturally to him the first time. As I expected, he punched nearly straight into the cow's face. When I reset the rigging for Stone, she did the same thing, though with a lot more force.

As I recalibrated and readjusted the machine, I explained what I wanted next. "I'm looking for a downward angle," I said, pointing to the bridge of the cow's snout. "Aimed right about here."

As I would have predicted, this was a bit more awkward. Devon had to jump into the air a bit, and he brought his hand down karate-chop style. Stone used an overhand double-fist that I thought showed the most promising damage.

However, just to be a completist, once they'd finished that, I had them try with shovels. That produced the most disgusting cow head pancakes I'd ever seen in my life. The accompanying bone shattering and goo splattering nearly put me off my lunch, as well. I was suddenly grateful I hadn't had time to fetch donuts.

However, it was now obvious that whatever struck the cows wasn't nearly as strong as a vampire or a golem.

When the two cops showed up with the zombie's body, I waved off their apologies for being so late. They'd had some kind of trouble sneaking the body in the back door. However, I left the zombie pushed into the corner for the moment, because I wanted Peterson to try bashing the cow with a shovel.

His partner wanted a go, so I let him try, too.

We were having so much fun that none of us noticed when the zombie got up and walked out the door.

EIGHTEEN

When the door swung shut, I looked up and saw the empty wheelchair. "Oh shit!"

Not bothering to pull off my splatter apron, I ran out into the hall. The zombie had only made it a few feet. He was hampered by the modesty sheet clutched around his body like an oversized toga. His gait was floppy and weirdly out of sync, reminding me of a marionette. One bare foot slapped along the polished concrete floor.

I stopped when I realized how slowly he was moving. The two human cops were the next out the door, hands on their guns, followed by Devon and then Stone. They skidded to a halt behind me. We all stood in a clump watching the zombie shuffle quietly toward the exit.

"We should follow him," Stone said, removing her splatter gear and handing it to me. She quickly closed the distance with three powerful strides. Once she caught up with him, the zombie gave her a sharp, annoyed glare and then tried to quicken his pace with a little hop. Unfazed, she walked alongside him patiently, her hands folded behind her back, like a mother with a dawdling toddler.

"You have time to clean up and join us, I think," Stone suggested. She watched as the zombie slipped on the edge of the sheet. He struggled, sliding on the slick concrete, until Stone finally put a hand on his elbow and bent to untangle the cloth from his pant leg.

"Me?" I asked, looking at all the other law enforcement around me. I was sure I should really stay and examine the findings from the experiments, but I had to admit I was deeply curious about where he was going.

"Yes," she said in her matter-of-fact way from where she crouched at the zombie's feet. He'd gotten his foot loose and was making a shambling forward progress of a sort. "He's your patient."

They had only made it as far as the parking lot by the time I'd stored all the results in the freezers and cleaned up the biggest messes. Despite her assurances that I had plenty of time, I hurried as quickly as I could. I was out of breath by the time I caught up with Stone and her zombie charge.

At some point, she must have taken pity on him, and rewrapped the sheet. Now it was draped over his shoulders like an overlong shawl. She also had her hand crooked like a gentleman, and the zombie clutched it for support.

"Where's Devon and the others?" I asked.

"I sent Peterson and Hanson to report this new development to Spenser. Devon," she said with a shrug, "is not my responsibility."

I suspected that meant they'd finally had whatever

argument had been brewing outside the morgue. Falling into step beside Stone and the zombie, I took in a deep breath. The sun shone warmly on my face. Snowmelt had darkened the sidewalks. Beyond the parking lot, patches of muddy grass were visible in the expanse of the capitol's lawn. Geese honked their noisy return, flying in a lopsided V pattern overhead.

"Why do you and Devon fight so much?" I asked as we ambled along.

Stone helped the zombie negotiate the curb. "We have a difference of opinion as to whether or not kabbalah is maleficium."

"Kabbalah is the magic that made you?" I took the zombie's other elbow when he careened in my direction. Once he was righted I let him go.

"It is," she said. It was warm enough that, though she wore the heavy leather, lined police jacket, it was unzipped.

"Maleficium," I repeated slowly, considering. "Is there a difference between that and the unnatural?"

"No, not really," she said. The sunlight brought out reddish highlights in her hair. She still had terribly disorganized bangs, but she'd pulled the rest back into a tight ponytail. "Maleficium is more overt in its opinion." When I looked at her curiously, she added, "It means bad magic."

The zombie groaned noncommittally.

I had a much stronger reaction. I kicked at a frozen chunk of gravel on the sidewalk. "Bullshit."

"No," she said, insistently, "it really does mean that."

"That's not what I'm reacting to," I said, sending more rocks and ice flying. "I thought that everything would be okay once I found out magic was real, but it's not, is it? I'm not the right kind of magic. That's just awesome."

A bird cawed from an overhead wire. It was a cuff-wearing magpie—perhaps one of Sarah Jane's gang. I wondered if it would report back to Jack, or if it was just making a comment of its own.

Stone, meanwhile, had nothing to say, no words of comfort or reassurances that it was no big deal to be one of the unnatural ones.

The zombie, however, reached out and gave my hand a squeeze. I looked into his clouded eyes and wondered why I had his sympathy. Did he simply feel badly that I was angry at this discovery? Or, did he agree that there was an unfair bias against those classified as unnatural? Given that he was the victim of unnatural magic, I suspected the former, which just made me angrier.

I didn't want a zombie's pity.

Because, despite how people reacted to those who were labeled unnatural, I still believed what Jack told me. Where my magic came from wasn't nearly as important as what I did with it.

Stone studiously avoided looking at me, which suited me just fine—I would have glared at her, anyway. I began to understand Devon's feud with her. She was so desperate to be one of the "good" guys, trying to pass as one of them. I could see why he took every opportunity to poke her about it.

The zombie continued to lead us forward. We made our ambling way down a shop-lined street. A man in his mid-forties sat on a rocking chair in front of a place selling antiques. He smoked a pipe, and nodded to us as we passed. Stone gave him the small-town cop nod. I wished him a good afternoon. The zombie moaned politely.

He took no further notice of us, despite the fact that the

zombie's funeral suit sagged due to the split up the back and he was dragging a dirty sheet behind him.

Unfortunately, the zombie seemed to be leading us back to Big Tom's. I wasn't sure if we should let him go back, considering how upset the police chief had been at the idea of zombies there. I looked to Stone. "Should we let him go to the diner if he wants?"

She nodded. "If he's drawn here, there's a reason."

"I'm not so sure," I said. "He told me he's a red herring."

I may have actually surprised Stone. She didn't quite sputter, but there was real emotion behind her question. "He what?"

"When he was dead . . . er, more dead, he spoke to me."

The zombie's expression stayed vacant, but I thought I sensed him leaning toward us, as though listening intently. It made me wonder if the person who reanimated him was doing the same.

"Zombies can't talk," Stone said resolutely. Planting her hands on her hips, she paused. "Their mouths are sewn shut."

"I know that," I said. "It was very garbled, but he told me he was a distraction—at least that's what I assume he meant by 'red herring.' I thought, at first, that he was far too helpful to be telling the truth, but now I wonder if he was desperately trying to give me information before the necromancer took control again."

When I checked to see if the zombie was still interested in our conversation, I noticed that he'd stopped his slow, plodding progress. The modesty sheet slipped from his fingers. It slid off his shoulders into a heap on the sidewalk.

I didn't have a chance to warn Stone before the zombie leaped forward in an attack.

Not that it mattered much. She saw him coming and

raised her arm in a block. Though she did little more than move her fist a few inches, the power of the blow sent the zombie flying backward into the bakery window. He bounced against the glass hard enough that I heard the impact of the back of his skull.

I winced, but the zombie didn't.

He recovered quickly and pounced forward again. This time his arms led the charge, flailing wildly. Stone did some kind of smooth martial arts move that had him stumbling past her.

Unfortunately, that put him right in front of me.

Hands closed around my throat. Though his skin had the velvet softness of old age, plenty of power crushed down on my larynx. I would have screamed if I could get any air. His face, inches from mine, was slack and empty of any expression. The mortuary makeup was starkly garish in the bright sunlight.

I struggled against his grip. Stars began shooting around the edges of my vision. Just as I was sure I'd pass out, I felt Stone coming up behind me. She pried his hands from my throat.

I took in a deep, shuddering breath. He reared back to head-butt me, but I managed to duck out from under Stone's arms. Awkwardly, I stumbled to my feet, still clutching my bruised throat.

"Run," Stone said calmly. "The problem with zombies is that they're relentless."

"But what about you?" I gasped.

She still gripped his wrists, and held him, literally at arm's length. He began kicking at her shins. "I'll be okay. He's the problem. I don't want to damage him," she said. I heard a popping as his shoulders dislocated as he struggled.

"Damn it. I'm going to need backup. The precinct isn't far away. Run."

Even though I had no sense of which way to go, I took off. I felt a little cowardly leaving her there, but it seemed pretty obvious by now that Stone was impervious to damage. I, however, was a liability. My throat ached. I would be sporting serious bruises tomorrow to match the burn mark on my cheek.

I ran until I was several blocks away. Out of breath, I fished my phone out of my pocket. Finding Jones's number on my recently dialed list, I punched SEND. He answered right away. "Twice in one day, Connor. More good news?"

"I wish," I said between gasps. I managed to tell him that Stone was holding off the zombie near Big Tom's. He seemed ready to hang up, but I held him on the line. "Be careful. It's a distraction for something, I'm sure of it."

"Witch instinct?"

Was that even a thing? "No, the zombie told me himself."

"When he was dead?"

"Yeah, it seems I can talk to dead people."

I was sure Jones would get all tight-lipped and snarky and say something about how this was proof positive that I was an evil witch of galactic proportions. He surprised me by asking, "How long have you been able to do this?"

"Since I got my new tattoo," I said, though I wondered at the truth of that. Was it that the tattoo gave me that power, or did all the magic surrounding me the past few days wake up a latent talent of mine?

Jones apparently had no comment or criticism. "I'll keep my eyes open. You be careful and get back here as soon as you can."

He hung up before I could ask him for directions.

* * *

I was lost. I'd run out of downtown a couple of blocks ago, and when I tried to double back the way I thought I'd come, I must have gotten even more turned around. When I called Jones, it rolled directly into voice mail. Though Jack said he'd left me his phone number, I couldn't find it anywhere. I leaned against someone's retaining wall and tried my GPS app again.

It seemed to think I was in Iowa.

Luckily, the weather was nice and the entire town couldn't be any bigger than thirteen square miles. When I heard a caw overhead, I thought maybe Sarah Jane was coming to my rescue. Turned out it was a plain old crow.

Disappointed, I picked a random direction and headed out.

Sweat prickled under my armpits by the time I came to an intersection that looked promising. There was a church on one corner, a bar kitty-corner, and a funeral home across the street. The church was classic: white-painted slats and a tall steeple. The marquee in front told me that the Reverend Iverson would be preaching at 8:00 and 11:00 on Sundays, and reminded me that Jesus saves. The bar, which had the clever name of Hole in the Wall, had a sign in the window promising a different kind of saving: TWO FOR ONE AT HAPPY HOUR. The door to the bar was propped open slightly, and I could smell stale beer as I passed.

The funeral home was actually one of the nicer ones I'd seen. It was an old house, a stately Victorian, painted white as though to match the church. It had a turret and a large portico over a driveway, probably originally used for receiving carriages. The name on the front read: MILLER. What really caught my attention, however, was the hearse parked there, as if ready to receive a coffin in a few hours.

Though it was true that on an average day, worldwide, 10.8 people died per second, that number reduced radically the smaller the population pool. I could imagine that one to two people might die every day here, depending on the median age of Pierre. Still, what were the odds that someone other than our zombie was having a funeral today?

Could this be the funeral home that the zombie had come from? The easiest way to find out was to go online. At least my phone managed to pull up the *Capitol Times*. I checked the obituaries. Many of the online entries were frustratingly sparse—no pictures and only the barest information about when memorials would be held. Only a couple mentioned visitations at funeral homes and none listed for today or last night at Miller's.

This was probably a dead end. Still, the presence of the hearse kept niggling at me.

I should check it out.

I tried Jones, but got voice mail again. I left him a message telling him that I was following a hunch at the Miller Funeral Home. Just as a precaution I read the cross-street signs and reminded him that I was utterly and hopelessly lost.

And on my own.

Standing by the church sign, I wavered in my resolve about going in alone. I had just decided it was too risky when a young woman came out the front door of the funeral home. Blond and petite, she had a broom in her hand. She had on a thick wool sweater and jeans, a knit scarf wound around her neck, and matching thin gloves on her hands. She began sweeping the floor of the open-air porch. When she noticed me, she gave a little wave of hello. "Beautiful weather, isn't it?"

"Yes, very," I said, feeling emboldened to cross the street and walk up the front steps to join her on the porch. "Are you expecting business today?" I gestured at the hearse with my thumb.

Her smile faltered. It took me a second to realize that she must have noticed the snake on the back of my hand. Her hands gripped the broom handle tighter. I anticipated the sudden swing, but not the muttered Italian or Latin that came with it. I was similarly unprepared for the explosion of light before everything went dark.

NINETEEN

I woke up in the dark. At first, I thought that I'd been dreaming. After all, it was warm and sort of comfortable with the silk pillow under my head and velvet all around. When I tried to roll over to go back to sleep, however, I couldn't. The space was too small to do it easily.

I was in a coffin.

I could only pray that I wasn't already buried.

I felt my pockets frantically. My phone was still there. I pulled it out. The light of the display showed the white cloth of a much-too-close ceiling. I closed my eyes when I felt myself hyperventilating. Panicking was the worst thing I could do. I touch-dialed Valentine's number from memory. The silence of the lack of signal was loud in the confined space. Even though I hadn't been able to get through, I put the phone back carefully. I would try again if everything else failed.

Pulling my elbows in, I awkwardly tried to push the lid off. I couldn't get enough leverage. I began to inch myself over onto my stomach, with the thought that if I could get my back into it, I might have enough strength.

I was almost in position when I heard a female voice with a trace of a Southern accent. Given the steel and padding between us, it was surprisingly clear. "You're a cooler customer than most. By now, people are usually screaming their fool heads off."

Wasting oxygen, I thought. But, at least it seemed as though I was still in the funeral home. That could be either good or really bad news—depending on whether or not they were also a crematorium.

"You smell like a witch," she continued. I could imagine her bent over the coffin, her ear pressed close to hear any answer I might give. Though, she could just as easily be using magic to throw her voice from somewhere far away. For all I knew, she'd gone back to sweeping the porch. "But I haven't seen hide nor hair of a familiar. Yet you're strong enough to steal my brother's protection talisman."

So that was what the snake was? That explained why it had acted the way it had in the apartment when the spiders had attacked.

"Stupid boy," she muttered to herself. "He's messed everything up."

I arched my back experimentally. It would be hard to get my knees under myself, but I had to give it a try. From what I remembered from a PBS special on the subject, I had only about two hours or so of usable oxygen.

"Still, the snake charm should have easily defeated most witches," she continued. "Unless, of course, you're one of those unfortunate unnaturals who are fettered by that disgusting half-fairy."

Despite myself, my breath hitched at the mention of unnatural.

"Oh?" She sounded both delighted and curious. "Perhaps we won't have to waste your talents, after all."

That sounded promising. Maybe I could just agree to go to the Dark Side long enough to get released from this coffin. I'd gotten my knees up as far as they could go in the cramped space.

"You know, of course, everything they told you is a lie," she purred. "Unnatural does not necessarily equal evil."

Coming from a woman who clearly had a skewed sense of right and wrong, this would be ironic, if I hadn't already heard this from Jack. Still, I played along. I put a mix of skepticism and surprise into my voice. "Really?"

"Careful," she hissed. "Don't waste your breath. Just listen."

I could get behind that. Speaking of, mine was ready to try a big heave-ho. I waited, not wanting to squander my one chance with bad timing. If she was going to release the casket's seals for me, I could surprise her with a big push, maybe even knock her back a step or two.

"Good," she said to my silence—or my plan, but she didn't seem particularly adept at reading minds. "The other thing they lied about was that the power source treats us equally. Think about it. They're so fond of the river metaphor, let me use it as well. Tell me, which generates more power: an inner tube floating with the current or a dam that forces water to spin its turbines?"

"B" was the obvious choice. However, there was a flaw in her analogy. While floating created no energy, it also used none.

"Have you ever noticed when they have to do something big, they start talking about actions and reactions?"

I did remember Jack worrying about "devilry" he may have unleashed after trying to pull the snake from my arm.

"It's because they can only do so much before they have to start tapping the unnatural. The polarity shift causes a ripple."

I'd felt that. Jack had called it a shift, I think.

"They're so high and mighty, yet they use the same energy in the same way we do." I could hear the hurt in her voice. It reminded me of Devon's anger, and, if I was honest, my own.

Even though it meant using a bit of oxygen, I had to ask, "Your solution for bigotry is reanimating corpses?"

She laughed; it was a light, genuine sound. "No, that was my stupid brother's idea. He was obsessed with breaking the fourth wall, thought it would give him unlimited power. Just got him dead, didn't it?"

I would have agreed if I had any idea what she was talking about. My muscles were starting to cramp up, and I felt a little light-headed from claustrophobia. I was ready to break when my phone rang. Because of the odd way I was wedged, I almost couldn't pry it from my pocket in time to pick up. As it was, I answered on the last ring. "Hello?"

"If you called to have me take out more garbage I will grow very tired of you."

Valentine!

"A phone?" I heard my captor shriek. "No!"

Before I could begin to explain the situation to Val, I heard the hiss of the seals being broken. With all my strength, I pushed my back against the lid of the coffin. It popped upward. As soon as I could see a sliver of the outside,

I tipped to the side and let gravity pull the heavy steel to the floor.

I heard a shriek, but I had no idea if I managed to knock down my captor or not. The sudden influx of air to my lungs and light to my eyes completely disoriented me. My arms and legs shivered with exertion.

Tinny and distant, Valentine's voice from the iPhone speaker asked, "What's going on?"

"It's okay," I panted. "I'm okay."

"Not for long," the necromancer's sister snarled.

This time, I moved fast. I didn't know if you could actually dodge magic, but I was sure as hell going to try. As blind and clumsy as I was, the best I could do was bail out. I tumbled onto the floor, arms and legs thrashing. My graceless exit from the coffin sent a number of other display models rolling. One of the carts must have hit a wall of urns, sending ceramic explosively crashing to the floor.

Despite the chaos, I didn't manage to do much to stop the necromancer's sister. When I finally blinked the tears from my eyes, I discovered her standing over me. Her face was flushed red with anger, and her long hair was disheveled. She muttered in Latin and her hands massaged the air as if kneading invisible bread.

I had a feeling I was about to get a serious magical smackdown.

Closing my eyes, I cringed, waiting for the inevitable. "Ah, fuck all," I muttered.

A clap of thunder forced my eyes open. A burst of light blasted the necromancer's sister off her feet. She was thrown backward, and tumbled up and over a mortuary table. I heard a crash as she knocked into a medical cart. Steel instruments rained down on top of her.

When she didn't get up right away, I struggled to my feet. I glanced around to see who it was who had come to my rescue.

There was no one.

Picking my way around the broken shards of urns and tipped coffins, I found the necromancer's sister pinioned to the floor by surgical instruments. Scalpels and scissors had landed precisely along the edges of her sweater and jeans. A roll of medical tape unraveled over her mouth.

She glared angrily at me and struggled against the makeshift bonds.

"Weird," I said. Glancing over my shoulder, I still expected some accomplished wizard to step out of the shadows to take credit for this.

Another blast of wind, icy this time, came from the stairway. I pivoted, ready for some new danger. The shadow on the wall showed batlike wings that, before my eyes, folded into the figure of a man. Valentine glanced carefully around the room, his cell phone still close to his ear.

"Oh my God, thank you," I said, leaping over the detritus to envelop him in a big hug. "I thought I was dead."

His arms went around me slowly, as though surprised by my gratitude. "You're thanking me for arriving too late?"

I pulled my head from his chest to frown up at him. "No, for the rescue, the big magic bang—that was *you*, right?"

"I believe that was *you*," he said dryly.

"Me? But all I did was—"

Curse.

Just like when I "stole" the necromancer's snake protector. If this was how my power manifested, I was going to seriously have to watch my mouth from now on.

There was a commotion upstairs. I could hear pounding and voices shouting, "This is the police! Open up!"

Valentine gave me one of his self-satisfied grins. "Ah, I see the cavalry has arrived."

Of course, Jones got all weird and confrontational when he saw Valentine, which meant Valentine got that smug expression on his face that I was beginning to interpret as "I could eat you all in a single bite."

"The important thing," I said in my loudest voice to get Jones's attention, "is that we have the necromancer's sister."

"Brooklyn? What? Where?" Jones's eyes frantically searched the room.

Jones knew her name?

I was about to comment on that, when Valentine pointed down to the floor. Jones followed his gesture, and his eyes went wide with—sympathy? Concern? Whatever it was, he quickly schooled his expression to coolly inspect the still intensely pissed off and struggling woman pinned to the floor. He knelt down and examined the various instruments holding her in place. "Spontaneous improbability magic?" He shot a surprised look at Valentine. "I didn't think that was your species' specialty."

"It's not," Valentine said, with a proud glance in my direction. "It's hers."

"You?" Jones sounded incredulous as he gave me a measured inspection. "You did this?"

I shrugged. "I guess."

Jones gestured to an officer with his chin. The officer must have known what Jones wanted because he came over and began unsticking the necromancer's sister, while holding up some kind of talisman that he pulled out of his cop utility belt.

Standing up, Jones pulled me to the side. "Tell me what happened."

Valentine shadowed us as Jones led us to a mostly undamaged section of the basement, next to the crematorium furnaces. I was horrified to discover they'd been turned on.

"Start at the beginning," Jones prompted. "What brought you here?"

I explained how I'd gotten lost and everything up to the final "fuck all," as it were. He listened intently, looking progressively more irritable. Valentine, meanwhile, couldn't keep the smile off his face.

"You're sure that's all you did?" he asked. "No accidental gesture? No . . . Latin?"

"Unless cringing counts as a gesture, yes, I'm sure."

Jones looked at Valentine and shook his head. "Well, we can clean up here. Why don't you take some time off?"

I wasn't sure that was a good idea. "Do you know her?" I asked Jones, gesturing with my chin in the direction of where they were still dealing with the necromancer's sister. "Only I noticed you called her Brooklyn."

"Oh, I did?"

That was the most unconvincing lie I had ever heard in my life. Jones couldn't even keep his eyes from sliding away from mine.

"Yeah, you did."

He shrugged. He even managed to refocus on my face. In the outer circle of his green irises I saw a faint glow when he spoke. "It's a small town. A very small town when you're magical."

Valentine sneezed. "Ugh," he said, waving his hands in front of his nose dramatically. "Your blarney stinks of overripe pineapples. Turn it off."

So Jones was trying to use his magical powers on me just now? What was he trying to convince me of, exactly, I wondered?

Jones ignored Valentine. He kept his eyes locked on mine. "You've had quite a scare, Alex. You should go home and rest."

I blinked. In my inner ear, I heard a soft strain of music so beautiful that my heart ached. Suddenly, I felt exhausted. The rush of excitement drained completely, leaving me feeling limp. All I wanted to do was go home and curl up under the covers.

Valentine's voice sounded harsh in comparison, though I was grateful for the support of his arm around my elbow. "We get the hint, fairy princeling. We're going."

Valentine steered me toward the stairs slowly, as my legs seemed sort of sluggish and there was a lot of broken pottery to step around. At the foot of the stairs, I caught a whiff of cool, fresh air. The strange cobwebs in my brain cleared.

I hadn't even realized how heavily I'd been clinging to Valentine, until I stood upright. "Hey," I said, suddenly really angry to have been overcome by Jones's magic.

Valentine squeezed my arm slightly—a warning.

Jones looked up with a dark expression in his eye. He started toward us. I remembered that he told me he had to keep in close proximity for his glamour to work. I swallowed what I wanted to ask, and tried to sound casual when I asked instead, "Hey, uh, what about the body from my morgue, the guy we've been calling the necromancer?" *Whose name you have probably* always *known*, I added silently, before continuing, "Where's he? Or his body?"

Jones stopped, clearly relieved I didn't call him out. "Oh. Well, obviously, we'll see if his sister is feeling talkative,"

Jones said. He waited a moment, as if waiting to see if I would say anything else. When I didn't, he turned away from us and headed over to where Stone seemed to be putting charmed cuffs on the woman in question.

"Try not to kill the prisoner this time," I joked.

Jones shot me a look that made it clear he did not find my humor to his liking.

I stood for a moment trying to decide what had just transpired here, and what it all meant. My head was too foggy to make much sense of anything at the moment, however. Maybe it was a good idea to go home for a little while. I headed up the stairs. Valentine trailed behind me.

"I do believe the fairy princeling is jealous," Valentine said once we were out of the mortuary's back door. I noticed that the wood had been staved in by something very, very strong.

"Jealous? Of what?" I leaned against Valentine's arm. My head was beginning to pound from the extended period without fresh air.

"Of you," Valentine said. "Of your magic and your friends."

"You *are* pretty cool," I said with a fond smile.

"As are you."

Valentine had a phenomenal sense of direction and knew exactly how to get to Robert's place. Turns out, I hadn't been terribly far from home. We walked the distance easily, though I was exhausted by the time we got back. The shock from the whole experience caught up with me in a rush.

I must have looked as droopy as I felt because, once inside, Val insisted that I shower while he cooked some late lunch. He promised not to burn the place down this time.

The hot water was heavenly on my bruised back and neck. I knew I should probably use cold to decrease the swelling, but I wanted the luxury of the heat. Scrubbing everywhere, I tried to remove any trace of the horror of the experience from my body and my mind. My skin was rubbed raw, but my hands still shook.

Nearly incinerated inside a coffin. *Gah.*

The reflection in the steamy mirror looked like a scared little girl with blue bruises on both sides of her neck. The impression of the zombie's fingers was distinct. The burn on my cheek from the spent casing seemed like decoration in comparison.

I wrapped myself in my terry cloth robe and padded out to find the dining room decked out with Robert's best linen and candles. "Oh" was all I could say, as Valentine pulled the chair out for me.

Valentine had also raided the china cabinet for Robert's grandmother's Wedgewood. He saw my expression and halted my reprimand with a raised hand and an innocent shrug. "I can't resist pretty things."

I had to admit that in the candlelight the setting was gorgeous. It wasn't like he'd allow any of it to break; Valentine did always take good care of the things he coveted. The thought made me ask, "How did you know to come? When I first tried to call I couldn't get a signal."

The soup that he poured into my bowl smelled of beets and beef. Borscht?

"You have my number in more ways than one."

I remembered that Jack could call Sarah Jane with his mind. "So it's telepathy?"

He shrugged, and sat himself down. "I call it instinct."

The soup was good. I had several sips before I asked,

"Where were you headed? Did I take you away from something important?"

In the dim light Valentine's eyes glittered darkly. "Nothing is more important than you."

If that were true, he would never have left this morning. I didn't want to push things, so I let him have his secrets. I groped for a safer subject and found work. "Why do you think Jones used his glamour on me?"

Valentine shrugged. "The fairy wanted us out of the way."

"You don't think it was something more sinister? You don't think it was weird that he knew my attacker by name?"

He picked up the fancy bowl with his hands and took a big gulp of it. I smiled. It was so like him to be strangely uncouth while surrounded by expensive things. When he set it down, he said, "Stranger to me was his desire to cover it up. This *is* a small town. Moreover, as a princeling it would not be unusual for him to know all the magical in his region regardless of their—shall we say, orientation."

"I don't think he tells a lot of people that he's a half-fairy prince." I pushed the soup around in the bowl, thinking.

"How can they fail to notice?"

"Not everyone has dragon senses," I reminded him. "One thing I did notice, though, is that Jones doesn't seem to be a very good cop."

Valentine snorted. "Now, that surprises me. Fairy love honor and justice, or at least pretending at it."

"Jones is definitely heavy on the pretending, then." I scowled.

"No," Valentine said, picking up the bowl to slurp up the contents again. "You misunderstand. When a fairy pretends, it is a thing of beauty to behold. I would say he gives it his whole heart, but fairy have none. Which is why they fake everything with a passion."

"I don't really understand," I admitted. "All I know is that Jones is the worst cop I've ever seen and the rest of his team is no better or too busy squabbling with each other to notice that nothing's getting done. As far as I can tell, I'm the only one trying to crack either case."

"Either? You have two?"

I ticked them off on my fingers. "The missing necromancer/ grave robber. The cow mutilations." Then, I shook my head in frustration, and added another finger. "Maybe three; it depends on if the sister is working with her brother or against him."

Valentine drew his brows together, as he ladled himself another helping of borscht from Robert's grandmother's soup tureen. He took his time filling his bowl, clearly admiring the way the silver glittered in the candlelight. "Perhaps the fairy is just lazy," Valentine offered, but didn't even buy his own suggestion for very long because he added, "Though he seems awfully young to have slipped into the indolent stage already."

I nodded, even though I couldn't say I easily followed Valentine's assessment of fairy character. I had, at first, considered the possibility that Jones was one of those people who had grown comfortable doing the least amount of work to get the job done. But is it lazy to make your inhuman partner, who isn't very good at talking to people outside the magical community, explain that there might be the equivalent of a spell bomb inside a corpse?

Or is it criminal negligence?

Or something worse?

There was something else niggling at the back of my

mind that I wanted to ask Valentine about. I took another spoonful of soup while I tried to formulate my thoughts in an organized way. "Even though I think they started that way, I don't think the brother and sister are working together now. She didn't have a high opinion of him, and she seemed baffled by his motivations. She said something about a wall."

"A wall?" He was clearing the plate from me. I hadn't even remembered emptying the bowl, but my stomach felt satisfied and full.

"Some number . . . fourth wall . . . or was it fifth? I didn't understand it. But, she said that he thought that if he could break it, he would have a lot more power."

From the kitchen, I heard the plates go next to the sink. "It's an interesting theory."

"You mean you know what she was talking about?"

Valentine came back out and leaned his hip against the doorjamb. "Her brother is a 'Tinker Bellist'—so named after the fairy in *Peter Pan* who could be healed if enough people believed. It's the idea that the more people accept the reality of magic, the stronger magic becomes. The assumption is based on the supposition that magic was easier to tap before the Age of Reason and, in fact, the whole movement to equate magic with superstition and madness was a conspiracy by those who would seek to contain the power."

"So what's the thing with the wall?"

"It's a theater term. To break the fourth wall is when the actor intentionally destroys the illusion of distance between himself and the audience. He addresses them directly, reminding them they are watching an actor playing a part. I suspect, in this case, it means using magic in public, making it impossible for regular people to deny or ignore."

Given everything that happened in this town, you wouldn't think there'd be many people like that left.

Maybe that was the point.

"Do you think it's true?" I asked. "Does it really work that way?"

"I don't know," he said. Valentine began moving around the room, snuffing out the candles with his fingers. "But I do know that there is something special about this place. You spent years in the company of a powerful demon and you never saw her for what she was. In fact, it didn't take much for the doctors to convince you that you made it all up. I could never have revealed myself to you in Chicago, but here . . . ? You've been here, how long?"

"Four months."

"Yes, hardly any time at all." Leaning toward the tall taper in the center of the table, Valentine blew a thin breath of air. Ice crystals, like a miniature snowstorm, streamed from between his lips. They swirled and danced around the flame before dousing it. "Now you not only see the magic you used to ignore, but you can *use* it."

"And you think that's because a larger percentage of the population in Pierre believes magic is real?"

Valentine sat down across from me. "I didn't say that. It is, however, one possibility."

So the necromancer might be sending zombies into the diner just because it was the single most disruptive place to do so. Also, picking the recently deceased, someone the towns-folk would remember, would only heighten the inability to ignore the dead elephant in the room, as it were—only it was dead grandpa. Before I moved here, I researched the size of Pierre. There were only about fifteen thousand people living here. "What would happen if everyone in town believed?"

"Well, those who subscribe to the Tinker Bell Theorem say that a hundred percent buy-in could cause a kind of magical pulsar, with massive bursts of energy going off regularly."

"Which, presumably, a skilled magician could use to his or her advantage?"

"Absolutely."

"Do you believe in it? The Tinker Bell Theorem?"

"It's difficult to prove one way or the other," he said with a lift of one shoulder. "There are very few places in the world without skeptics. But there *are* communities where magic appears stronger. Is it the conviction of the practitioners or some other harmonic convergence? Perhaps, as some believe, the magic is in the earth itself, and some places have the right kind of mountain ranges or lakes or rock formations. I don't know."

Even so, I thought this theorem seemed like a strong possibility for a motive. It might explain the zombies and possibly even the attack on the rancher's cows. Jones was concerned that word of the cow mutilations not get out to the public. Yet it had.

Could that have been the work of the necromancer as his sister suggested?

"Okay," I said, desperately trying to remember my forensics classes. "That could be motive, what's the other thing we need?"

"Opportunity," Valentine supplied with a crooked smile that showed a bit of sharp canine.

"Seems to me opportunity decreases dramatically when you're dead."

"For normal people, yes," Valentine observed dryly.

"Is being dead an advantage in magic?"

Valentine lifted a shoulder. "If you die under the right circumstances, it can be. Vampires are stronger than living men. Zombies are more—"

"Tenacious," I said with a shiver.

He inclined his head. "Just so."

I chewed my fingernail, trying to puzzle it out. Valentine continued to clean up around me.

Yet somehow I didn't think we were on the right track. When I met the necromancer, he didn't seem particularly powerful, like he'd achieved some altered state beyond death. He was just plain dead.

Well, not exactly. I looked at the snake on my hand. This had sprung out of him. He hadn't turned into it, though, the way a human might become a vampire or a zombie. I supposed, like the severed head said, it was a part of him.

No, from the moment everyone saw it or interacted with it, they called the snake a *spell*. It might have started out as his, but it was clearly mine now. I stroked the head, remembering how it had helped me, tried to save me from the spiders.

The spiders were like some kind of booby trap, too, weren't they? Jack and Jones couldn't even enter his apartment; they said it was so strongly anti-naturally warded. Wards were like a protection, too, right?

Why did the necromancer need all these security measures?

All these defenses seemed less like the actions of a man on the verge of becoming something greater than those of one under siege.

So who was he protecting himself from?

Were we looking at murder, after all? Was someone trying to stop the necromancer from gaining his goal?

Which was . . . ?

The Tinker Bell thing?

If so, the sister certainly seemed to think he was pretty stupid. She seemed to want something else entirely, but what, exactly?

And how was Jones involved?

I started thinking out loud, because I wanted Valentine's take on all of it. "The zombie talked to me when he was dead . . . Well, his mouth was sewn shut so I thought he'd said, '*He* hates Spenser,' but I wonder if the zombie meant, '*She* hates Spenser.'"

"There's a lot to hate," Valentine agreed, heading for the kitchen with the last of the silverware.

This time I followed, pulling my robe tighter around my waist as I got up. "I suppose. I mostly find him cantankerous. I'm not sure he always treats Devon fairly, and he has some serious mommy issues. But the sister seemed very stung by someone who *hates* unnatural magic."

Valentine opened the freezer and pulled out a quart of ice cream. "You think it's Spenser?"

Was it? After all, what was it that everyone around Jones continually fought about? Natural versus unnatural. Stone desperately wanted to be natural. Devon revelled in being unnatural, mostly, I began to think, just to poke at Jones.

Heck, I'd felt the sting of his disapproval myself.

I pulled bowls from the cabinet while he got out the syrup and a can of whipped cream. "He seemed particularly irritable at the funeral home, didn't he?"

"I assumed that was because I was there," Valentine said, scooping out a large spoonful for himself. "And because you kicked magical ass."

I laughed slightly at that. I dug out my own helping and

added lots of toppings. "Well, that's the most obvious option," I agreed, taking a bite. I savored the chocolate before continuing. "You'd think he'd have mentioned a connection to the necromancer's sister before this."

Valentine said, "Perhaps he didn't know they were related."

"I like that better than my own theory."

"What's that?"

"That he's kept the information from us on purpose."

"What purpose would he have?"

I didn't know. This was where all my theorizing ground to a halt.

Valentine pulled the spoon from his mouth in a rather suggestive manner. "They're lovers!"

"What?" I wagged my spoon at him. "Now who's pretending?"

"He knew her name," Valentine insisted mischievously.

"So?" I grimaced at him. Trust him to go to the basest possible option. "You said yourself that it made sense in a small town, in a tiny magical community. Anyway, they could just be friends."

"That's much less interesting," Valentine insisted with a petulant pout. "My theory is more fun."

"But it's a really wild theory."

"I still like it. Humans get very tangled over love and sex. They kill for it almost more than any other animal."

I did remember that from my forensics class. Nine times out of ten, husbands killed wives or vice versa. Valentine had a good point. Sex was often the lowest common denominator. "This town isn't that big," I noted, playing along with his hypothesis. "The dating pool among magical people must be tiny."

"Minuscule," he said, taunting me with the way he used his tongue to lick the last bit of ice cream melt from his spoon.

I blushed, and tried to stay focused on the conversation. "Do you suppose it's considered dirty to date someone from the 'other side'?"

Valentine shrugged.

If it was, then the number of eligible partners dropped significantly—assuming that it mattered to you if you dated someone with superpowers like your own. I could easily picture Jones as that type, however. Most of my ice cream had melted into slush, but I tipped the bowl to my lips and drank it up.

"Is there a magical way to kill someone without leaving any physical trace?"

Valentine lifted his eyebrow. "Many. Humans are stunningly easy to kill, magically or otherwise."

I ignored the shiver that crept up my spine at the ice in Valentine's voice. "What about a way to neutralize someone's magic without entirely killing them? Or," I said, thinking about how hard it had been to go after my own family, even my evil stepmonster, "what about an accident? Could you put someone in a state of suspended animation with a botched attempt at magical murder?"

"I wouldn't know. I rarely miss."

A theory was percolating in my head, but I had no proof to confirm it yet. I put the bowl down. I wanted to get dressed quickly. "What if the necromancer's sister was angry at her brother for stirring the pot with this whole fourth wall thing—especially since it made things worse between her and her lover?"

"Her *current* lover? Not ex?"

Of course, I didn't know. This was all theory and conjecture. But, the fact remained, Jones knew the necromancer's sister well enough to call her by name. Glamour or not, we had to find out what he knew.

"How quickly can you get me into the office?"

"If we fly, a matter of seconds."

I dressed as fast as I could, throwing on jeans and a sweatshirt. The look was a little less than office casual, but I was in a hurry. We stood outside Robert's house, and Valentine was studying my face. The sun had melted most of the remaining snow, and my Converse sneakers were thin protection against the wet and cold. "Are you sure you want me to do this?" he asked

At first, I didn't understand his hesitation. But then I saw that expression in the worry lines between his brows. It was the same one he'd worn when he had been forced to transform in front of me the first time. "Are you embarrassed by what you are?" I asked. Before he could answer, I quickly added, "Don't be. I think you're beautiful."

Though I noticed his face soften, he sniffed. "Don't be ridiculous. I'm worried about you. I'll have to carry you." He held his hands out to show me, and I tried not to picture the sharp talons, as clear and long as icicles, that they would become.

Oh. I'd kind of hoped to ride on his back, like they always did in the movies.

He must have seen my wistful expression, but his hardened. "You would need a saddle. I will *never* wear reins."

Right, of course.

I let out a long breath, and I tried to stay focused. "Jones is with her right now. I don't want him to do something stupid."

"We don't have to get involved," he noted.

Actually, I did. Not only was it my job, but I was beginning to care about these people. What worried me more was busting into the precinct headquarters full of conjecture and accusations. I had no real proof, only a bunch of hunches and circumstances that fit a wild theory.

"I just want to be there," I said, telling myself that I didn't have to go in with guns blazing and pointing fingers. "If I'm wrong and Jones is hiding nothing, it will be a relief. Let's just do it."

"As you wish." Valentine nodded, and ducked his head down toward his chest. Instantly, he began to transform. Clothes disappeared. White scales covered his skin as he began to expand. Arms and legs became haunches, while a tail sprouted and twitched itself into a long coil. Wings unfolded gracefully. His face narrowed and elongated, a proud snout filled with rows of dangerously sharp teeth. A spiky mane of ice rose from his head and snaked down his spine.

When he finished, he was nearly as tall as the house on all fours.

A cock of his head implied that I needed to make myself ready. Even so, I wasn't quite able to keep the gasp from escaping when his claw reached for me. The padded paw that encircled me was softer and gentler than I expected. As the joints clasped together, I found I could sit against the curve of the fingers and hold on to knuckles. It felt as safe as an amusement park ride, which wasn't saying much. Still, I trusted Valentine not to drop me.

His body tensed and was followed by the massive upswell

of air as he beat his powerful wings. We went up briefly. Then we went down, and I felt my stomach drop. I thought we were falling until he'd flap his wings again and we'd bob back upward. I had trouble enjoying the flight, because the whole experience was nauseatingly jerky.

The wind stung at my face, bringing tears to my eyes. I blinked them away to watch the houses moving below us. The Missouri glittered beautifully. If I could get used to the up and down motion, it would be lovely to travel this way.

But, I hardly had the opportunity. He was right; it took little time before the precinct house was below us. From above there was no illusion. I could see the courtyard clearly, as we began a gliding spiral downward.

A gang of magpies appeared in the air beside us. They darted around us—joyfully calling to each other, playing in the wind eddies caused by Valentine's wings.

I closed my eyes as the ground came toward us. Skillful use of wings and muscles absorbed the impact. I felt ground beneath my feet. I stood on my own as the shape of Valentine's hand changed. Soon I felt the more familiar sensation of his arm around my waist and his body behind me. The magpies continued to flit around him, almost protectively circling him, as if they had adopted this giant flying reptile as a member of their crew.

I ran to the courtyard door only to find it locked from the inside. Valentine stepped around me. He took the knob in his hand and gave it a simple twist. I heard the lock break. He pulled the door open with a slight bow, as if he was a gentleman opening it for a lady.

Which he was—most definitely, dragon or not.

I leaned over to give him a quick but passionate kiss on his lips. "I owe you."

"Hardly," he said, and with a smile he fell into step behind me. "Dramatic entrances are reward enough."

Inside, I was surprised to find Jones was alone with the necromancer's sister.

One of the vines that seemed to cover most surfaces in the room was wrapped around her, like manacles, surrounding her wrists and ankles. She wasn't struggling. Her face was flushed with emotion, though with which one I couldn't say.

Whatever Jones had been saying died in his throat. His mouth hung open as I walked in the door.

"I think there's something you're not telling us," I said to him.

"Me?" Jones pointed to his chest, belligerently. "What the hell are you doing here, Connor? I told you to go home and rest."

"Yeah, well, rest got me thinking," I said. I hadn't meant to be this belligerent about my theories, but Jones's attitude irritated me. I wouldn't be dismissed. So, I ignored Jones and looked at the necromancer's sister. "Are you two dating?"

"I wouldn't call it dating so much as sleeping together," she said, with a dark glance at Jones.

"What?" Jones sounded genuinely startled. I thought my entire theory was going to go out the window until he said, "We broke it off months ago. What relevance does that have to this case?"

"Everything, possibly," I said to him. To Brooklyn, I asked, "Why? Why did you break up?"

Her blue eyes narrowed. I thought that if she could have hurled a curse, she would have. Instead she said, "I think you know why."

"Because you're unnatural?"

She looked away, and I thought her body language

answered my question quite clearly. Jones, meanwhile, was getting angrier. He stepped forward threateningly. "You need to tell me what the hell is going on here."

Valentine lifted his gaze just enough that Jones noticed.

Jones hesitated and lowered his voice a bit. "Let's go into my office. If you have some accusations to make, I'd like to hear them. Privately."

I could think of no reason not to grant his wish. "Sure," I said. "We could go to your office."

"Let me just get someone to guard Brooklyn," Jones said. Skipping lightly up the flat, wide step/seats of the amphitheater, Jones stuck his head outside the door to talk to whoever was standing right there. Stone? Some other guard?

Reaching over, I gave Valentine's hand a little squeeze.

He nodded, as if he understood my trepidation. "I'll be with you," he said. Then, he added, with a little self-congratulation, "I told you sex would be part of the equation."

I snorted a small, fond laugh.

Together we walked up to where Jones held the door for us, his face nearly contorted with uncontrolled rage. I didn't like the look in his eyes, as we stepped out into the hallway.

"Can you take a fairy?" I whispered to Valentine after we were a few steps in front of Jones.

"Easily," Valentine assured me.

TWENTY

Everyone in the precinct hushed when Valentine and I followed Jones into the main room to his office. By the time he closed his door, you could have heard the proverbial pin drop.

Jones had a large oak desk. On it was an old-fashioned blotter filled with doodles and scraps of information, a few thick paper case files in battered manila folders, and a sleek laptop. There were two classic steel file cabinets against one wall and a bookcase full of old, leather-bound volumes. Some of the books even had binding that looked hand-stitched and tooled. A framed pen-and-ink illustration showed a fully armored knight leading a horse with two maiden riders, both looking behind them at an old woman's face peering out from the forest trees. There was some kind of inscription below, but I didn't have a chance to inspect it more closely.

Jones put the desk between us. He put his hands on the

back of his chair and gestured at the two seats, but no one sat down. Valentine found a darkened corner to settle into. Jones gave him a wary glance, and then focused his attention on me. "Explain yourself, Connor."

"Okay," I said, taking in a deep breath. "I don't think you're a bad guy necessarily."

"Necessarily?"

His sharp glance made me want to back down, but instead, I said, "Yeah, not necessarily. At the very least you've been negligent. First, you walked away when you should have been the one to tell me about this." I held up the snake-covered arm.

Jones flinched almost imperceptibly. I didn't know if his reaction was due to guilt or the fact that I'd felt the snake wake up with an angry buzz when we stepped into the interrogation room.

He didn't try to defend his actions, so I continued, "Second, it should have been routine police work to search the necromancer's apartment, but I had to think of it. What's his name, anyway? You do know, don't you?"

"Steve," Jones supplied. He sounded neither defeated nor chagrined. In fact, he seemed a bit irritated. "Everyone knows his name. It was on the police report."

That took a tiny bit of wind from my righteous sails. Not only that, but I was having a lot of trouble reimagining the necromancer as some guy named Steve. It was such a commonplace name, so harmless sounding. With some effort, I got myself back on track. "Did you know he was related to Brooklyn?"

"Of course," he said, again without any guilt.

"Um, okay," I said, feeling myself starting to flail a bit.

"Isn't it a conflict of interest to be dating the sister of a known grave robber?"

The leather backing on the chair bulged under his fingers. "I'm not the first person to make a poor choice in lovers, but, as far as I know, it's not a crime to be stupid. Besides, I broke it off well before we had Steve in our sights as the possible perp of the grave robbing."

I put my hands on my hips. Jones sounded so reasonable. Could I have been this wrong about everything?

I heard Valentine sniff the air.

Was Jones using his glamour? I tried to look into Jones's eyes, to see if I could spot the telltale glow around his irises, but his head was tipped in a way that cast them in shadow.

"I *know* there's a connection between the three of you," I insisted. "You do, too. When the necromancer, uh, Steve, woke up, he said your name. I have that on tape. Plus, your name was mentioned again when the zombie from the diner said, 'He hates Spenser.' Or 'she.' I couldn't understand him very well, so it could be either of them," I admitted. "But it was *your* name."

"So?"

"So jilted girlfriend makes for an excellent crime of passion," I said.

"Or an overprotective brother," said Valentine from the back of the room.

"Sure," Jones agreed, though skeptically. He released his death grip on the back of his chair somewhat. "But a motive for what, exactly? You came in here ready to accuse me of something, but I don't see what it could be. What crime do you think I've committed?"

I suddenly couldn't think of one either, but I wasn't ready

to back down yet. "You tell me. If you knew about the connection between the necromancer and your ex-girlfriend, why didn't you pursue it? When Nana Spider mentioned relatives, you never mentioned Brooklyn. Again, when I showed you the Twitter account for @Skull_lady, you never even suggested that Steve had a woman in his life who was close to him. Why not?"

Jones pressed his lips together. His glance flicked first to Valentine, and then back to me. "Have you ever had someone in your life that you know is bad, but—well, you don't want to believe it?"

Did I? I managed not to sneak a look over my shoulder at Valentine. "Are you admitting that you didn't pursue leads that pointed to Brooklyn?"

Jones broke my gaze to stare down at the chair in front of him for a long moment. "I guess I am."

Well, there it was. The confession we came here to get. I let out a breath, and wondered why I didn't feel more satisfied.

Jones's shoulders were bowed. "I should have gone after all the clues with all my strength," he said. "I just—didn't want to believe she was involved, even when it was obvious. I'll resign from the case. Perhaps I'll have to put in for a transfer."

The puzzle pieces I thought I had gotten together rearranged, and the picture fell apart again. I finally pulled out the chair Jones had offered, and dropped into it. I was disappointed by the simplicity of his motivations, and it left me completely baffled as to how Steve the necromancer had ended up dead.

Jones seemed lost in his own thoughts. He'd begun rearranging some files on his desk. He was muttering to himself about how he'd probably get reassigned somewhere dreadful like Minneapolis. "Bad weather and such a huge town to be lost in."

How funny that for Jones the worst transfer would be to the bigger town. It was usually the opposite in the ordinary world.

That reminded me. "Do you know about the Tinker Bell Theorem?" I asked him.

"Of course," he said, sounding surprised by the sudden shift in conversation. "Do you?"

"Honestly, I just found out about it," I said. "Because Brooklyn told me that her brother was trying to break the fourth wall."

"What? Why?"

"Well, that part I don't know," I said, though my mind was churning. Something about the way Jones had reacted about the idea of a transfer made me consider, "What if this really *is* still all about you and destroying your hold on this town? I mean, I originally thought that the two of them were working at odds, that maybe the necromancer had confronted his sister about her relationship with you, and that had led to an argument where he wound up dead." I used my toe to twirl the chair on its base, embarrassed by how my theories sounded out loud. "But what if the whole thing was a setup to expose you, while breaking down the fourth wall at the same time?"

"I'm not following," Jones admitted.

Truth was, I was making all this up on the spot as well. All sorts of thoughts were hitting fast. "Did you read the police report?"

"Yes," Jones said with a hint of his old irritation. "I'm not entirely incompetent, you know."

"It kind of seems like a setup, doesn't it? Steve is moaning and moaning and moaning right up to the moment the police break in. The cops break in to try to help him, but the instant they do, he's dead as a doornail. A faked altar and fake poison to make everyone assume he's dead, while the real magic is hidden."

"Under the floorboards in the closet," Jones noted, following along.

"Everyone thinks Steve is dead, but what if he was never supposed to be? You said you smelled something really specific on him, right, Jones? If I broke the rib cage, it would incapacitate me. Are you usually able to smell such specifics in spells?"

Jones frowned. "No, not really."

"Right, so that was planted to keep me from performing the autopsy. They're hoping either I'll listen to you, or I'll be like my predecessor and be lazy. Either way, no autopsy. After some time in the freezer, Steve wakes up and walks out."

"Except he doesn't, because they didn't know about you," Jones said.

"*I* didn't even know about me," I said.

"It's convoluted, but it has some possibilities." Jones was frowning, but I could tell by the way he was chewing his fingernail he was considering as well. "Let's go ask her," he said, finally.

I followed him as he barreled back out the door toward the interrogation room. "What are you going to do about your reputation?"

"I'll throw that troll off the bridge when I get to it."

The necromancer's sister gave us a hostile glare until Valentine stepped into the room. At that point, she looked terrified.

"I am certain," she said shrilly, "that being interrogated by a dragon violates the Stonehenge Accord."

Jones sighed. "Settle down, Brooklyn, you're not a prisoner of war."

"Bullshit," she snapped. For emphasis, she lifted her vine-bound hands out of her lap.

"You're under arrest for assault," he said patiently. He pointed to me. "You attacked our coroner and put her in a coffin."

"Battles!" she insisted. "In the ongoing war."

Jones rubbed the spot between his eyes, and then looked at Valentine for help. "You know what? Why don't you go ahead and take over?"

"As you wish," he said quietly, his eyes locking on where Brooklyn squirmed. He moved forward, unhurried, but in a manner reminiscent of a predator stalking prey.

All the color drained from Brooklyn's face as he settled himself on the stone step across from her. The koi darted to the other side in the pool and huddled together in a tight mass. She cowered, leaning away from him, looking like she wanted to join them.

He carefully folded his hands on his knee.

She stared at his interlocked fingers as if he'd just pressed a knife to her throat.

Jones and I stayed at the back of the room and watched. Jones cocked his head slightly and whispered, "I'm glad he's on our side."

I nodded, but I knew better. Valentine was on no one's side but his own. He was doing this because it amused him to do so.

Valentine said nothing for what felt like an awfully long time. He sat, patiently, with his hands on his lap and stared at her. For her part, Brooklyn started to sweat. I could see the sheen of perspiration on her brow, even from this distance.

"I never meant to hurt your witch," she finally blurted.

"I'm sure you didn't," Valentine agreed quietly.

"She brought it on herself."

"Careful," Valentine hissed.

Brooklyn shrunk back, and her whole body trembled. The remnants of an icy draft drifted up from the sunken pit.

"This is all Steve's fault," Brooklyn said suddenly, a quiver in her voice. "If I'd known about your witch, I would have worked much harder to convince Steve not to do it. I told him he had no guarantee that the new coroner wouldn't do an autopsy. But did he listen to me? No. He was so sure that Spense's sense of justice would protect him. He said over and over that the fairy would never let anyone be harmed if he caught a whiff of a spell. Honestly, he thought Spense wouldn't even take his body to the morgue, but somewhere else to try to despell him first."

Wow, he'd totally read Jones wrong. I was sort of offended to think that Jones didn't take my safety more into consideration. I gave Jones a sidelong glance to discover he'd been looking at me as well. He looked away guiltily.

"Regardless," Valentine pressed. "The whole plan was flawed. A hundred percent is a fool's game."

"It's not," she said, her sudden interest for this topic showing in the shift of her posture. "We've run the calculations. It was over half before we even began. I'll bet we're well into the sixties now."

"Yes," he said, encouragingly. "I've seen eighty and higher, but no one has cracked a hundred. You'll never cause an event."

"It's happened. You . . . You're Russian, yes?" When he

gave the barest nod of acknowledgment, she said, "The Tunguska Event."

Valentine let out a sniff of a laugh.

I looked at Jones, who put his hand to my ear. "It's that big, mysterious explosion in 1908 that knocked down all those trees . . . ?"

I nodded, shushing him. I'd seen a documentary on it, but it had been clearly determined to be some kind of meteorite collision.

"I suppose that means you believe you're a more powerful witch than Matrioskha? That you and your brother could contain an event of that magnitude, when she and her familiar could not? There were three hundred and seventy-two people in that community. There's more than fifteen thousand in this."

She said nothing, just pressed her lips together stubbornly.

"Fool." He shook his head. "A small and petty mind such as yours should never be allowed such power."

She took the bait. "Petty? We're trying to win the war, for us." She used her bound hands to make a circle that included Valentine. "The so-called unnaturals."

Beside me, I felt Jones stiffen and take in a sharp breath.

"Very grand, indeed," Valentine consented. He turned his head to look up where Jones and I were standing. The bright sunlight behind him, his eyes were hooded and shadowed. "So you begin by removing this obstacle? This bastard princeling, who himself is no witch, but who keeps a vampire-werewolf on a leash like a surrogate familiar?"

She spat on the ground. "Yes!"

"Hey!" Jones said at the same time.

Valentine stood up, slowly, deliberately, and turned to face the challenge in Jones's voice. "I believe motive has been established," he said, and I heard the finality in his tone. He was done playing torturer for Jones. He came up the stairs and greeted me with a light kiss on the cheek. "You were right, it seems, on both accounts."

Jones was fuming, but I couldn't help but smile at Valentine. *Bastard princeling?* I mouthed.

Jones had begun to head down to where Brooklyn sat, but Valentine's hand shot out and slapped hard on his shirt, just below his collarbone. "You," Valentine said calmly, but succinctly, "owe me."

Jones looked ready to argue, but, instead looked down to where Valentine's flat palm rested inches over his heart. "Don't threaten me."

"No threat," Valentine said without removing his hand. "But I am not your beast of burden; you will pay for services rendered, little fey."

Jones's face tightened, but he nodded. Tersely, between clenched teeth, he whispered, "Fine."

Valentine let him go.

Stepping back into the precinct office, we nearly bowled over Jack. His ear had been pressed to the door. From his kneeling position he gave us a guilty wave. Standing up, he flicked imaginary dust from the thighs of his jeans. "So, uh, how's it going in there?"

"Good," I said, holding the door partway open. I'd come to believe that Jones's guilt was little more than a desire to not get an ex into trouble, but I didn't think he should be left alone with her, anyway. I wanted Stone around to keep an eye on him. "Where's Stone?"

"Didn't she come back with Jones?" Jack asked.

"I don't know," I said, trying to remember if I'd even seen her at the funeral home when Jones had burst in for a belated rescue. The last time I could be sure I'd seen her was when she was fighting the zombie. "We've got to find her."

I must have sounded panicked, because Jack reached out to touch me. I saw his eyes stray to where Valentine stood behind me. He pulled his hand back quickly. "Uh, just relax. I'll see what I can do," Jack said. He caught the attention of a passing uniform. "Hey, can you get Dispatch to find the whereabouts on Hannah?"

The cop grabbed the microphone from her lapel and spoke into it. After identifying herself, she said, "I need the ten-twenty on Officer Stone."

There was some back and forth with Dispatch, most of which was in number code. There was something about a 10-39 and questions about whether Stone was 10-10. Not understanding what they were referring to just made me more anxious. "What's going on?" I asked Jack.

"No one can find her. She's not coming to the radio, and Dispatch just suggested that maybe she went off duty without telling anyone. Her radio is switched off, and there's no answer on her cell."

"That's not like her." Hell, I could hardly even imagine her off duty at all.

"I know," Jack said. "Where did you last see her?"

I tried not to stammer, but I felt so guilty having left her in the middle of a fight like that. "She . . . she was with the zombie. He was attacking. She told me to leave. I called Jones for help. I assumed that was where he was while I was stuck in the coffin."

The cop who had been helping us covered her radio with her hand and said, "That was outside of Big Tom's again. I responded to that. At one point there were six of us on it, but then it went down hard and didn't get back up. Stone said she was going to take it to a cemetery."

"A cemetery?" I asked her. "Why not back to headquarters or to the funeral home?"

Jack answered, "Graveyard dirt. It's to make sure the zombie stays dead this time."

"She's an efficient person," I said. "Which graveyard is closest to Big Tom's?"

"Riverside," said the officer, reaching for her microphone again. "I'll send a car."

"I could fly over, if you wish," Valentine said into my ear.

I almost said yes without thinking. I was worried about Stone, but she was a golem. I didn't know if that meant she was indestructible, but she *was* tough. The police were headed that way already, I could hear their chatter on the radio. "Only if you want," I said, turning to give his cheek a light stroke. "You've done so much already."

He leaned into my hand. "I don't mind when you ask, love."

"It would be very easy to take advantage of you," I said, letting my hand drop.

A wicked smile flashed briefly on his lips, and then he leaned very close. "I dearly hope you will. Later." He nipped my ear playfully. Breaking contact, he said, "I'll check on your friend—unless, of course, you wish me to keep an eye on our bastard prince?"

Jones would *hate* the idea of Valentine babysitting him, and for some reason that tickled me. "Ooooh," I said with a mischievous smile of my own, "do that!"

* * *

Jack and I ended up in the back of Peterson's squad. The sirens blared and cars moved out of our way as we raced down the street. Though Peterson was a careful driver, I held on tightly to the roll bar and kept my eyes straight ahead.

Staring at the back of Peterson's head reminded me how much fun he and his partner had smashing cows' heads. I wished I'd thought to have Valentine ask Brooklyn why she'd killed Olson's cattle. I supposed that their mutilation could have been part of the plan to get one hundred percent, but Olson's ranch had been far outside the city limits. Though all his neighbors agreed that they'd seen lights, it seemed to me that crop circles were the sort of thing that drew a lot of skepticism. Most people understood them to be hoaxes, and those who didn't thought they were the work of space aliens, not magicians.

If Brooklyn and her brother didn't kill the cows, who did?

The car slowed as we hit the unpaved Cemetery Road. Ahead, two Pierre patrol cars were parked on a small berm in front of the wrought-iron fence that surrounded the cemetery grounds. Through the slats, I could see a series of plots. They were fairly modern, shiny granite squares placed in orderly rows. There were few trees, so the snow had completely melted to reveal thick, well-manicured sod. The blades had even begun to green in places.

Devon met us on the gravel road leading to the gate. "That's Spenser's squad all right," he said, nodding to the car positioned closest to the gate. "I found my bottle hidden in it. Stone must be here somewhere."

Hanson, who'd come out of the other patrol car with

Devon, said, "I called the cemetery director. He said this place is about thirty-five acres."

Jack pulled his Yoda hat from the pocket of his coat and scrunched it onto his head. "There are two likely options," he said. "If this was the cemetery the zombie was supposed to be buried in later today, Hannah would try to find his plot. Dirt from that specific spot would be the most powerful deterrent. However, if she just picked this place because it was closest, then she'll go for the oldest section. The older the dirt, the stronger the magic."

"Let's split up," suggested Peterson.

"Let's not," I said. "Let's be smart about this. There's no way Stone would assume that she'd luck out and hit the very cemetery the zombie belongs to. Plus, it's impractical to fireman-carry a corpse from plot to plot hoping to stumble upon an open grave, which might not even be the right one. If you talked to the cemetery director and he didn't mention talking to the cops already today, then she's gone to the oldest section. Let's all go together. If the zombie is awake, she might need all our help."

Jack called up the cemetery's website on his phone. He found a map and showed it to us. "Looks like we're headed there."

I might have guessed that direction, anyway. In an otherwise barren expanse, cedar and yew bushes grew to tall, spiky spires marking the spot someone had once planted a small offering to a loved one. The gate was open, so we followed a curving path. The wet had turned the gravel into a tan slurry. Stepping into a water-filled rut, I wished I'd worn boots instead of Converse.

"You didn't bring the dragon," Devon noted, coming up alongside me. He was a little less disheveled than he had been this morning. He'd changed into a clean white T-shirt and a brown bomber jacket. He had dark sunglasses over his eyes. With the shades, he *almost* looked the part of vampire.

"Why would I need him when I have such a strong, capable vampire-werewolf like yourself?"

Devon grimaced at my over-the-top fake flirt. "I'm beginning to think he doesn't really exist."

"Oh, he does," Jack piped up from behind us, sounding a little morose about the fact.

I was about to ask him what he meant by that tone, when a loud caw came from the clump of trees ahead. Several magpies zoomed toward us, zipping this way and that, clearly agitated.

Jack started to run toward where they circled. "I sent Sarah Jane ahead. The Outlaws must have found Stone!"

Devon could move faster than the rest of us. I was just beginning to trot when I heard him say, "Oh shit."

We came into the clearing a moment later. Devon knelt beside a pile of dirt. I thought, at first, we'd found an open grave. My eyes slowly made sense of what I saw. A muddy hand, an arm stretched out imploringly toward something it couldn't quite reach, attached to a body not made of flesh and bone, but dust, clay, and dirt. It was the hair I recognized: a tangle of ungainly dry brush. Wild and messy, I wanted to fix it for her.

It was Stone.

TWENTY-ONE

Devon's hands shook as he reached out to touch the mound of dirt's shoulder. "Someone did it," he said softly. "They finally did it. They erased your letters. Fuck."

Jack suddenly gripped my arm, pulling me back from the mud-body. A bird screeched in fear. "The zombie couldn't have done that. Not even accidentally."

"Why not?"

"You need magic," Jack said.

I heard the snaps of holsters opening. Peterson and Hanson pulled their guns and began scanning the area. Jack gripped my elbow tightly, as we frantically searched for the culprit among the marble obelisks and eroded, listing limestone markers.

A mausoleum's door hung open, crooked on broken hinges, its lock shattered. I pointed it out to Jack. We crept forward. Noticing our movement, the two officers flanked us, training their weapons on the opening.

My snake tattoo constricted. That was all the warning we got before a magical pulse knocked us off our feet. It felt like a slap of a giant hand. My butt landed in the squishy grass and the cold shock dazed me.

A figure emerged from the vault.

Leaving the morgue had not improved the necromancer. He was naked, except for the torn and filthy Tweety Bird pajama bottoms, which he'd wrapped like a loincloth around his privates. His chest cavity had been sewn closed with clumsy, wide stitches. The tattoos met unevenly now, like two sections of badly aligned wrapping paper. Stringy, dingy blond hair clumped around an ashen face. Eyes were dark pits, empty and hollow.

The zombie had looked more alive.

Shots rang out as Hanson emptied a clip into him. The necromancer staggered. I could see flesh tear as bullets exited, but there was no blood spatter. A rigor mortis grin jerked onto his face, as he righted himself. The voice that came from his mouth was not generated by functioning vocal cords. It sounded like the garbled static you hear as you dial past radio stations. The words were unintelligible, but the effect was immediate.

A howling wind slammed us down. The impact forced the air from my lungs. Pressure pushed against my chest, sinking my back deep into the spongy grass. I couldn't seem to catch my breath. I choked.

Out of the corner of my eye, I sensed movement. Devon flew at the necromancer, tackling him. The moment the necromancer's skull cracked into the marble of the crypt's wall, I was able to suck in a huge gasp of breath. Jack and the cops did the same.

The fight was not over, however. Though it looked like

Devon slammed a limp, unresponsive body repeatedly against the stone structure, I could feel a deeper, magical battle. Dark clouds gathered and wind swirled in every direction. A moan alerted me to the approach of the zombie.

He'd brought friends.

At least a half dozen slow-moving but tenacious zombies shuffled toward us from every direction. Devon might be strong, but he could never keep that many zombies at bay. Not if we had any hope of keeping the necromancer from being able to focus his magic again.

Jack clasped my hand. He knelt in the grass and helped me sit up. "We've got to do something," he croaked.

But I didn't know what. I knew that swearing made my magic come, but I had no idea how to direct it at someone or something. Even so, I tried an experimental, "Shit."

Nothing.

Hanson reloaded. From a pouch on his utility belt he pulled a handful of glittering bullets. Silver? I looked at Devon and the necromancer. They were a tangle of arms and legs. Would silver stop zombies? Would it hurt Devon, too? I hoped to hell that Hanson was a crack shot.

His partner, Peterson, meanwhile, took the direct approach. He pulled his nightstick from his belt and went in swinging. His stick cracked against fragile bone and sinew.

The magpies seemed to approve of Peterson's strategy. With a triumphant caw, they dived and swirled, picking at zombies, pulling hair and plucking at eyes.

Still holding my hand, Jack closed his eyes. "We can try to use our power together," he suggested. "Clear your mind."

How was I supposed to do that with all this chaos? But I tried. Remembering how it had felt in the necromancer's apartment when I'd seen the words on the trapdoor, I let my eyes unfocus.

I felt nothing.

To be perfectly accurate, I did feel the water seeping through the fabric at the knees of my jeans. I also had a strong sensation of the wind whistling past my ears, and the horrific sounds of the battle raging all around me.

I couldn't even sense Jack's power shifty-thing.

We were doomed. "Ah, hell," I whispered, completely dejectedly.

That, apparently, was the right thing to say.

Sort of.

A pulse of light, like a shock wave, blasted from where I sat. It moved outward in an expanding circle. Unfortunately, like a bomb, it knocked down everything in its path. Jack was thrown off his feet, along with the cops and the zombies. When the negative air pressure rushed back toward me, even the magpies fell out of the air.

With a surprised and horrified glance in my direction, the strength drained from Devon and he faltered, crumpling. He clutched desperately at the necromancer and consciousness before collapsing in a heap.

The only people left standing were me and the necromancer.

Oops.

When the necromancer turned his deadened eyes toward me, I started swearing up a blue streak. I used every word that my father had told me ladies never uttered in polite company. I tried out adjectives I'd only heard on the Comedy Channel and combinations of verbs that I knew for certain were simply not physically possible.

Why wasn't it working?

The necromancer continued to advance. I screamed obscenities into that death grin. I scrambled to my feet, but not before his hand closed around my wrist. His grip was like a vise.

I heard a strange rattling hiss. Like the last time the necromancer cast a spell, it seemed to come from some otherworldly place. I braced myself, expecting another blast of magic. Instead, I felt the tattoo under my skin squirm and stretch.

As the necromancer dragged me toward the open mausoleum door, the snake's head pulled itself from the flesh of the back of my hand. I could see it slowly taking on dimensions, the black scales filling and expanding.

The necromancer never noticed it until it reared back and sunk its fangs deep into his forearm.

TWENTY-TWO

The noise that shook the trees sounded like the universe unraveling. My arm felt as though someone had shoved a hot poker under my skin all the way up to my shoulder. I added my feeble scream to the din.

In front of my eyes, the necromancer . . . dissolved. Like an old film melting in a projector, holes of light dotted his body and began to grow. Soon, there was nothing left. The bright, hot white light faded. My arm felt scorched; it hung uselessly at my side.

I dropped to my knees. Then I let myself fall the rest of the way to the ground. Exhausted, I closed my eyes.

When I opened them again, Valentine smiled down at me, his head cocked to the side like a curious dog. "You need to start inviting me to these little parties of yours," he said drolly, as he helped me to my feet. "I'm getting tired of arriving late."

"Yes," I said. "Sorry." I carefully removed my coat to examine my arm. It was numb, though the sensation of pins and needles slowly returned to my fingertips as I massaged them. The tattoo remained, resettled into its usual position. There was a red-gold sheen along the curve of its body, as if it were still burning slightly.

Hanging on to Valentine's shoulder, I watched as Jack and the others were similarly helped upright by a troop of officers and paramedics. A group of the latter clustered around Devon, who cupped his eye as though it were injured.

I overheard someone tell him, "The loss of vision in that eye is likely temporary."

Christ, I'd blinded the vampire.

"I need to figure out how to control my magic," I told Valentine.

"Obviously," he drawled.

"Is everyone okay?" Before he could even reply, the image of the pile of mud and twigs came rushing into my mind. "Oh! What about Stone? Is she . . . Can they fix her?"

"Probably," Valentine said casually. "At least, it's possible if they call the right person. The question is, will they?"

"What? Why wouldn't they?"

"Your fairy princeling seems to think it's unethical."

My anger gave me the strength to pull away from the shelter of Valentine's arm. "Are you fucking kidding me?"

"Careful," he said with a tease in his voice. "Watch your language. You don't want to blow the place up again."

"Oh, we'll see about that," I fumed.

*   *   *

My anger only spiked when I found Jones crouched next to Stone's remains. His head was bowed and his hat was against his chest, as if in respect. Bile rose in my throat. "Jones, you piece of . . ."

Valentine's hand clapped on my shoulder, cutting me off. "Seriously"—this time there was real warning in his tone—"be careful. We don't need a war with fairy over his untimely demise, as satisfying as that might be."

"His mom doesn't even like him." My eyes fixed on a spot on the back of Jones's uniform. If I could control my magic, I'd be burning a hole right through his heartless chest.

Valentine's voice sought to soothe, calm. "Regardless, the good folk are capricious in their affections; Maeve might hate him today, but still choose to avenge his death with a mother's fury."

I didn't want to talk about reasons to spare Jones's life. I stood over him, careful not to disturb a single rock in Stone's pile. My hands balled into fists at my hips. "What is wrong with you?" I demanded. "She was your friend. Wasn't she? At the least she was your partner."

"She died in the line of duty," he said. His voice was scratchy with emotion. "It's an honorable death."

"Bull—" At the harsh intake of Valentine's breath, I stopped myself. "That's just a copout. You don't want her reanimated because she's unnatural."

He didn't deny it. Instead, he stood up to look me in the eye. I could see wetness at the edges, but his expression was tightly controlled. "She was an exemplary police officer. She deserves an honorable end to her career."

"If her career is so awesome, why end it at all?"

Jack and Peterson joined us by Stone's body. Devon, led by Hanson, made his way into the grove as well. Everyone watched Jones.

"I don't want to," he said. He scrubbed his face and his shoulders slumped. "But she's rogue."

"What does that mean?" I asked.

Jack answered, "When her maker died, she was supposed to die as well. Traditionally, golems don't have souls. They're made for a purpose, and when that job is over . . ." He shrugged, not looking at the dirt at our feet.

"She obviously had a soul," I said.

Devon surprised me by adding, "And a purpose."

When I turned to regard him, I could see the damage my magical blast had done to his eye. The iris had whitened and the pupil had shrunk to a tiny pinprick.

"Serve and protect," Devon said, quoting the police officer's pledge.

Jones's eyebrows jerked upward slightly, and then he stared down at the muddy human shape for a long moment. Slowly, he began to nod. "Yes," he said. "I'll make some calls."

Several of Stone's brothers in uniform volunteered to stand as an honor guard over her body until a rabbi could be found who was willing to perform the magical rite to reanimate her.

The rest of us agreed to meet back at the station house for debriefing. Though I expected he'd take off now that the excitement was over, Valentine stayed. Somehow he, Devon, and I all ended up crammed in the back of Jones's squad.

Jack sat in the front, in Stone's usual spot. The dent of Stone's finger was still visible in the center of the Refocus.

The moment Devon sat down beside me, I blurted, "I'm so sorry."

"Don't be," he said. Of course, he happened to sit with his bad eye closest to me, so he had to twist around awkwardly to see. "You burned the magic out off all those zombies. It was awesome." Then, as if an afterthought, he added, "It'll heal eventually. Maybe even the next time I feed. Of course, if you feel really guilty about it, you could volunteer a little blood."

"Funny," Valentine said in a way that made it clear he didn't find Devon's offer amusing on any level. His head tilted back against the seat, his eyes closed, he sat with his hands resting lightly in his lap. The pose reminded me far too keenly of how he'd looked the last time I'd seen him in the back of a cop car. "Considering your current predicament, I'd think you'd be wiser about your choices in dinner companions."

Devon bristled. Trying to get a good look at Valentine, he asked, "Excuse me, do I know you?"

"Oh, I guess you two haven't officially met," I said, feeling very much in between these two men in more ways than just physically. "Devon, this is Valentine. He's my, uh . . ."

"The dragon," Devon said, his eyes widening slightly. "So you *do* exist."

Valentine lifted his head and opened one eye. "There was some question?"

"No," I said. "Devon's just being a jerk."

"Nothing new," Jack muttered from the front.

Jones just shook his head, obviously concentrating on driving and thoughts of his own.

Valentine lay his head back down. Devon turned his bad eye to me, and watched the buildings pass through the window.

"I hope Stone will be okay," I said to no one in particular.

"It's hard to say," Jones said, fiddling with the heat knob on the dash. "The rabbi I talked to had a few concerns. If you're right"—he found my eyes in the rearview—"and Hannah has a soul, she could be restored exactly the way we remember her. But he thought it could be an illusion. If that's the case, she could come back nothing more than an automaton, a robot."

I frowned. In that scenario, it might have been better to let her go. It would be ghoulish to see her walking around the office devoid of her personality. It'd be like having a zombie in her clothes.

Valentine squeezed my thigh.

He looked at me, imploringly, sympathetically. He didn't have to say anything; I knew he had my back no matter what. Anyway, I was sure she had a soul. I should hold on to hope.

We turned into a Dunkin' Donuts parking lot. I was about to make a joke about cops and their penchant for sweets when I realized that it was less than half a block from the precinct house. It was actually a clever place to leave a police car.

Jones and Jack got out and opened the doors for us.

We fell into a kind of order as we made our way along the sidewalk. Jones and Jack walked side by side in the front, leading the way, Valentine and I in the middle, and Devon in the very back. When we approached the door, Valentine slowed to walk beside Devon. He leaned in closely and murmured something. Whatever he said shocked

Devon into doing a double take, and coming to a complete standstill.

Devon watched Valentine walk away with his mouth hanging open and a deep blush creeping up his collar. He smiled dopily, like he'd just found out he'd won the lottery.

I held the door open for Valentine. "What did you say to him?" I whispered.

"I told him I know of a spell that may free him from his bondage to the fairy prince."

The atmosphere in the conference room was muted and somber. Everyone turned out, however, to hear the news about Stone and the necromancer case. The crowd parted to let Jones through to the front, where he started to remove all the photographs and notes from the dry-erase board.

Valentine and I found an empty spot near the door. Most of those gathered watched Valentine with concern and gave us a wide berth. Across the room, Denis, the George, caught my eye and waved. I almost thought he might come over and chat with us, but Valentine glared at him and he stayed put.

Someone bumped my elbow. I turned to see Boyd, who I recognized from his freckles and the fact that he was holding the necromancer's toe tag. "I guess we won't need this, eh?"

"Yeah," I said, but I frowned at him. Had he picked nothing up from it? Jack had been so excited that I'd remembered to grab the tag; it seemed strange that Boyd had never even gotten around to reading the vibes or whatever it was he did. I shrugged. It seemed my autopsy had really messed up the necromancer. He hardly seemed human at the graveyard. I didn't know how Boyd's powers worked. Maybe he could only read human traces. It was possible there wasn't much residue of anything coherent on the toe tag.

Jones finished putting away the last photo. The only thing left on the board was the cow mutilations. He started to erase those, but stopped. He turned around and raised his hands for everyone's attention.

"First, because I know most of you have probably heard that something happened to Officer Stone, I can confirm. Unfortunately, it is true. The word was erased from her forehead."

The room erupted in gasps and murmurs of concern.

Jones lifted his hands to quiet the room. "I can only say that, while there is a chance she can be reanimated, we won't know how successful it will be until after the ceremony is performed," he said, sadness etched in his face.

He paused, leaning both hands heavily on the table. "I'm afraid there's more bad news. Devon has been blinded in one eye, and, effective immediately, I'm putting myself on administrative leave, until Internal Affairs can make a full inquiry into my conduct on this case. Alex," he said, looking up and pinning me with his gaze. "Why don't you take over this meeting?"

In the stunned silence that followed, Jones sat down and bowed his head.

Everyone shifted to look at me. Beside me, I felt Valentine bristle defensively.

"It's okay," I told him. Even so, he followed as I made my way through the parting crowd to the front of the room. Jack gave me a smile as I passed him. Even Devon gave me a little nod of a salute, though maybe it was for Valentine, since he beamed almost goofily at him as we continued on.

It was weird to be the focus of so much attention. From

this perspective, the room was populated by an inordinate amount of blue police uniforms. That was disconcerting to say the least, especially since I wasn't even sure where to begin. I was grateful I'd have the whiteboard to write on. I chose a blue dry-erase marker from a group on the table, and wrote, "Steve, the necromancer," in squeaky letters across the top of the board.

Valentine settled against the back of the wall, like my shadow.

"We still need to confirm a lot of what happened before we can close the case," I said. "But it seems that Steve has . . . uh . . ."

"Dematerialized," Jack offered helpfully from the sidelines.

"Right, dematerialized, and Brooklyn, his sister and accomplice, is in custody."

An officer I didn't recognize raised his hand and simultaneously asked, "How did that happen, the dematerializing?"

I looked to Jack, who shrugged. Right, he was passed out. "I'm not sure," I admitted. My fingers traced the still aching edges of the snake's body. The outside, which had been rimmed in red, had faded to a yellow. I turned to Valentine. "The snake bit him, the necromancer, I mean. Could that have caused it?"

"A paradox, perhaps?" Valentine suggested, looking to Jones, who had perked up at this part of the conversation. "Spell bites creator?"

Jones nodded, as though thinking through the implications of Val's suggestion. "Combined with her spontaneous improbability?"

"Could work," Jack agreed. To me: "You cursed him, I presume."

"Six ways from Sunday," I said. "But I didn't think it was working."

"Spontaneous improbable magic can be unstable and unpredictable," Jack said. "It's the magic of miracles."

I tried to keep my eyes from rolling. It would be my luck to get magic that was hard to control.

"So that's it then," Boyd said from the back, still sounding relieved, but in a strained way. "The necromancer is gone. Threat neutralized."

"Why is Spenser resigning?" someone else wanted to know. A lot of others took up the same question.

"Uh . . ." I looked at Jones, but he was studying the wood grain in front of his interlaced fingers where they rested on the tabletop. I supposed I could go through all the instances of Jones's negligence, but it didn't seem right, especially since he was going to have Internal Affairs look into the case.

"I passively obstructed the case," he said, his eyes still cast down, but his voice clear.

A lot of people seemed truly shocked by this revelation.

He stood up, slowly. "I'm sure people still have a lot of questions, but the team needs to go over the case. I'm appointing Peterson as the acting head of the precinct; I'll answer any questions you have, privately."

It was clearly a dismissal for everyone but the team working the necromancer case, but it took a long time for the room to clear. People seemed to be in a daze, and clung together in a clot, as if for comfort.

It shouldn't have surprised me, but it seemed that Jones was well liked and respected by his colleagues.

When everyone finally filed out, the room felt expansive and empty. Devon and Jack took seats on either side of

Jones. Boyd, still clutching the toe tag, hung near the back of the room.

"Look, I've got that other case, guys," he said apologetically, glancing at the still-open door.

"Sure," Jones said, apparently forgetting he wasn't in charge anymore, and waved him off.

Boyd all but dashed out.

He certainly was an odd one. "We should have asked him to say," I said. "He's the one who wrote the initial police report."

"Are you sure?" Jones said. "I thought it was Peterson."

I was beginning to wonder if Boyd had some kind of forget-me glamour, or if he was really that unremarkable. I dug my phone out of my pocket, and opened up my e-mail app. "See?" I showed Jones.

"Huh," Jones said. "Well, you've got the report, at least. I'm sure we can reconstruct everything."

I supposed he was right. "Did you get any more of a confession out of Brooklyn while we were looking for Stone?" I asked.

"Oh, yes," Valentine said, from his spot against the wall. "Though Jones wouldn't let me use my freeze breath on her."

Everyone paled at the idea, except Devon, who attempted a little nervous laughter.

"So, what did she say?" I asked, choosing not to comment.

"It seems you were on the right track," Jones said. "Their plan had been twofold. They wanted to trigger the Tinker Bell Theorem, and, if possible, get rid of me as chief investigator, as well."

I blushed. I'd inadvertently helped them achieve one of their goals. I had to swallow the urge to apologize to Jones. Luckily, Jack raised his hand.

Once he had our attention, Jack lowered his hand and asked, "Has anyone told her that her brother is dead?"

We all looked awkward about that.

"No. I will," Jones said. He shook his head. "It'll be hard but she's already grieving him. He's been half-dead since the autopsy. She revived him as much as she could, but, well . . ."

I shivered at the memory of his badly stitched-up chest. "Did I kill him?"

"Which time? Twice, I think," Devon said.

Valentine came up behind me, and put his hands lightly on my shoulders. "As good as he was at appearing dead he was a conversely poor judge of character."

Right, he'd thought Jones would spirit his body away rather than put me in the crosshairs. I wondered what Internal Affairs would make of that.

A tense silence passed.

"Let me get this straight," Jack said. "The necromancer, Steve, faked his death, which became partially accurate." We all nodded along as he recounted the facts. "But, why, again? How does faking his death cause the Tinker Bell Theorem to be triggered?"

"It doesn't," I said. "That was part of a plan to discredit Jones."

"How?" Jack asked.

"Uh," I started.

In his usual half-interested pose, with his head resting in his hand, Devon casually said, "Spense and Brooklyn were hot and heavy for years."

Years?

"Oh, you dark horse," Jack said teasingly.

I'd say, though it explained Jones's reticence to go after Brooklyn. In fact, given how close they must have been, I actually was impressed with Jones's behavior. As far as I knew, he'd never gone to her with the precinct's plan or any of that. If it had been Valentine, who knows to what lengths I would have gone to protect him?

"I broke things off when we started to suspect Steve of grave robbing. Sometime after that they must have added discrediting me to their list of to-dos."

Jack continued to ponder the case. He tapped a long-boned finger against his lip. "The zombie at the diner. That was for the Tinker Bell."

"And, I think, the grave robbing," I added. "I've been wondering: How did you guys hide those crimes from the public?"

"It's taken all my efforts to keep it off the web," Jack admitted.

"I've been tempted to just send a forget-me spell bomb to the local newspaper," Jones admitted.

"It's been extremely tough," Jack continued. "The families always knew. They've been harassing the chief about the case almost continually. Why do you think he was so livid about the zombie?"

I hadn't known. "So, it's been working?"

"Sounds like it," Valentine murmured. His hands had been unconsciously massaging my shoulders slightly.

"Are the cow mutilations related?" Jack asked. "The officers said it was really difficult to get people to forget they saw lights. And it made it into the paper."

My gaze strayed to the whiteboard and the words *fairy ring* under the cow mutilation case. I thought back to the crazy visit to Jones's mother. He'd said the whole house was some kind of fairy ring and that without the salt we could be lost in time.

"What do fairy rings do?" I asked.

"What?"

"When we visited your mom, we were in a completely different place, weren't we? Can you use a fairy ring to travel in time as well as space?"

Jones, who had been stuffing the loose papers and notes into a case file, considered it. "I suppose. They connect places, but they could connect times, too, if there's one in the future or the past to connect to. Time is pretty meaningless to fairy."

"Could we use one to go back and see what killed the rancher's cows?"

"Theoretically, but you'd need a fairy with a spare ring . . ." he started. He must have seen my idea glittering in my eyes, because he shook his head. "It's not happening, Connor. I'm off the job."

"You are *now*," I said. "But you weren't then."

Jack smiled at my nerd logic, but Jones continued to shake his head. "I'm on leave."

I tapped my finger on the remaining open case on the whiteboard. "Wouldn't you rather go on leave with all the mysteries solved?"

I knew I'd gotten him with that. "Fine."

Jones told us to meet at his place after dinner. He had a fairy ring in his backyard we could use.

In the meantime, Jack offered to give Valentine and me a ride back to Robert's place. On the way, he told us that he was headed back to the cemetery to take his turn guarding Stone.

"How long until the rabbi comes?" I asked.

"One is driving in from Iowa right now," he said. "He'll be here sometime tomorrow morning."

I tried not to be astonished that Iowa had a kabbalah-practicing rabbi. After all, I would never have guessed South Dakota had so many zombies. "Let me know if there's anything I can do."

"Solve the case," he said. "I think Hannah would appreciate coming back to that."

A little lump formed in my throat at the thought that if she didn't it would make a fitting memorial. "Okay," I managed to say.

Before getting out, I touched Jack's sleeve. "What's the deal with Boyd? Why can no one remember he was the police officer at the scene?"

"It's the Dakotas, man"—Jack cut me off with a little laugh—"everyone around here has a name like Peterson, Olson, Hanson, Johnson. Hell, it's tough for me sometimes."

"Uh, Boyd sounds nothing like Hanson," I noted.

"Oh," he said, sobering suddenly. "I can keep an eye on him for you, if it's important."

"Very," I said. "But be subtle, okay?"

He tried to look offended, but failed. "I'll do my best."

When I talked to him at dinner, Valentine was adamantly against coming with me through the fairy ring.

"You've proven yourself very capable." Valentine yawned. He'd curled up in a spot of fading sunlight on edge of the bed. We'd had cheese and green pepper quesadillas, salsa, and the few crumbs of tortilla chips I found in the bag I pulled from the back of the top shelf in the pantry. Shortly after eating, Valentine had settled in like a satisfied cat.

"You don't need me. Besides, fairy magic is smelly. It makes me sneeze."

I was worried that we'd find something terrible on the other side of the ring, like a gryphon or hydra or other ancient monster. "I could bring Kleenex," I said, trying not to sound as desperate as I felt. "Plus, I'd enjoy your company."

He gave me a little smile for effort. "I'm sure you would," he said. "But you can enjoy me even more when you come home."

"You really don't like Jones, do you?"

Valentine stretched his legs and propped himself up on his elbow. "You don't either or you'd have learned to call him Spenser by now."

That was probably true. "Are you sure I can't convince you?"

"I don't like being trapped in a fairy ring. They're small and stinky. Not unlike prison, honestly."

Oh.

"You can stay."

It was weird to see Jones out of uniform. When he answered the door, my first impression was that he didn't quite know how to pull off "civilian." He looked vaguely uncomfortable in slacks and a polo shirt.

"Come in," he said. Looking over my shoulder into the night, he asked, "No dragon?"

"He seems to think I can handle this on my own," I said.

"He's probably right." He stepped aside to let me in. "Besides, the fairy ring will protect us."

The décor of Jones's house could have been plucked straight from *Field & Stream* or *Sports Illustrated*. It was a man's house, full of manly things. There was even a deer's head on the wall.

If I didn't know him better, I'd think he was trying too hard.

I didn't get much chance to inspect the rest of the place, though, as I was only invited in long enough to walk straight through to the glass doors at the back. Outside, he had a wide wooden deck, complete with chunky woodsy patio furniture and an industrial-strength gas grill. A light on the garage illuminated a lone crab apple tree in an otherwise well-cared for lawn. A pile of snow melted in the drive in front of a beat-up truck.

He led me down the wooden stairs to where the deck shadowed the side of the house. There, just on this side of a gravel garden, delicately thin mushrooms grew in a perfect circle. I almost didn't see them, their stalks were thread-thin and their brown caps so round and tiny. Though it was dark, I got the distinct impression of green in the center of the circle. I could smell summer: blooming clover and freshly cut grass.

Jones put out his hand to stop me from accidentally breaking the ring. I hadn't even realized I was moving toward it.

"Careful," he said, digging into the pocket of the Windbreaker he'd grabbed on the way out. Pulling out a familiar glass vial, he gave it to me.

I gripped it tightly.

"This is going to be trickier than the last time," he warned. "Fairy magic is capricious and chaotic at best. We're trying to go somewhere in place and time that's very specific. We may have to spend time in-between until I can connect to the exact time that the fairy ring was created at

Olson's ranch. You can't break the line until we've found the connecting ring."

I nodded, even though I had no idea what "in-between" was. The concern in Jones's face made me ask, "You've done this before, right?"

"When I was younger," he said. "And more foolish."

That must have been a long time ago, because I couldn't even imagine the Jones that would even consider anything foolhardy. Still, I was comforted to know he'd had experience with this and was still alive to tell about it. "Okay," I said, taking in a deep, steadying breath. "Let's do this."

He offered me a hand. When I didn't immediately take it, he said, "It's very disorienting."

"Right," I said.

My snake tattoo protested a little when we clasped hands, but it must be getting used to my friends because the ache was tolerable.

"On three," he said. "One . . . two . . ."

"Three," I said with him, as we stepped together over the slender, unimpressive-looking line of mushrooms.

But my foot never touched the ground on the other side. Instead, I fell into a dark, endless pit. I let Jones's hand go in my panicked tumble. Darkness swallowed me whole.

TWENTY-THREE

The sound of pounding hooves hammered through the inky darkness. Slowly, as if from a great distance, I made out the sound of voices. A man with a voice like my old psychologist's said something about catatonic delusion.

Was I dreaming?

The voices returned, talking over me, about me, about diagnoses and treatments.

My stepmother's voice, shrill, but firm, explained to the doctor, "She's intentionally driving a wedge between us with her fairy stories."

When I tried to deny it, the doctor reminded me that my denial and sense of entitlement were all part of the symptoms of the grandiose and persecutory types of my disorder.

It was happening all over again.

Or . . . had it never stopped?

Was Pierre all part of some hallucination?

I tried to scream but couldn't. Terror crushed my stomach.

No.

I was not insane. I'd left that place, hadn't I?

A snake hissed angrily. A horse whinnied, like a cackling laugh.

I tumbled downward until something solid gripped my wrist. A yank, and then, suddenly, I could make out dim shapes. Dots of dark against dusty white, coming closer, and then my body slammed into hard-packed dirt.

My eyes began to clear. Soft flakes of snow drifted lazily from the sky, melting on contact with my hot and flushed face. The sound of my breathing was harsh in my ear. My entire front stung from the impact with the ground. I held on to these real sensations and clutched at stalks of brittle hay with my trembling fingers.

"Is this real?" I whispered, tears of fear in my eyes.

A hand rested, heavily, solidly, against my shoulder. I looked over to see Jones kneeling beside me. "Yes. Sadly," he said, inspecting the remains of a spattered cow pie on the elbow of his Windbreaker.

"But . . . I heard . . ."

"Lies," he said, pulling himself to his feet. He offered me a hand up. "Lies so awful they seem real, but you also heard the Night Mare's hooves." To my horrified expression, he added, "Tell me about it. I fucking hate fairy."

With his help, I pulled myself into a sitting position. I revelled in each ache and pain and future bruise because they grounded me. The snow melted into wet on the butt of my jeans, a very annoying physical sensation.

I still felt unsettled, though.

It didn't help that all around us lights danced, like fireflies, flickering on and off, but always staying within the confines of the circle. The ground began to warm as shoots of green hay unfurled and began to grow.

"Please tell me you didn't drop the salt," Jones said, once I'd made it all the way to my feet.

"Crap," I muttered. It wasn't in my hand or my pockets. I glanced around, beginning to get nervous, but, miraculously, found the vial on the ground inside the circle.

"Next time I hold on to it," Jones said.

"No next time for me, thank you," I said, handing it over. The dancing lights dimmed to pale streaks before disappearing entirely. I didn't even want to go back if it meant returning to the dark place where my worst nightmares had come true.

I shivered. It was colder now than it had been at Jones's house. I supposed that was because it was the day the cows got mutilated—two nights ago?—and not tonight at all. Snow drifted down in lazy, light flakes onto the field. Cows lowed in the pasture on the other side of the barn.

"We're not going to be able to see much from here," I noted. A light on the side of the building cast a bright yellow spotlight on the barn door. Snow glittered in the beam. It was difficult to see much in the night beyond, and the structure of the outbuilding blocked most of our view of the highway and the field where the cows roamed, anyway. With a heavy sigh, I muttered, "This is great."

Jones didn't take my disappointment personally. With a shrug, he said, "This is where it ended up. I'm just glad we seem to be here at the right time and the right place."

"And I don't suppose we can just walk over there?"

"Nope," he said. "We have to stay inside the lines until it's time to go back."

I shoved my hands into my coat pockets and shifted from

foot to foot to try to stay warm. The hay had grown up to our toes already. I strained to see or hear anything beyond the barn. "How long until something happens?"

Jones didn't check his watch, but instead looked at his feet. "Do you remember how tall the hay was?"

Almost knee-high. The stalks shimmied as they grew, like images of stop-motion. I estimated it wouldn't be longer than ten minutes. "Will . . . whatever attacks the cattle be able to see us?"

Jones shook his head. "Not from here."

"I guess that's some comfort."

"What are you expecting?" His breath wafted from his lips like smoke.

A dragon? Some other flying mythical beast? "I'm not sure," I said. I held my hand up with my fingers pressed together firmly and mimed hitting something straight down. "What's taller than a cow and has a long, flat paw that could go like this?"

A small bulldozer, like a Bobcat, chugged down the highway. I saw the bucket at the same time Jones remarked, "That."

I was glad I couldn't see the action when I heard the first sickening crunch. I distracted myself by asking Jones, "A bulldozer! Why didn't we see the treads?"

"The ground is frozen solid, and it's snowing. Besides, Olson had his tractor all over this place."

"So, what do we do now?" I asked, wincing at the sounds coming from beyond the barn.

Jones pointed to the hay, which had nearly reached knee-high. "Go back," he said.

I shook my head. "I can't."

Jones nodded. "There really is no other way. If it's any consolation, you already did this."

"What?"

"We're the ones who made this fairy ring in the first place," Jones said. With a little rueful laugh, "Just like my mother said. I was the only fairy here."

"But, I just, the Night Mare or whatever, I don't think I can take it."

"That's what I'm saying. We already made it home safely. Look at the hay. If we hadn't left, it would have kept growing. We have to go back this way." He withdrew the vial from where he'd stashed it. Uncorking the top, he put his thumb over the opening. He spun around. As he did, he lifted his finger. Salt sprayed out. When it hit the edges of the fairy ring, sparks flashed, as bright as lightning.

The salt burned through the magic in a second. Jones grabbed my hand and stepped over the edge.

And we fell into utter blackness, as dark as unconsciousness.

This time I clung on tightly to Jones. My fingernails dug into the flesh his palm.

Out of the darkness came a horse. It was huge. Its mane was silken black. As it galloped, stars twinkled along its haunches. Eyes like red-hot pokers bored into my soul, trying to tease out my greatest fear.

I crushed Jones's fingers in a death grip, but no voices came. No one tried to convince me that my life here was a fraud and that, in reality, I was huddled in some corner in a padded room mumbling to myself.

The night horse thundered past. As the clatter of the hooves receded, I thought I heard: "Are you sure?"

My stomach clenched as laughter reverberated in the emptiness, but I held on. We seemed to flip head over heels in the zero gravity of fairy space. Passing through something gauzy, like a curtain of cobwebs, we stumbled into Jones's lawn. More practiced at this, Jones turned his tumble into a graceful roll. Partly propelled by his momentum before he let my hand go, but mostly due to my own clumsiness, I tripped over my own feet and went facedown.

Again.

At least I didn't drop into any cow manure. My coat and the knees of my jeans were grass stained. Wet seeped in everywhere, but I lay there, hugging the ground. I would have kissed it, but Jones was already giving me a funny look.

"You want some hot chocolate or something?" he asked. When I stayed on the lawn, unmoving, he offered: "Or a hot toddy?"

I'd never had a hot toddy before in my life, but I knew it had alcohol in it. "That sounds awesome."

Jones invited me into his kitchen. He put a battered teakettle on the gas stove. I took a seat on the stool near the island counter. The walls were a cream color that the yellow overhead light made soft and inviting. Herbs grew in a box near the window, and a philodendron flowed over the top of the refrigerator. He didn't have a lot of kitsch or other decorations, but the room felt homey.

"This is nice," I said. It seemed much less like something from a magazine, and I wondered if this was Jones's favorite space.

"Thanks." He set two mugs on the counter. Brown with bright white streaks, they were handcrafted and sturdy-looking. From a bottom drawer Jones pulled out a bottle of whiskey and splashed a bit into each cup. After digging around on the spice rack, he added a clove and a stick of cinnamon. "This will settle your nerves."

I started to protest that my nerves were fine, but my teeth chattered. I was still trembling from our trip through the fairy ring. I wanted reassurances that I wasn't dreaming all this from some psych ward. I knew Jones would give them to me, but I was afraid I'd start wondering if it was all just the rationalizations of my own insanity. So, I focused on something sure to distract. "I'm sorry about, well, the resignation and everything."

The teakettle whistled, and he took it off the burner. He poured the boiling water into the mugs with the whiskey and spices. He shrugged. "I brought it on myself. I suppose if I wasn't such an asshole, people wouldn't be in such a hurry to get rid of me."

"I think people like you more than you realize." At least more than I realized. I didn't know what else to say, so I added, "Two cases closed. That must feel good."

He pushed the mug in my direction. "I guess. I still feel like we're missing something critical in the necromancer case, but I can't put my finger on it."

"Do you think it's something to do with Boyd?" I wrapped my hands around the pottery, letting it warm my fingers. The hot whiskey and cloves had an almost medicinal scent, but I took a cautious sip. It was powerful enough to clear my sinuses. It burned down my throat, and settled like an ember in my stomach.

Jones watched my reaction to the drink and then said, "Boyd? He was on the team?"

Now I was sure there was something strange going on

with Boyd. "Yes," I said, taking another swig of the toddy. It went down a little smoother, though I coughed a bit when the powerful liquid hit the back of my throat. "Everyone keeps forgetting he was, but I have an e-mail from him."

"Oh, yes," he said, as though uninterested. He seemed to search for something at the bottom of his mug for a few moments. Then, his eyes returned to me. "All right then, who do you think was driving that bulldozer that took out Olson's cattle?"

I wondered at the sudden switch in topic, but I rolled with it for now. "I think it's one of two possibilities. Either it's a disgruntled neighbor, or it was the rancher himself."

"For the insurance money?"

"Right." I finished off my drink, careful to leave the clove bud at the bottom.

"I'm sure Peterson's already on that," he said, reaching for where his phone was plugged into the charger. "But I'll text him a reminder."

"It's going to be hard to stay out of precinct business, isn't it?"

His thumbs paused over the keyboard. He shut the phone and set it back down. "Hell yeah."

Jones and I left his house at the same time. When I asked him where he was off to at this hour, he told me that he planned to deliver some coffee and donuts to whoever was on duty guarding Stone's body.

There was an awkward moment of silence that hung between us, as a thousand different responses spiraled through my mind. Eventually, I just said, "That's nice."

"Don't get high and mighty on me," he said warningly. We were standing on his stoop, while he finished locking up. "I've known Stone a lot longer than you."

The alcohol fueled my audacity. "And yet you would let her die?"

"I would," he said, his eyes flashing. "I don't think there's anything she'd want more than to go out a hero, honorably. If she comes back a soulless automaton, I will see it as my duty to take her out. Stone wouldn't want to live that way."

I flushed. I could understand his point, but I wasn't finished arguing by far. "Why do you hate the unnatural so much? If you were more open to it, you would never have gotten into trouble with your girlfriend. She would have nothing to blackmail you with."

He turned sharply and put a finger in my face. "It's personal."

His hand had dropped and balled into a tight fist. I didn't think he'd really hit me, but I could tell that it was a struggle. I put my hands up, as if in surrender. As I walked to my car I could only think that some unnatural must have really fucked him over.

Maybe it was his mom.

I wondered what visions the Night Mare gave him.

I came home to discover my roommate flirting outrageously with my boyfriend. They were sitting at the kitchen table. The house smelled of baked apples and cinnamon. Robert had made his famous apple crumble without me!

"I was just telling Valentine he'd make an awesome dragon," Robert said as I was hanging up my coat.

I nearly choked. "What?"

"In *ElfWars*," Robert said. "I was just telling him how great the game is."

"I'd rather be an orc," Valentine said.

"You're far too intelligent and elegant to be an orc," Robert insisted. "If you really don't want to be a dragon, I could see you as an elf."

Valentine made a face. "Elves remind me too much of fairy. Speaking of, how was your date with the little prince, Alex?"

Robert looked shocked and offended so before I answered, I said, "He's talking about the ones with pixie wings, Robert." I pulled up a chair and sat down. "Things with Jones went okay, I guess. We've determined that the cows were killed by a bulldozer. Then we got into a fight about Stone."

I wanted to tell him about the Night Mare, but with Robert in the room with wide, curious eyes, it would have to wait.

"Bulldozers." Valentine sounded disappointed. "Nothing more interesting?"

"Nope," I said. "Just bulldozers."

"Who would kill a cow with a bulldozer?" Robert wanted to know. "That's awful."

Given that I could still remember the sound of shattering skulls, I had to agree. "That's the only real question we have left: 'Who done it?'"

The boys plied me with leftover crumble and ice cream, and we stayed up another hour or so talking over the merits of elves versus orcs. Somewhere around one thirty, I crawled into bed with Valentine.

When we had snuggled under the comforter, I held him tightly against my body. Into his ear, I whispered, "Tell me you're real."

His fingertips brushed my ribs, causing a quiver all the way down through the core of my body. He smiled at my response. "Is this real enough for you?"

"Not nearly enough." To show him what I needed, I tightened my grip until my fingernails left marks in his skin.

"Ah, I see," he said. "Then I'll have to show you a lot more."

I'd just fallen asleep when the phone rang. Nearly falling out of bed, I dug in through my pants pocket to find it. The caller ID told me it was Jack. I answered, "What's happened?"

"Breakout," he said. "Someone sprung Brooklyn."

"Boyd," I whispered.

Beside me, Valentine murmured a sleepy, "Wha . . . ?"

"There's an APB out for her," Jack said. "There's not much you can really do, but I thought I should warn you. Who knows what she's up to, but she might be coming your way."

I hardly had a chance to thank him when the bedroom door snapped back on its hinges and a bolt of magic shot out, aimed directly at my chest.

TWENTY-FOUR

In a blur of inhuman speed, Valentine moved to block the blast. It hit him in the face so hard that he was knocked backward. Dazed, he fell against me, pinning me under his weight.

"Bind the dragon, quickly!" Brooklyn screeched. "If I hold him unconscious for too long he'll begin to transform."

She didn't try to keep her voice down, so I could only assume that Robert was under some kind of spell. At least I hoped that was all they'd done to him.

Without the lights on, it was difficult to see anything more than the shape of the man who came scurrying in to do her bidding. He carried a loop of some material that let off a faint, bluish glow.

I clutched Valentine protectively, at least as best as I could with both my hands stuck underneath him.

The man hesitated at our bedside, uncertain what to do with my obstruction.

"Oh, just tie them both up!" Brooklyn shouted. "If he gets too big I'll have to let him go anyway."

Beneath my fingers, I felt Valentine's flesh begin to harden into scales. The springs of the bed squeaked as his body expanded slowly. Underneath him, I felt my body being squeezed.

As the man climbed onto the bed and bent over us, it was impossible not to identify Brooklyn's minion in the magical glow of the wiry rope. "Boyd!" I shouted in horror. "I knew it! But why?"

Kneeling over us, he threaded the cable under Valentine's arm. Boyd looped it around Val's neck. I tried to push him and bite at him, but Valentine's body had me well pinioned.

In his semiconscious state, Valentine hissed as the rope's strange material contacted his skin. I smelled the sickening odor of burning flesh.

"No! You're hurting him," I shouted, struggling to get loose. I was able to shimmy an arm out from under Valentine's waist and bat frantically at Boyd. Tucking the wiry rope against his body, he pulled duct tape from his jacket pocket. He tore a piece from the end and slapped it over my mouth.

"No swearing," Boyd admonished.

The tape was sticky, but also gritty like it had sat in the trunk of someone's car too long.

I slapped him uselessly in frustration. Unfortunately, he took the opportunity to catch my wrist in a tight knot. Boyd yanked my arm down so that it was lashed against Valentine's stomach. Then he took the coil, dropped it down over the edge of the bed. I wondered what he hoped to accomplish with that, until I saw it come flying over the other side. Magic had looped it around the underside of the bed.

Boyd coiled more rope around Valentine. He tied his wrists to the bedposts and his legs to the baseboard. Trapped beneath him, I felt Val's transformation slow and reverse as if he were trying to shrink away from the pain.

In my mind, I was cursing up a blue streak. Apparently, my superpowers only worked when I could speak out loud.

"How fitting," Brooklyn said. She leaned her hip against the doorway, casually. "The two lovers bound together. Perhaps we can make it look like a crime of passion."

Boyd stopped his wicked, random tying long enough to glance up angrily. "A coverup? No. We need to leave a giant, rotting dragon corpse in the middle of town. How else are we going to achieve the singularity?"

"It's more important to dispose of these two."

"No, that's not what I signed up for."

Valentine groaned, waking. He thrashed, his backside grinding into my hips. His head hit mine, and the old, curled edge of the tape caught in his hair. I felt the glue bond peel up a little, but his hair ripped before the tape gave way.

The pain must have roused Valentine because he let out an earsplitting roar. The windows rattled.

The sound shocked Boyd off balance and nearly deafened me. But it also gave me an idea.

"Damn it," Brooklyn cursed in surprise, pushing herself upright. "I've never tried to bind a dragon before. He's stronger than I expected. Finish quickly, so I can close the spell."

While Boyd scrambled to his feet, I stuck my cheek up against the short hairs at the back of Valentine's head. The moment I felt the tape catch, I turned my head sharply. The seal ripped from my mouth.

The pain made the swearing come naturally.

I tried, however, to imagine not hurting Valentine. The last time I let loose one of my swear bombs, I cut down everything in my path indiscriminately. Though I was never very good at visualization, I tried to imagine a bubble of protection around him.

His roar, on the other hand, made me suspect my attempts had failed. Ice crystals fogged the room. Lacy lines expanded across the glass panes of the window.

When I watched my magic skitter through the air, spiking along the frost, like an electrical current, I wondered if, instead, Valentine roared to help focus my magical blast. As the magic zipped through the icy air, it seemed to grow in size and potency.

All of a sudden, a discharging zap rang out as Boyd and Brooklyn collapsed. Valentine fell back against me, knocking the air from my lungs.

The magical wire still held fast.

For a moment, I wondered if all I'd managed to do was knock everyone out again. I'd be stuck here at the mercy of whoever woke up first.

Valentine moaned softly. "I'm going to have a bald spot."

The tape still stuck to one side of my mouth. "I'm going to have a nice square welt on either side of my mouth."

"I guess we're even. Just once, though, I'd like to rescue you," he said.

"I wouldn't have been able to do it without you. Or your hair, anyway."

"Nice." He rolled slightly, and I yelped as he pressed my numb arm farther into the bed. "Sorry," he muttered. "I'm trying to undo this. We've got to get loose before your chronically late cavalry arrives."

*　*　*

I'd just pulled on some sweats when Jack pounded frantically at the door. Unfortunately, Robert got to it before I could. He flung the door open, irritated, only to be greeted by several uniformed police officers and Jack, in a black *Matrix*-style trench coat and Yoda-ear hat.

"Police," Jack said, showing a badge I hadn't known he possessed.

Sarah Jane came swooping in, frantically cawing. She swept past Robert, who let out a nervous little scream. The bird was noticeably relieved when she saw me. She flew happy circles around the living room before perching on the back of the dining room chair.

"Oh, thank God you're okay," Jack said, barreling past the stunned Robert to catch me up in his arms. He was cold from the outside, but I hugged him tightly in return.

Valentine came out into the living room. Jack let me go almost guiltily. Valentine was wearing jeans and a pair of gardening gloves of Robert's. Bright red swollen marks crisscrossed his chest wherever the cord had touched it. "They're in the bedroom," Valentine told the uniformed cops. He stripped off the gloves and set them on the doily-topped end table. His wrists were nearly bloody with welts.

"Who?" demanded Robert.

"We had some intruders," Valentine said. "But it's okay now."

"Oh my God!" Robert's hands flew to his mouth. "I slept through it?"

"It all happened pretty fast," I said. I led Robert over to the couch and sat him down.

He put his head in his hands. "Things like this aren't supposed to happen here," he said.

"Yet they always do," I muttered quietly to myself. I patted Robert on the back reassuringly. "I know," I said. "I'm sorry."

The uniforms dragged out Brooklyn and Boyd. They were still unconscious. Valentine had wrapped the glowing cable around their wrists and ankles. One of the cops looked at the material. "Dragon's bane?"

Her companion gave her a little nudge in the direction of where Robert sat, dazed, on the couch.

"Oh," she said. "Er, good job subduing the villains, but next time you should leave fighting crime to the experts."

"Yes, ma'am," Valentine said on script.

We didn't sleep at all for the rest of the night. Instead, we made Robert tea and inspected the window that Brooklyn and Boyd had broken in order to gain access to the back door. "I never heard glass break," I remarked to Valentine.

Robert insisted on cleaning up right away, and fetched a dustbin from the pantry. He swept the shards into a pile.

Valentine leaned in. "Magic muzzle. It prevents human ears from perceiving sound. It's what woke me."

"Then they must have known you'd be ready. Brooklyn probably never intended to hit me with that blast."

"No, she knew I'd protect you instinctively."

"Instinct again," I muttered. Just once I wanted him to defend me because he wanted to, or . . . loved me.

"It's a good thing," he said, nuzzling my neck. "Don't knock it."

I shrugged out from his attention to help Robert with the trash bag. When I came back, Valentine went off to the garage to find a suitable piece of wood. He returned muttering about how he'd never seen such a clean and organized garage in his life. We didn't get much of a chance to talk about anything important until the window was boarded. Robert had finally fallen asleep on the couch, shock having worn off.

Valentine was in the kitchen, wrapping his wrists with medical gauze.

"Let me do that," I said, when he fumbled with the tape. "It's over now, finally. I suppose you can go back to . . . wherever dragons go."

I didn't look at him, afraid to give away my emotions. I knew it was smarter not to get attached to him, but I couldn't help it. I didn't want him to go anywhere, but I didn't know how to ask him to stay.

"Dragons go where they want," he said quietly.

I looked up then, and was surprised to find him staring intently at me. I couldn't read his face, so I asked, "And where do you want to be?"

"With you."

I started on his other wrist without looking up again. I could only control my voice at a bare whisper, "For real or because of instinct?"

"Instinct doesn't keep me here. You do."

Tears sparked in the corners of my eyes. "I do?"

His kiss was firm on my trembling lips. "You do."

Peterson ran a very different morning meeting. I'd settled into my usual spot near the back, a large mocha in hand as an antidote for my fuzzy head, just as he asked everyone to bow their heads for a moment of silence in honor of Stone. "The rabbi arrived early this morning," he explained. "Let's pray for the best possible outcome."

I normally wasn't much for prayer, but I did silently hope that Stone not only had a soul, but that it had waited around long enough to be revived by the rabbi. My gritty eyes appreciated the few seconds of relief that being closed afforded.

"What are you even doing here?" Jack asked in a whisper.

"I wanted to see this through to the end," I said, opening my eyes reluctantly. Besides, I had left Valentine sleeping.

Peterson asked everyone to also keep Jones and Boyd in their hearts. He said that our brothers in uniform deserved our concern, especially when they were led down the wrong paths.

I was beginning to feel like I was in church. I rubbed my eye, and leaned toward Jack. "Was Peterson a preacher in a past life?"

"Ask Beth, she's the reincarnation expert."

I laughed. "Of course."

After a few more platitudes about loyalty and duty, Peterson finally got around to the business at hand. Pointing to the last remaining case, he told the gathered group, "After the evidence gathered last night by Spense and Alex, we're turning this case over to the *ordinarium* cops."

The room was agog with questions and surprise.

One of the uniforms in back raised her hand. "What about the dancing lights? Isn't that still our jurisdiction?"

"It was us," I explained. I looked to Peterson to see if it was okay with him for me to tell the story. He gave me a nod, which I took to mean that I should go ahead. "Jones and I used the fairy ring to go back in time to see if we could tell what kind of creature killed the cows. Turns out, it was a Bobcat, like a bulldozing one, not a magical one."

In fact, I was planning on heading back to the lab after the meeting for one final experiment with the cow's head. I'd already made arrangements with the works department to borrow a Bobcat. All I needed to do was set up my cow simulation contraption. The chief of police had sounded pretty surprised by my request to cordon off part of the parking lot, but he'd agreed. I got the sense he thought the whole idea was kind of cool, very *MythBusters*. I wouldn't be surprised if half the regular police department just happened to take their lunch break in the parking lot today.

The disappointment was palpable in the room. I could hear mutters of irritation about the normal cops taking our case from us.

Peterson gave a shout for us to settle down. "I know this stings, but it really is their case now. Hanson and I are still going to act as part of the investigation team since we did a lot of the legwork already. I have a feeling we're going to discover that this was an irritated neighbor, but the list was long. Rancher Olson isn't very well liked."

He invited Hanson up to the front of the room, and we got a rundown on all the suspects. There were three likely culprits, including Olson himself. My money was on an inside job, honestly. It seemed to me that a neighboring rancher would stage a cattle-rustling con rather than something so brutal as cow bashing. I was glad to hear that theory floated around during the discussion.

I sipped my coffee and tried not to let my attention wander too much as Peterson wrapped up the thoughts on the case.

"How's Valentine this morning?" Jack leaned in to ask.

"Oh." I was a little surprised at Jack's concern over his rival, but I said, "He's sound asleep. I think he's planning to hibernate until the welts heal."

"He might," Jack nodded, though I'd been facetious.

"Do dragons really do that?"

"Hibernate? Well, not in the scientific meaning of the word, but they are rather fond of sleeping—at least by reputation. I . . . er, I guess I thought you knew."

"I know nothing about dragons," I said. "Trust me."

Jack looked as though he might say something else, but we were both distracted by a question that someone had raised in the back of the room. "What's going to happen to Pete?"

I frowned. Who the hell was Pete?

To my confused expression, Jack answered, "Peter Boyd."

We all turned to Peterson, expectant. He hooked his thumbs on his belt, and rocked on his feet a moment before answering. "I'm not exactly sure. I suspect there will be a trial."

"Are you mad?" Jack asked.

All the heads in the room turned to glare at him.

"Oh, for oak's sake," he said. "If they're Tinker Bellists, that's exactly what they're hoping for—a big circus trial."

Peterson frowned sternly at Jack, but it didn't have Jones's gravitas. "There's no way the media is going to get wind of any of this. A trial of their peers would mean magical folk. We may have to have a change in venue in order to find a magical judge, but the legal team is coordinating that. Rest assured, the precinct is very aware of the special circumstances surrounding this case."

It was clear by his tone that was all there was to say on the subject and the meeting was adjourned.

Jack walked with me out the door. He looked a little like I suspected I did in my first days with Precinct 13—a little lost and at loose ends. So, I said to him, "I could use your help setting up one last cow experiment."

He pointed to his chest like he couldn't believe I meant him.

"Yes." I smiled. "Come on."

I insisted that I drive because my car had a working heater and radio. I could tell, however, that Jack was mildly unimpressed with the boring lack of character my modern vehicle exuded.

Once he'd buckled in and we were on the way to the courthouse, I asked, "You seem to know about this Tinker Bell Theorem, right?"

"A bit," he said.

"Does it work in reverse?"

"How do you mean?"

I wasn't sure exactly, but I'd been thinking about my stepmonster a lot lately. I'd been trying to reexamine that part of my life with a magical eye. It was difficult to push past all the pain and accusations, but Valentine had said Gayle was a threat because she blocked my "call" to him. At first, I'd wondered why, but after the nuclear option in the graveyard and everyone's reaction to the "spontaneous improbability" of my curse spells, I figured I knew. Lately, instead of why, I'd been wondering *how*. "Well, can you make magic weaker by not believing?"

Jack played with his earring as he thought about it. "If the theorem works at all, I would say that, yes, it's bound to be true in both directions."

I nodded. I remembered Valentine had also said something about how equating magic with superstition and madness had been a tool for those who wished to contain the power. That seemed to have worked for society, but what about individually? "So, you could potentially control a witch by telling her that magic wasn't real?"

"Are you thinking of your stepmom?"

"I am," I said.

We'd arrived at city hall. I turned to enter the underground lot, since I knew the above spots would be harder to come by thanks to my experiment.

"I think we should make sure that, as soon as we're able, we send someone to Chicago to check on your father," Jack said. "This demon sounds like a real piece of work."

I could hardly disagree with that.

As I predicted, the parking lot was full of gawkers when the Bobcat cracked down on the cow's head. The entire crowd made a sound of disgust that sounded like, "Ewwwww."

But when the Bobcat backed off and I compared the skulls, it was a clear match. The crowd applauded.

Afterward, while Jack and I were cleaning up, the chief came over to shake my hand. I had to remove my glove before getting a hearty, knuckle-crunching squeeze and pump. His smile was as bright as the gold horseshoe belt buckle glistening at his crotch. "Old Franklin never did anything like that."

It took me a few minutes to remember that Franklin was the name of my predecessor. "No, I imagine not." I managed to extricate my hand before he pulped it.

He nodded approvingly. "You're all right, Connor."

"Thank you, sir."

He stood with his hands on his hips, nodding approval at our work. "You should really consider occupying that office of yours. You know we'd love to have you here at city hall."

I'd already been thinking along the same lines. "I like being able to work for the county *and* the precinct."

"We're lucky to have you." He nodded and slapped me heartily on the back before heading back inside.

Genevieve separated herself from the remaining loitering crowd to join us. She didn't say anything, she just pulled on a pair of gloves and started helping Jack with the cleanup.

She was smiling, too. I got the sense that I'd won over a lot of hearts with my science today, including hers.

The best part of the day, however, was when I dropped Jack back at the office. We walked in to a party. Or so it seemed. Everyone was making happy noises, drinking champagne from plastic glasses. Jack pulled a uniform aside. "What's going on?"

He smiled. "You haven't heard? Stone's back."

Despite everyone's obvious jubilation, I was nervous as we approached the conference room. I could see the wiry, messy curls that escaped from under her cap from across the room. She had her back to the door, so I hadn't seen her face yet. Just seeing that wild hair made my heart skip.

Would it really be her?

Jack and I made our way through the throng of well-wishers. We just made it up to her in time to hear Vito ask, "So, um, if you're not doing anything this weekend, I'd love to take you out."

Her smile could have lit up the room.

That was when I knew she was in there. It was our Stone. She was really back.

When it was my turn, I gave her a great, big hug. She held her arms out stiffly, with surprise, but when I didn't let go, she wrapped them around me awkwardly. When I was finally able to let go, I told her with a tear in my eye, "You and me, we're going to get your hair done properly."

Her eyes sought the spot that Vito had retreated to.

"Yes," I said fondly. "Before your big date."

Jack and I went out to lunch, as friends, and he promised to help me work on focusing my swearing powers. "Though," he said, "with spontaneous improbability, it's difficult. Part of the magic is that it's somewhat wild and uncontrolled."

"I just don't want to have to go nuclear every time." I felt a little twinge of guilt when I thought about Devon's eye.

"I think we can manage that," Jack agreed with a grin.

The only sour note in the whole day was overhearing Peterson's raging argument with the department he called "Infernal Affairs." We all heard his bellowing voice as he insisted that they didn't need to investigate Jones. Given the way he stomped around the office after slamming down the phone's receiver, it was clear he lost that point.

I'd heard from Hanson at the end of the day that the regular cops had tracked down the Bobcat's rental information. With that in hand, they were able to get a full confession from Olson himself. It seemed that the way Olson ran his organic farming was extremely cost-inefficient and the ranch was hemorrhaging money. He'd hoped to get a good insurance settlement, but hadn't counted on magical fairy rings and smart, capable, if nonmagical, police officers.

I was proud to be part of both departments.

Tired, but happy, I went home to discover Valentine still in my bed. Kicking off my shoes, I stretched out beside him. I stroked his hair, careful of the rough patch by the short hairs in the back. "You're still here," I murmured.

"Yes," he said. "This, my dear, is a very interesting town. I may be here quite a while."

I thought I would be, as well. Tomorrow, I planned to move my spider plant and some of my files to the big office, upstairs. The plant would appreciate being in the light.

I thought, for once, I might, too.